The Amethyst Necklace

Susan Griffin

This novel is entirely a work of fiction. The names, characters and incidents portrayed in it are the work of the author's imagination. Any resemblance to actual persons, living or dead, events or localities is entirely coincidental.

First Published in Great Britain 2020 by Tanzanite Press.

Cover Art by: Berni Stevens Book Cover Design.

ISBN: 978-1-8382742-0-7

For Shaun

Thank you for your support

Prologue

Reilly's heart raced and his limbs shook, desperation to flee clawed at his insides. How had it come to this? He was trapped in the middle of a never-ending nightmare.

He looked across at Ned who was sitting in the spectators' gallery, a frown etched on his face. Ned had once been a friend. Even so, he had been quick to tell the police what he had seen that day, but he must never know the truth.

Pain throbbed across Reilly's brow and his eyes burned in their sockets, but somehow, he lifted his head and made eye contact with the Court Clerk.

'Reilly Brownlow, you have been charged with manslaughter. How do you plead?'

The Clerk's voice faded out across the room as time slowed down. Reilly had to give his answer, state his case, and own up to the crime. But he was unable to speak as regret, ugly and dark, stabbed relentlessly at his chest. Now was the time to confess, the moment to tell the world the truth, of what really happened in the mill that fateful day.

His gaze was drawn across the room to Ruby, and

as their eyes met, something melted inside him. She looked glorious today with her hourglass figure, dark hair piled up on her head, and the amethyst necklace around her neck. However, even from this distance he could see her dark eyes, so full of fear, were red and swollen.

Reilly shut his mind to the thought of being locked up for so long. With those thoughts came dark memories of another time when he had been incarcerated against his will. Somehow, God willing, he would get through what was to come, serve his time, and eventually be reconciled with his family again.

He tore his eyes away from his true love and turned back to the Clerk. 'The plea is Guilty,' he answered into the hushed courtroom, lifting his chin and closing his ears to the heart-breaking sound of Ruby's weeping.

Chapter One

May 2018

After unlocking the front door, India found herself standing in a long dark hallway, and after a moment of adjustment, took in her surroundings. Directly in front of her at the end of the hallway was a wide staircase, and on either side of that were closed doorways.

Stepping to her right, she opened the first door and found herself in what would have been the front parlour or drawing room in Victorian times. She could immediately see how the overgrown foliage across the large bay window was blocking out the light. Once this was cleared, it would be a much brighter room.

India smiled to herself; already her interior designer mind was hard at work, and the knowledge she had gained at Stafford-Designs would stand her in good stead for the task ahead.

Pausing for a moment, India realised there was perfume in the air. When she had first opened the front door, a musty smell had assailed her nostrils, which she had expected in a house like this which had been shut up for a while. But in this room there was another more pleasant smell, and it was a sweet musky sort of scent.

Beans was now making so much noise that India bent down, unlocked the cat carrier, and let him out. Suddenly he went deadly quiet, poked his nose out of the carrier slowly, and looked at her uncertainly. She left him to find his way while she perused the room with its old, brown leather sofa and heavily patterned wallpaper.

Squaring her shoulders, India walked through another doorway and found herself in a small utility room leading onto a large kitchen area. Despite Ruby's house needing some serious renovation, India could see there had been some changes for the better here. This was a lovely room, and one she wouldn't need to change at all.

Again, she could smell the slight musky scent here, and she could hear the ticking of a clock. The whole area had a very modern feel to it compared to what she'd seen of the rest of the house, and had obviously been a much lived-in and loved room. The large, oblong-shaped area had once been two rooms, a breakfast room and a small kitchen, India realised, because she could see where the dividing wall had once been.

The ivory coloured units looked a cross between modern and old-fashioned with their silver handles, and the walls were painted in a warm lilac colour. At one end of the kitchen was a small alcove, with a two-seater settee wedged into its recess. Above it on the wall was the ticking clock, with its large, modern, light coloured face.

As India's eyes fell on the heavy oak table in the middle of the room, she noticed there was an old-fashioned snakeskin handbag lying on the table, next to a beautiful crystal vase. It was as if Ruby had simply walked out of the door, leaving her handbag behind, and India felt a cold chill run down the back of her neck.

She recalled the solicitor explaining that Ruby had left something for her in the house, so this must be it. A handbag. What a strange thing to leave for someone.

Her curiosity piqued, India undid the clasp, dipped her hand into the bag and felt around. Her fingers curled around something cold and smooth, and she lifted it out. It was a glass phial, an exquisite looking bottle of scent with the words '*Soir De Paris*' along its front, and below in small letters was the word, '*Bourjois.*'

She pulled the stopper off the bottle and sniffed the fragrance. It was a mixture of jasmine and musk –the same scent she had noticed in the front parlour and here in the kitchen.

Placing her hand back into the handbag and peering into its depths, she at first thought it was empty, but then caught sight of something wedged down the side of the mink satin lining. As she pulled it free, she gazed at an old black and white photograph, and realised there was something slightly familiar about it.

The young mixed-race man was posing in an army uniform. He was staring seriously into the camera lens, and despite the folds in the image, India could see how very handsome he was. He had jet-black hair and a generous mouth, but his large dark eyes looked clouded with worry. *Was he about to go off to war, like so many others of his time?* she wondered.

She placed the photo back on the table and had just moved the crystal vase out of harm's way, when a loud noise coming from the direction of the front door echoed through the stillness. At the same time, her phone began ringing. Glancing at the caller ID, she saw it was her friend Izzy.

'Not now, Izzy,' she whispered, vowing to ring her friend back later, and hurried through the hallway towards the front door. However, despite her haste, the caller had vanished by the time she got there.

Returning to the kitchen, she switched on the kettle to make a cup of tea and opened a cupboard in search of a mug. An urgent tapping sound made her jump, and glancing up she saw a man peering anxiously through the window at her.

India opened the window and blinked at the man. 'Can I help you?' she asked. 'Sorry if you've been knocking for a while. I need to install a doorbell as soon as I get around to it.'

She couldn't help noticing the man's vivid blue-green eyes, and how they were staring at her in a slightly strange way, almost as if he were studying her features.

'That's alright, no worries,' he said quickly. 'I'm Jez from Carlisle Landscaping. We're in the middle of putting a fence up in your neighbour's garden, but we'll need access to yours,' he explained. 'Would that be okay?'

'Yeah sure, no problem, just go ahead,' India told him.

'Thanks, we'll be as quick as we can,' he said then paused, again with that strange look as if he were studying her. 'How you settling in here in Isfield?' he asked.

'Yeah, okay so far, thanks,' India told him thinking how nice he was, and how people were probably way more friendly out here in the countryside than where she'd moved from. Then she wondered if he had known her grandmother Ruby.

Jez nodded at her and then disappeared quickly out of the gate. Something about him made her pause at the window while she waited for the kettle to boil. She saw him return a moment later with a woman in tow.

The woman, who was dressed in combat trousers and had short spiky hair, then helped him as they began banging fence posts in the ground between her and next door's garden.

Before turning from the window, she glanced around Ruby's garden, and noticed for the first time that it was in dire need of attention. It occurred to her that perhaps she could hire Carlisle Landscaping to do the work for her, as she'd never get around to doing both the inside of the house and the garden before selling it.

Remembering the contents of the handbag, she dismissed the garden maintenance from her mind and turned back to the kettle.

After locating a bone china mug and a canister of teabags in one of Ruby's cupboards, India retrieved the milk she'd brought with her, and made the longed-for cup of tea.

Sitting down, she picked up the photograph of the soldier and turned it over to find the words *Dearest Reilly, I will love you forever xx* written on the back. Then in capital letters was printed the date: *March 1941*.

India's mind went back to the letter and necklace the solicitor had given her from Ruby, and she decided to have another look at them. Removing them both from her own handbag, she sat down and placed them on the table. The envelope had her name, India McCarthy, written in black ink; the blue velvet jewellery box sat alongside it.

She raised the lid on the box and a strange feeling

came over her as she looked at an oval-shaped amethyst stone. It was as if its deep violet colour were mesmerising her.

When the solicitor had given her the gifts left to her by her grandmother, India had been surprised at Ruby's generosity – someone she had never known. And she couldn't help wondering what her grandmother could possibly have to say in the letter that would be of any consequence, after so many long years of silence.

Taking a deep breath, India pulled the letter out of the envelope, laid it flat on the table, and began to read.

Dearest India,

I am nearing the end of my life, and by the time you find this letter I will be gone from this earth. My dear granddaughter, for many years I have yearned to see you but alas it was not to be – family complications would not allow this. Life is not always how we want it to be.

You may wonder why I have left everything to you; it may seem that way, but I have kept something back, something very valuable. Your father has it in safe keeping for the day you are reunited. I know the two of you have lost touch, and it's always been my dearest wish that one day this will change, and you will find each other again.

Also, I hope by now you will have the necklace. A dear friend of mine, Scarlett, passed it on to me at the age of twenty-one, and I've treasured it ever since. Maybe you will love it as much as I did.

Yours forever,
Your grandmother,
Ruby McCarthy.

India put down the note, thinking about its vague contents, and took deep breaths in an attempt to calm her racing heart. After so many years thinking her father was dead, she still found it hard to realise that somewhere in the world he was alive and well.

The thought left her feeling elated one minute and downcast the next, and there were times she wished she could turn the clock back and not have the knowledge of his existence. At least then, life had been simpler.

Her thoughts returning to the letter, she couldn't deny she was intrigued by Ruby's reference to the 'valuable' item she'd kept back for her. What could it be? Straightening her back, she picked up the necklace and walked back through the utility room into the drawing room.

As she stood in front of the mirror above the fireplace, India lifted the necklace and placed it around her neck, then stared at her reflection in the mirror. It was a stunning piece of jewellery, as well as a precious gift from her grandmother, and she might also enjoy wearing it as purple was her favourite colour.

Feeling slightly better, she smiled at her image and told herself to take one day at a time. As she turned away from the fireplace, her gaze fell on an old sepia photograph on the mantelpiece.

India stared intently at the photo, and could see the woman in the picture must be Ruby when she was a young woman, probably around her own age. The likeness between herself and her grandmother was uncanny. Ruby had the same thick, dark hair, brown eyes, and rounded figure as India. She was posing with her arm around a small boy of around five years of age, and India knew this must be her long-lost father Noah, as a child.

Picking up the gilt-edged frame, she gazed at them longingly; a pang of regret stabbed at her chest, and tears filled her eyes. They both looked so happy and were smiling into the lens of the camera, but they were also an enigma. India knew nothing at all about her grandmother, the woman who had left her this house, and her memories of Noah were hazy and vague, like looking through a thick fog.

Ruby obviously wanted India to be reunited with her father, and the 'valuable' item in her letter seemed to be the carrot she was dangling in front of her.

India knew she could certainly do with more financial help, as the small lump sum Ruby left and her redundancy money wouldn't last long. But knowing that Noah had never once tried to get in contact, hurt her so deeply that she found it hard to bear the pain. Seeking him out now seemed like a bad idea, even if she did know where to begin her search.

India felt her chest tighten with resentment. Lifting her chin, she decided there and then to treat the house as a financial proposition. She would get it into good order then sell for the best price and move on with her life.

Even if she didn't seek out her own father, India was intrigued to find out more about the man in the photograph called Reilly. Could he have been her grandfather? Looking into a bit of family history might be an enjoyable distraction while renovating the house, and she'd always liked a little mystery.

India's musing was brought to an abrupt halt as Beans suddenly shot through the hallway and skidded to a halt by her feet. Reaching down, she lifted him into her arms, where the cat meowed loudly.

'Calm down, Beans,' she admonished. But the cat

glared at her as he struggled to be free. 'Have it your own way then,' she said.

Putting him back down on the floor, India opened the front door and watched as he dashed outside into the overgrown garden, just as Jez was about to disappear out of the gate.

'Excuse me,' she called loudly, while opening the door wider and hovering in the doorway.

Jez turned at the sound of her voice and walked swiftly back towards her. As he stopped in front of her on the doorstep, she became aware that those turquoise eyes of his were staring at the necklace around her neck.

India felt uneasy under his watchful gaze. Unconsciously, she lifted a hand to cover the amethyst stone, but then quickly removed it, telling herself it was her grandmother's gift to her and was rightfully hers.

She was confused by the look on his face, which was a mixture of shock and sadness, but at the same time she couldn't help noticing how attractive he was. Jez Carlisle was tall, big, and muscular, but in the nicest possible way. His hair, which was slightly dishevelled, was fair, thick with waves and flecked with gold, and those eyes were quite striking.

To cover the embarrassment of the way he was staring at her and frowning, India ploughed on with her request. 'Could you leave me one of your cards, please?' she said, trying to smile at his strange expression. 'I'll need help with this jungle of a garden, as it'll likely need a complete overhaul. My grandmother let it go to rack and ruin, you see.'

India knew she was babbling now and wondered why she had mentioned Ruby. It had obviously been the wrong thing to say, because his head shot up and the frown deepened.

'Did you know my grandmother?' she said, the words were out of her mouth before she could stop them. She wasn't even sure why she'd asked him.

Jez held her gaze for a moment and then glanced around him, his expression serious, as if noticing the state of things for the first time.

'Nope, I didn't know her,' he said vaguely, while delving into his pocket for a card. 'Right, here you go,' he held out his card to her. 'Let me know if you want us to do the garden, and I'll let you have a price and some available start dates.' Then suddenly he grinned at her, turned on his heel, and was gone.

India felt rather unsettled. From the moment she'd set eyes on Jez, there had been a shifting feeling near her heart. She watched him disappear out of the gate, and acknowledged that she was deeply attracted to him, which startled her, coming so soon after her break-up with Archie.

She also had the very odd sensation that Jez Carlisle had somehow taken exception to her living here in Ruby's house, and she couldn't for the life of her understand why that would be.

Chapter Two

November 1940

The deep, penetrating wail of the air-raid siren tore through the air of Hanningtons Department Store, sending icy shivers racing up Ruby's spine. Next came the urgent announcement over the loudspeaker system they had all been dreading.

'All staff make your way to the air raid shelter located in the basement of the building, and don't forget your gas masks!'

It was early evening and Ruby and her colleague Harriet were working an extra late shift at the store, for stocktaking. The shop floor, which had been ordered and quiet only a moment ago, was suddenly transformed into a mass of employees all heading in the same direction.

As Ruby's heart thudded wildly in her chest, she dropped the box of hats she'd been holding, grabbed her gas mask, and dashed over to Harriet whose face was white and pinched.

'Hurry along there!' came the authoritative voice of their line manager as she chased up the stragglers. Then, stopping in front of Ruby and Harriet, she glared at Harriet who had made no move to obey her command.

'What's going on here? Get into the shelter now, both of you!' she exclaimed.

'Don't worry, we're flipping going!' Ruby told the manager, who quickly moved onto the next person.

Grabbing hold of Harriet's arm, Ruby began pulling her towards the exit, trying her best to ignore the stricken look on her friend's face.

'For God's sake, Harriet,' she said, as they got to the door and Harriet planted her feet refusing to go any further. 'We need to go now, there's no time to waste,' she told her urgently.

Cries of 'Get out of the way!' and 'Don't stop there!' echoed around them, as Harriet and Ruby were jostled and jarred by other employees desperate to get through the doorway and down into the shelter. Ruby quickly moved to the side to allow the others to pass and Harriet mutely followed her.

The girl's eyes were wide with fear. 'Sorry... Ruby,' she murmured, her bottom lip trembling. 'You know I can't go down there. I just can't do it, not after what happened before...' she clutched agitatedly at Ruby's arm as she spoke.

Shaking her head, Ruby's mind whirled as she tried to think what to do. Taking a deep breath, she squared her shoulders and looked directly into Harriet's eyes.

'Harriet, you need to listen to me, the shelter is the best place right now,' she looked around the empty shop floor and then back at Harriet. 'It's not the same as that day in the cinema,' her voice trailed off as Harriet continued to stare at her in a dazed fashion, and Ruby knew she wasn't listening.

Retreating into herself, Harriet squeezed her eyes shut and placed her hands over her face. Ruby saw her chance. Taking advantage of her friend's lack of resistance, she grasped her elbow and steered her quickly towards the now empty stairway.

However, just as they got to the top step, Harriet sprang into life and, wriggling free of Ruby's grip, she began fleeing towards the double doors at the front of the store. With no concern for her own safety, Ruby raced after Harriet, shouting for her friend to stop. But the girl was deaf to Ruby's warnings and was now in the grip of blind panic as she reached the double doors and quickly disappeared from sight.

As Ruby emerged from the building into the black night, she stopped and shivered as the cold November air hit her face. She clutched at her side and took a great gulp of air into her lungs then looked rapidly around in the darkness for Harriet.

'Harriet, Harriet!' she called urgently. Harriet's silhouette emerged through the dark a few feet ahead of her. She was standing on the pavement outside the store, staring up towards the sky.

Ruby rushed towards her just as the deep thud of a bomb exploding nearby ripped through the air, and the ground shook beneath her feet. Struggling to ignore the distant sound of chaos and mayhem in the wake of the explosion, Ruby took Harriet by the shoulders and began to shake her, hoping to shock her friend into common sense.

Harriet's face, though, was a blank mask, and she was as limp as a rag doll as her head bobbed up and down with the force of Ruby's actions. She stared in terror at Ruby, just as the loud droning of an overhead plane filled the air. For a second, they were both frozen in time, their eyes drawn skywards, where searchlights swept high into the air in an attempt to pick out the enemy aircraft.

As the terrifying sound of a bomb whistling towards them filled the air, Ruby tore her gaze from the sky. 'Get down!' she screamed to Harriet, but her warning came too late, as the explosion lifted her off the ground and threw her back down with a sickening thud.

The deep ear-splitting noise was crashing all around her, as Ruby's head slammed into the pavement. Everything was black, then colours blurred into one another. She tried to breathe but couldn't; she was aware of lying face down on the pavement, her nose squashed hard against the cold concrete.

Ruby was suffocating, unable to move, and her head was as heavy as lead while her nostrils were filled with an acrid smell. She lifted an arm and shoved at her head with her elbow. Then, gulping at the smog-filled air, she somehow managed to push her face free of the pavement.

Something wet and warm was seeping down Ruby's face and into her eyes. The salty taste of blood filled her nose and mouth. Rolling her painful body over, she rubbed at her eyes, and forced them open, still aware of blood pouring from somewhere on her head.

Thick smoke filled the air and the world had gone strangely silent. Her eyes were now open but all she could see was a hazy thick fog. As she stared sightlessly around, shapes began to appear. Windows had been blown out of the front of the department store, fire burned in the distance, and there were shards of glass and debris scattered everywhere.

In the chaos of the explosion, Harriet had disappeared and Ruby was desperate to find her, but the searing pain in her head was paralysing. 'Harriet, where are you?' she croaked, as the energy drained from her body and everything began fading away.

A final image of Scarlett's letter containing the warning of disaster, flashed through her mind, just as blackness finally sucked her into its comforting depths.

Chapter Three

'Mum, why did you lie to me?' India said, forcing her voice to sound even.

She took a deep breath and waited for Miranda to answer, reflecting on how this subject was too painful, especially as she'd hidden the hurt for so many years from her mother and everyone else. Uncovering it now felt like too big a mountain to climb, but it was time to face the truth.

Miranda sat up straighter and two spots of colour appeared on her cheeks. 'I didn't lie to you, India. I told you your father had disappeared, that he was lost to us and would never return, which of course was true at the time,' she said solemnly.

India struggled to contain her annoyance. 'When I was young, though, you did tell me my father was dead, and I want to know what really happened.'

India knew her mother had misled her over the years and was desperate to get to the bottom of why. However, a little voice in her head told her that at last her mother was talking to her about her father, which was progress after so many years of silence.

'You always said he left without a backward glance, but the thought that all these years he's been alive when I thought him dead… is heart-breaking.' India felt the familiar ache in her chest and dipped her head, sensing hot tears threaten at the back of her eyes.

Her mind went back to James Saville, of Saville and Sons Solicitors, explaining that Noah McCarthy was definitely still alive. She'd watched him as he had sat back in his leather chair, formed his fingers into a steeple, and given her a sympathetic look.

He didn't understand, of course he didn't, how India had been deceived all these years by her own mother. And she didn't understand either how this could have happened. It made her feel as if she didn't know her mother at all, just as she'd never known her father.

Miranda leaned back in her chair and regarded India thoughtfully. 'I'm sorry about that, India. I really am. But your father made the decision to leave us, not the other way around.'

India knew her mother had tried her best for her in her growing years, which made it all the more awful that she had also deceived her. They had been very close once, but that was a long time ago.

Miranda drew her mouth into a straight line. 'I'd planned on telling you the truth when you were older,' she said with a frown. 'But I never quite found the right moment somehow.'

India had been sixteen when Miranda met Michael, and India never took to her new stepfather. She was obviously happy her mother had found someone, but the mother and daughter relationship had deteriorated after that. As a consequence, India had built a barrier around her heart that no-one, except her friend Izzy, could see beyond.

India understood by her mother's closed look that she wasn't going to get any more explanation out of her today. 'Okay,' she said, 'but what really bugs me,

23

since finding out that he's alive, is why didn't he keep in touch with me?' India looked at her mother with a questioning gaze.

Miranda suddenly looked slightly awkward. *Was that guilt on her face?* India wondered. 'Mum, did he try to contact me after he left?' Her heart lurched and she held her breath as she waited for Miranda's answer.

Miranda shifted in her chair and tilted her head to one side. 'The thing is, I thought it best not to give you the letters, as I knew it might upset you…' her words trailed off and she sighed heavily. 'Maybe that was the wrong thing to do,' she added, looking thoroughly uncomfortable.

India felt the tightness in her chest again intensify and her limbs felt weak. She leaned on the worktop for support and stared at her mother. What kind of person would hide correspondence from an absent parent? Especially when Miranda knew how much her father leaving had affected her. 'So, he did write to me, after all?' she said, stating the obvious.

On learning that her father was actually alive, India had initially vowed to have nothing do with him, because of the deep hurt she felt over neither him nor Ruby, her grandmother, ever attempting contact with her.

But what her mother had just told her made India feel as if nothing was as it had seemed, and something had just shifted. She felt stunned, completely shell-shocked about the letters. 'Where are they now?' she said angrily, still unable to believe what her mother had done.

When her mother didn't answer, India added, 'Can I have them, or have they been destroyed over the years?' She sat back in her chair and shook her head sadly, knowing she wouldn't put it past Miranda to have got rid of the letters.

Her mother widened her eyes in shock at India's question. 'No, they haven't been destroyed!' she said indignantly. 'It's time you saw them, I see that now, but to be fair to me, I thought I'd done the right thing for your wellbeing at the time.'

India didn't know what to say. It seemed such an awful thing to do to your daughter, but maybe she had done it with the best intentions. She stared down at her lap, for a moment lost in thought, but then looked up as her mother began talking again.

'India, please remember you were very young when he left…' she paused and then, still holding eye contact with India, added, 'I was trying to protect you,' as if she were somehow justifying everything she'd said and done when it came to Noah.

After Miranda had gone, India sat down on the sofa and reflected on the conversation while stroking Beans. All those years India thought her father was dead, he had actually been writing to her. How could her mother have done that to her only child? Yet Miranda had looked so sad when she left that India concluded it must have been her mother's own issues with Noah which had led her to do such a dishonest thing.

So, she wondered now, *why did her father not inherit this house, instead of her?* That was something else she should have asked Miranda before she left. India remembered next to nothing about him, so it was all a mystery.

The photograph of Ruby and Noah came back into her mind and a new determination to find her father was born. Perhaps she needed to find out what happened to him and ask him for his side of the story. Instinctively, she knew that until she did these two things, there would be no rest for her.

Chapter Four

Ruby opened one eye slowly and then the other to find she was surrounded by a world of white. *Where was she? Was she dead?* Gazing around the room, she began to feel a distant memory hover on her subconscious. Something very bad had happened, she knew, but what?

Attempting to move her head, she tried to focus on recent events but the effort caused an ear-splitting pain to shoot unmercifully across her forehead. Quickly closing her eyes, a groan of agony emerged through her painful, swollen lips.

'Hello, my dear. How are you feeling?'

A woman's kindly voice penetrated Ruby's dulled senses, and once again she lifted her eyelids slowly. This time the face of a middle-aged nurse standing beside her bed swam into view, and despite the pain, she managed to keep her eyelids open.

'What's happened?' she croaked. 'I can't remember anything.'

'It's alright, don't try to move at the moment. You're safe now,' said the nurse, who was now moving around the bed, tucking in the sheets.

Ruby's painful head spun. *What was she safe from?* Using all her will, she tried lifting one arm to reach towards her aching forehead, but it was heavy and glued to her side. However, she found she was able to move her other arm.

As her fingers made contact with a thick wedge of dressing, Ruby let out an agonised cry of panic. 'Nurse,' she whimpered. 'Where am I?'

The nurse was immediately by her side. 'Shush now, don't distress yourself. You've been involved in a bomb blast.' She looked at Ruby, concern furrowing her brow. 'It's nothing that won't heal, my dear,' she said kindly.

An image of Hanningtons department store flashed through Ruby's mind, and then it vanished again. 'A bomb?' Ruby heard her voice disappearing and dread threatening to engulf her. Looking up into the nurse's eyes, she began racking her befuddled brain for information that might lead to answers.

Ruby remembered running from the store while bombs were exploding around her. Harriet wouldn't go into the shelter, so she'd run out of the building after her.

Looking anxiously towards the bed next to her, she saw it was crisply made but empty. 'Do you know where Harriet is, nurse?' she asked with a feeling of dread.

The nurse gave an understanding nod and laid a comforting hand on Ruby's uninjured arm. 'I'm sorry, dear, there was a woman brought in who didn't survive the blast.'

On the edge of hysteria, sobs bubbled up inside Ruby and a tidal wave of grief threatened to overwhelm her. She sensed rather than saw the nurse disappearing, and squeezed her eyes shut to block out the horrific thought that Harriet might be dead.

The next morning Ruby awoke to the same nurse taking her temperature. 'My name's Ella,' she said pointing to her name badge. 'I hope you're feeling better?'

Ella's comforting voice soothed Ruby's torment and she turned her sore head to look at the woman. Slowly, and for the first time, she took in the light-coloured hair under the starched nurse's cap and her peacock blue eyes. And because Ella was still looking at her in that concerned way, Ruby nodded her head and said she was fine.

But the truth was that everything in her body hurt, and the words 'Harriet is dead' kept echoing in her head. As she watched the nurse reading her chart, hope sprang in her chest.

'What was that poor woman's name that didn't survive the blast?' she asked Ella tentatively.

The nurse gave her a sympathetic look. 'Harriet Fairburn,' she said, lifting her eyebrows. 'Was she your friend?' she asked.

Ruby stared back at her solemnly. All hope that Harriet was still alive had now gone as she confirmed that was her friend's name.

Ella hesitated and then lightly stroked Ruby's hand. 'There were five bombs dropped altogether,' she explained. 'The second one exploded at the junction of East and North Street, outside of Hanningtons store, and it was nothing short of a miracle you survived.'

Waves of nausea came over Ruby as she remembered that terrible moment when Harriet disappeared and the bomb exploded, and she winced at the images in her head. She became aware of Ella pouring water into a glass and plumping up her pillows through her torment.

'Perhaps it would be good for you to have some visitors?' Ella asked in a gentle tone. 'I'm sorry, I must go,' she added, as another patient's cries echoed through the ward. 'But if there's anyone I can contact for you, let me know.'

Ruby watched Ella disappearing down the ward and thought about what she'd said. She didn't want her parents to know of her injuries, and could almost hear their words of blame. 'This is the result of your defiance,' they would tell her. However, there was one person Ruby simply longed to see in this dark time of her life.

The moment Scarlett's figure glided down the ward, the world looked brighter. Everyone – patients and visitors alike – turned to look at Scarlett, who was wearing a red tea dress nipped in at the waist, with a sweetheart neckline. The effect was stunning. How Ruby had missed her colourful friend.

'Oh hell, Ruby, you poor thing,' Scarlett said, running her gaze along the length of Ruby's body and finishing up on her bandaged forehead.

For a moment they stared at one another, and then Scarlett perched on the edge of the bed and waited for Ruby to speak. Feeling her eyes fill with tears Ruby opened her mouth.

'Harriet died in the blast,' was all she could say, as she stifled a sob.

Scarlett's eyes were wide with sympathy. 'That's terrible. What happened?' she asked, taking hold of Ruby's uninjured hand.

Holding tight to Scarlett's hand as if it were her lifeline, the words poured out of Ruby's mouth as if they had a will of their own, how she'd tried to save her friend, and how Harriet had suffered from claustrophobia.

'Harriet and George were at the Odeon cinema in Kemptown when it was bombed recently. You know the one, where fifty-seven people were killed?' she told Scarlett. 'And the trauma of that day left its mark on poor Harriet.'

Scarlett waited until Ruby was silent. 'I don't know what to say, Ruby. I'm so sorry, poor Harriet.' She held Ruby's gaze as she spoke. 'I know it doesn't seem like it right now, but in time you'll accept what's happened,' she said wisely. 'You know me, I often think fate plays a part in this kind of thing,' she added thoughtfully.

Ruby felt the dark clawing guilt grip her chest. 'Fate? Maybe...' she said falteringly.

'Fate can deal some pretty cruel blows. I should know.' Scarlett stared into the middle distance and seemed to be remembering another time and place. Then her gaze swung back to Ruby as she shook her head softly. 'Brighton's been lucky up till now; those poor sods in London are getting it something rotten.'

Ruby agreed with Scarlett. 'God, it must be bad living there right now,' she said, feeling her chest tighten. Daily reports in the papers told of relentless night-time bombing raids with thousands dead and countless fires raging in the capital. The tube stations were crammed tight with people every night, in a desperate bid to stay safe.

Lifting the amethyst necklace from around her neck, Ruby tried to draw comfort from its smooth purple stone. When Scarlett had gifted it to her, she'd told her the necklace had come from India and suggested it had special powers.

This made Ruby want to laugh out loud until she saw how deadly serious Scarlett was, telling Ruby it might keep her safe in Brighton while the war was on. Ruby had bitten back the retort that everyone was saying this war would be over in a few short months.

Now, Scarlett's eyes fell on the necklace. 'It's supposed to be a flipping good luck charm,' she said, rolling her eyes at Ruby. 'Didn't help you much, though, did it?' she said, staring down at her hands sadly. 'If only I'd known when the explosion were going to happen…' She looked up at Ruby thoughtfully. 'Did you get my letter, Ruby?' she asked.

Numb tears pooled in Ruby's eyes, as a hard lump of blame formed inside. If only she'd taken more notice of that letter. 'I didn't tell Harriet about your premonition,' she admitted, staring at Scarlett with grief-filled eyes, and ignoring the voice in her head telling her Harriet would never have believed in such a prediction.

Scarlett looked a bit taken aback. 'Was it because you didn't believe me?' she said, lifting her eyebrows. 'Understandable, really. And it probably wouldn't have made any difference,' she said with a small shrug.

Ruby had to say what was in her heart. 'The thing is, Scarlett, you've never mentioned anything like this before,' she told her truthfully. 'How was I to know it wasn't just those old fears of yours resurfacing?'

Scarlett gave a soft shake of her head. 'The truth is, I've never told anyone before.' She stared into the middle distance as she spoke. 'The first time it happened, I was just a child,' she said sadly.

Ruby reached out towards her friend with her good arm. 'You don't need to explain it to me,' she reassured Scarlett, but at the same time she wanted to know all about this strange gift of second sight her friend now claimed to have.

Scarlett sighed and set her jaw. 'I think it's about time I told you, Ruby. Good grief, we've known each other a long time and you're my best friend.' Her smile wavered as she spoke.

'Losing everyone in that influenza pandemic was the start of it.' She bent her head and wiped a hand across her eyes, and then looked up at Ruby with a sigh. 'It was after my father returned from the war, that was when it began.'

'It must have been such a tough time for you, Scarlett.' Ruby's heart ached for her friend to have lost so much at such a young age. Her own childhood had not been happy, but the thought of what Scarlett had gone through as a child, was so much worse.

Scarlett frowned. 'There's no denying it were hard, but somehow it made me stronger, able to look at things differently. You have to remember, Ruby, it's a terrible tragedy poor Harriet's dead, but life goes on.'

Lifting her chin, Ruby felt a new determination to survive surge through her body. 'You're right,' she said, and then dropped her gaze. 'If only I could get rid of the awful nightmares,' she murmured, not really knowing how she was going to face normal life again.

Scarlett pressed her lips together and looked thoughtfully back at Ruby with that turquoise gaze. 'Well, I think you need to go away for a while, have a change of scene. It would do you good,' she said, tilting her blonde head from side to side.

Ruby's heart jolted. 'What! I can't do that. Anyway, where would I go?' She bit down on her lower lip and clutched at the sheet with her good hand. 'Although the very thought of working in Hanningtons store again…' her voice tailed off.

'Flaming hell, Ruby. I think you're trying to look too far ahead. Couldn't you do a few more hours at the pub instead?' Scarlett raised her brows at Ruby.

Ruby felt a flutter of hope in her chest. She had enjoyed working evenings in The Fortune of War these past months alongside Harriet. But could she do it without her work colleague?

'Hello, ladies, how are we today? Sorry, I couldn't help overhearing your conversation.'

They both looked up as Ella appeared by Ruby's bed and began adjusting the pillows and generally tidying, while looking furtively around for Matron. She paused in her work to regard Ruby. 'Jude, she's my daughter, is studying with The Royal College of Art, and it's been relocated to the Lake District for the duration of the war.'

Ruby couldn't help wondering where this conversation was going, or what it had to do with her, but she waited for Ella to get to the point.

Ella continued to busy herself with her usual routine of taking Ruby's blood pressure. 'Jude was unhappy about this at first, as Ambleside's quiet after the liveliness of London life,' she said, while writing on Ruby's chart. 'She's settling in now, though, but I just thought to myself,' she lifted her brows at Ruby, 'that maybe you could go and stay with her for a while?' She looked across at Scarlett for approval.

The other woman smiled back and then nodded encouragingly at Ruby. 'That sounds a flaming good idea. What do you think, Ruby?' she said enthusiastically. 'Could be just what you need, to get away from Brighton for a while.'

The flutter of hope was getting stronger as Ruby

glanced at Ella and then down at her arm still in plaster. 'Perhaps... but when could I go?' she said, feeling confused.

'As soon as you start to feel better, dear, which won't be long,' Ella replied. Then, with a swish of her skirts she was gone, off down the ward to attend to her other patients.

Chapter Five

It was a warm day and Jez Carlisle could feel the sweat dripping down his back as he worked to uproot Mrs Appleby's redundant tree. It was long past its sell-by date, and she had instructed him to end its life today and plant up a new younger tree.

Porcupine Tree's *Lazarus* rang out loud in his earphones, spurring him on in his work, and he couldn't help remembering the last time he had been here, in Mrs Appleby's garden.

Jez had watched as India McCarthy approached Ruby's house opposite, and his heart had turned over. Noah had told him his estranged daughter would inherit the house, so it wasn't a complete surprise. He'd told Noah about India moving into the house later that day, and Jez felt sure he would call round to see his daughter. However, this didn't happen, and Jez found it very puzzling.

When he'd met India the other day, he had been struck by how attractive she was; he had seen photos of Ruby in her younger days, and India looked just like her – the almost black hair, the same dark eyes. The likeness was so strong that when Jez first saw her, it had been hard not to stare. It had also been a bit of shock to see her wearing Ruby's necklace, considering past events and all the trouble that necklace had caused.

If India McCarthy decided to give him the job of landscaping Ruby's garden, Jez knew that meant he would be seeing a lot more of her. And while on one hand the thought pleased him, it also dismayed him at the same time.

During the long hours of the night his head had been full of India McCarthy. Telling her that he hadn't known Ruby had been an outright lie, but under the circumstances, what else could he do? Once India started digging deep into the past, it wouldn't be long before she discovered the truth, and there was no way he could let that happen.

Focusing on the job in hand, Jez continued with his work, lifting the tree out of the ground using all of his strength. After a moment, he stood up and stretched out his back, feeling much better.

He took a drink from his water bottle and stared at the bright-red tattoo of Daisy-Duke, his Ducati bike, on his forearm. He wasn't normally one for tattoos, and abhorred how people looked when they'd had too many done. But after he'd bought his precious bike, it had seemed fitting to have this done of her. The love of his life would now live forever on his arm.

How he wished he were on her today, riding fast and furious, feeling the sun on his bare arms, with the blue sky and scudding clouds overhead. The landscape would be whizzing past him at top speed, and he would feel as if he hadn't a care in the world.

Jez loved his work as a landscape gardener, though. He knew that any negative mood would dissipate as soon as he began work, a satisfaction he would never have found if he worked in an office all day. And he knew he had only one person to thank for that.

***

India was sitting in the kitchen planning where she would start with the renovations today, when her phone rang. 'Hi, Izzy,' she said brightly. 'How are you and the baby bump doing?'

'Jeez, India, I've been trying to get hold of you for days,' her friend answered reproachfully. 'We're both fine, thanks, although I'm feeling fatter by the day,' she added ruefully.

'Well, you are pregnant, so you should be getting bigger,' joked India. 'Sorry, when you rang the other day I was busy, and would've rung you back, but the local gardener called round.'

'Okay, I'll forgive you then. Do you need a gardener for your grandmother's house then?'

'He wasn't calling round to do my garden, but for access to next door,' India explained. 'But now you mention it, the garden is a total mess.'

'So, what was he like then? You know, in the looks department.'

India knew Izzy was always on the lookout for a love interest for her, mainly because she thought India's current boyfriend was no good.

She paused briefly before replying. She was tempted to say 'very attractive', but the only other thing she could think of to reply was, 'He had bike tattoos all over his arms.'

Izzy laughed heartily down the phone. 'That doesn't make him a bad man, India,' she said between giggles.

'Course not. I didn't say that.' India remembered how there was something about Jez Carlisle that unnerved her, the way he had stared at her grandmother's necklace with those penetrating eyes, for a start.

Then dismissing him and the jungle of a garden from her mind, she explained quickly about the contents of the handbag she'd found in Ruby's house, and what the letter had said about Noah keeping a valuable item safe for her.

'Gosh, that'll give you motivation for finding Noah, won't it?' Izzy said.

India wasn't so sure. 'Maybe... I could certainly do with the money. But looking into who this guy Reilly was might be an interesting diversion when I need a break from the renovations,' she said. 'Actually, Izzy, I wanted to ask for your help.'

'Yeah, anything. What do you need a hand with?'

'Thanks. I'm moving the rest of my things out of my flat at the weekend, and wondered if Dimitri could help. I don't want you doing anything, not in your condition obviously, but maybe he could drive the van I've hired?'

'I'm sure he won't mind. I'll ask him for you. But isn't Archie around to help? What's going on with you two at the moment?'

Ignoring the tightness in her chest, India got straight to the point. 'We've split up, Izzy... after I found him with someone else. Please don't say anything. If you do, I might just cry. I know it's for the best, but it still hurts.'

India thought about when she'd first met Archie, how the glamorous side of what he did had drawn her to him, along with his charming good looks. She'd been excited by the prospect of a boyfriend who was going places.

But looking back now, she realised he was nothing but an ageing, wannabe rock-star, with a lined face and over-tight trousers. She used to find that blond, shoulder-length hair and bright blue eyes attractive, but realised now that she was glad she'd found the courage to kick him into touch and end the relationship.

Izzy had gone quiet on the other end of the phone, and India could imagine her biting back the words 'I told you he was no good'. Instead, she said eventually, 'I know it hurts, and I'm sorry to hear you had to go through that, India, but you'll find someone else.'

India doubted she would ever find a decent man, instantly dismissing how attractive she found Jez Carlisle. All her relationships ended on the scrap heap, but she refrained from saying this to Izzy, who knew this only too well, having been friends with India since they were at school.

When they finished their call, India walked through to the kitchen and rummaged in her handbag, where she found the photograph she always kept in her purse.

Memories came flooding back of the day it had been taken. As Archie's smiling face and wide blue eyes were peering into the camera lens, he had one arm wrapped around her, and India looked happy. It had been several years ago, at the start of their relationship, on a day trip to Rye. The future had seemed bright and full of promise and they had been so in love, but that was before everything went horribly wrong.

She wiped away a tear as events came flooding back, and Archie's ultimate deception had been discovered when she had walked in on him and another woman in a compromising position.

Feeling heat flush through her body, India tore the photo in half then shoved its tiny pieces into the kitchen bin. It was good riddance to bad rubbish to Archie and those baby blue eyes of his, because moving on from that relationship was long overdue.

Chapter Six

December 1940

Ruby ran her fingers over the oval-shaped amethyst around her neck. The smoothness of the stone was comforting, and made her feel safe as she travelled towards Ambleside.

Glancing down at Scarlett's unopened letter, which had been delivered the day before, she remembered when her friend had first moved in next door to her parents' house in Lewes.

Ruby's mother had lost no time in voicing her opinion. 'That young hussy has no husband in sight,' she'd said loudly. 'She's never short of men visitors and too brazen by far, if you ask me,' she'd added through pursed lips.

Ruby had been fifteen years old at the time, and loved Scarlett on sight. She saw a different person to her mother. To her, Scarlett was a breath of fresh air, with her brightly coloured dresses, red lipstick, and defiant attitude – a sharp contrast to Ruby's sombre life, with her rigid and deeply religious parents.

Now as the train chugged along, with the landscape whizzing by, Ruby thought fondly of Scarlett and how her guidance had helped her change her life. Feeling impatient to read Scarlett's news, she ran her finger along the envelope seal, and drew out the stark white sheet of writing paper.

Dear Ruby,

I hope the rest and fresh country air in Ambleside will help you recover from your ordeal in Brighton. But I miss you already, especially as Eric is not visiting me very often.

I must tell you, though, about a funny thing which happened last week. A young man turned up on my doorstep, said his name was Frankie, and handed me a letter.

I read the letter quickly, with Frankie staring at me in a strange way. Turns out, it was from Eric. I asked Frankie why Eric hadn't posted it, as he would normally. Frankie got angry and barged his way into my house. Eric, he told me, thought the letter had been posted. But Frankie had seen it on the hall table, and decided to deliver it by hand instead, wanting to see what his father's whore looked like!

Heated words followed, and I told him to leave. Hopefully, that's the last I'll see of him, but I'll need to warn Eric that his son knows about us next time I see him.

I thought about Eric once Frankie had gone. He explained to me recently how things had been very unsettled for him since the outbreak of war. Work's slowed down at the shipyard, since President Roosevelt put in place the building of the liberty ships. Of course, this is much needed for our country, to replace the ships lost in battle. But it also means Eric's shipyard is coming to a standstill.

To alleviate my loneliness and help the war effort,

*I'm going to volunteer as an ARP warden soon.
Hopefully, this means we'll see more of each other,
once you are home, as I'll be living in Brighton.*

Keep safe, and write soon my friend,

Scarlett x

Ruby put down the letter and thought about Scarlett. It sounded as if Eric's son might make things difficult for her, but Ruby was sure Scarlett would be able to deal with the situation in her usual capable, calm manner.

A while later, Ruby glanced out of the window to see the train pulling into Ambleside station. With her arm still quite sore, she found it difficult to carry her suitcase off the train, and was relieved when a gentleman passenger, who had been in the same carriage, helped her onto the platform. He also informed a porter she needed help, and the young man carried her case to the ticket barrier.

As Ruby filtered with the other passengers towards the barrier, a woman a few feet ahead caught her attention. Her dark curls were bouncing around her head as she chatted to her companion, and Ruby thought how very like Harriet she looked.

Pushing past people towards the disappearing woman, Ruby ignored the pain in her arm and the porter shouting at her to stop. Her thoughts were in turmoil; she knew this woman wasn't Harriet, but something inside was telling her that just this once she had to make sure.

With only one thought in mind, to reach the woman before she disappeared, Ruby was hardly aware of calling Harriet's name. Finally catching up with her, Ruby stopped and caught hold of the woman's sleeve.

'Excuse me…' she began, but the words died on her lips as the woman turned towards her.

'Can I help you?' the woman said, pulling her coat out of Ruby's fingers where they had been gripping it tightly, and giving her a strange look.

It was only then Ruby was jolted to her senses. 'I'm so sorry,' she said, as tears pooled in her eyes. 'It's just… I thought you were someone else.'

The woman shrugged and quickly headed into the crowd, leaving Ruby bereft. *What was the matter with her? How could she have thought that person was Harriet?* Taking a deep shuddering breath, she fought the feeling of panic threatening to engulf her.

'Miss, are you alright?' It was the young porter, now standing next to her and peering anxiously into her face. Ruby nodded numbly and let him lead her through the ticket barrier towards a bench.

Sinking down onto the bench, Ruby tipped the porter and watched him disappear into the crowd. Even though she was calmer now, she was aware of being alone in this unfamiliar place. Wrapping her woollen scarf closer around her neck against the bitter cold, she watched people going about their business. She preferred not to think what would happen if no-one came to meet her and she was left here alone.

Searching for something to do to take her mind off her worries, Ruby looked around noticing a poster on the wall behind her. Bold letters were emblazoned across it. 'Don't do it, Mother! Leave the children where they are,' it said.

The poster showed a mother with her children, sitting by a tree, with Hitler appearing as a ghostly figure behind her. Ruby shivered even though she had seen this billboard before. Over a million children had been evacuated in the first year of the war, but as no bombing had occurred, they had soon been returned to their families. The government was currently using this poster to encourage parents to keep their children out of London.

Ruby stared at the poster, thinking about all those poor mothers having to say goodbye to their children, when there was a tap on her shoulder.

'Hello there. Do you happen to be Ruby Summers, by any chance?'

Ruby looked up into a familiar-looking face and nodded at the young woman who must be Jude. She looked exactly like a younger version of Ella, her appearance only differing from her mother's in a sprinkling of freckles across her nose.

'Oh goodie, welcome to Ambleside then. I'm Jude by the way,' the girl said warmly, sticking out her hand to Ruby and tilting her head to the side. 'Walk this way. I have a car waiting to take us home,' she added enthusiastically.

Feeling rather shaky but much relieved that Jude was here at last, Ruby stood up. 'Pleased to meet you, Jude,' she said, her spirits lifting at such a warm greeting. 'Has anyone ever told you that you look like your mother?'

Jude laughed and her fair hair swung around her face. 'I'm always getting told that,' she said, while looking around for Ruby's suitcase. 'Are you all right? How was the journey? It's such a long way, isn't it?' she gushed.

Locating Ruby's suitcase, Jude picked it up and led the way swiftly towards a parked car. 'Sorry if I'm a bit late. Mother will kill me if I don't look after you,' she continued breathlessly, as she paused to let Ruby catch up.

Jude was asking so many questions all at once that Ruby felt a bit dizzy. 'I'm good, thanks,' she returned, thinking it might be best not to mention the incident on the platform.

Jude suddenly stopped and stared solemnly at Ruby's right arm. 'Oh gosh, you poor thing, did you injure that in the blasted bomb blast?'

Ruby was warming to Jude already, and she explained briefly about her injuries, pleased that her hair covered the deep red scar on her forehead.

Jude stopped alongside a black Austin and began waving to someone. 'Reilly, over here!' she shouted to a young man, who was standing nearby, chatting to a porter.

Reilly lifted his head and began striding towards them, and Jude looked from him to Ruby as he reached them. 'Ruby, this is Reilly Brownlow, he's our lovely chauffeur for today,' she explained, giving a mock bow.

Ruby thought 'lovely' was the right word, and became very aware of her own heartbeat as she shook Reilly's outstretched hand and took in his appearance. He was mixed race, tall and muscular, and as she looked into his large ebony eyes, her face flushed.

Somehow, she managed to find her voice. 'Good afternoon, Reilly, how are you today?' she said, trying to calm her racing heart.

Reilly's generous mouth curved into a smile. 'You alright, Miss Summers? I'm sound, thanks,' he replied. 'Your carriage is waiting,' he said, pointing towards the car, before lifting her case into the boot.

Jude opened the passenger door wide for Ruby.

'You sit in the front seat,' she instructed. 'There's a better view of the countryside there,' she explained, before climbing into the back seat.

When they were all settled, Reilly drove out into the traffic. Ruby couldn't help wondering who he was to Jude, feeling grateful the girl hadn't noticed her discomfort around him. With his honey-coloured skin and wide dark eyes, Ruby found it difficult not to stare at Reilly's profile as the miles sped by. She had never in all her life seen such a beautiful looking man.

'I hope you have a good stay in Ambleside, it's nice 'ere, Miss Summers,' he said, interrupting her thoughts. 'It's been me home for years.'

'Please, call me Ruby,' she replied, thinking it was unlikely he was a student if he'd lived in Ambleside a while. 'How far is the village from here?' She wasn't looking forward to another long journey, after sitting for so long on the train, but being next to this gorgeous man made it a whole lot easier.

'Not too far, only 'bout four miles up the road,' Reilly said, his beautiful eyes focussed on the road ahead.

Jude leaned her elbows against the back of Ruby's seat. 'I agree with Reilly, it's a nice part of the country,' she said eagerly.

Ruby was pleased to hear this glowing report of Ambleside, and found herself relaxing with the motion of the car. Focusing on the landscape, she watched miles of picturesque countryside pass by, while Jude pointed out various landmarks along the way.

'That's Lake Windermere,' Jude told her as they passed a beautiful stretch of very blue water to Ruby's left. 'It's England's largest lake, and there's also a small town named Windermere close by. Do you like walking, Ruby?'

Ruby thought about that question carefully. 'I've always lived in towns, so walking miles has never been something I've done in the past,' she said, turning towards Jude, who was now resting against the back seat, looking rather sleepy. 'But I expect there's some lovely walks around here,' she added.

'Ambleside is a sound place for a fell walk,' Reilly told her. 'I love walking in my spare time. I'd be happy to show you around the countryside,' he said, glancing across at Ruby and lifting those fine eyebrows.

'Thank you,' she said, feeling her face flush under his gaze. As he turned his attention back to driving, Ruby wanted to ask Reilly what he did in Ambleside. Jude had called him the chauffeur so maybe that's what he did, chauffeured people around for a living. Realising that Jude had gone very quiet, Ruby turned around to see the girl had fallen fast asleep.

'Has she nodded off?' Reilly asked, and when Ruby confirmed this, he smiled. 'Not surprising that she's not too sound,' he said. 'I heard she wore herself out until the small hours at a dance last night.'

Ruby could hear the amusement in his voice, and realised that if Jude had been at a dance alone, then these two were unlikely to be courting.

'What's that you're saying about me?' Jude's sleepy voice interrupted their conversation, and she sat up, yawned, and then leaned towards Ruby.

'Reilly was just telling me how you danced the night away last night,' Ruby said in a teasing tone, glancing back at Jude.

'No denying that. I love it. Do you like dancing, Ruby?' she asked.

Ruby tried not to remember Harriet, who had

loved dancing, and the times they had gone to dances together when Ruby had first moved to Brighton.

'I love it, too,' she said truthfully. *Or I used to*, she thought to herself, turning back to look at the landscape.

'You must come with me next time then,' Jude said. 'They're held in the village hall and there's one tomorrow night, as it's New Year's Eve. Will you come, Ruby?'

She wasn't sure she would ever enjoy dancing again, as it would remind her too much of Harriet, but she was aware that Jude was only trying to be helpful and she sounded so enthusiastic that Ruby said she would.

'This is the village of Ambleside,' Reilly announced as he drove the car through the small, quiet high street.

They passed quaint buildings and bright, inviting shops, and Ruby was relieved to see the absence of broken glass and rubble; so unlike Brighton these days. It was lovely not to see any boarded-up windows in the pretty Victorian properties, and she relaxed in the knowledge she had made the right decision to visit the Lake District, after all.

Chapter Seven

The sound of someone banging loudly on the front door jolted India out of her half sleep. She'd been dozing on the leather sofa in the front room, with Beans curled up in a round ball on her lap.

It seemed as if it had only been a few short minutes since she'd sat down with a much-needed cup of tea. The drink was stone cold on the coffee table by her side now, and glancing at her watch, India noticed that a whole hour had passed since Dimitri and Izzy had left.

She rubbed at her eyes as she glanced around the empty room. She'd hardly slept at all the night before. In the pitch darkness, she'd lain awake grieving for Archie and what could have been. The hot tears had fallen for the end of yet another romance, and the early hours of the morning brought India to wondering why her relationships with men never lasted.

Izzy frequently told India she picked the wrong men. 'You always choose the ones who can't commit,' she'd said in earnest. 'Maybe you feel you don't deserve commitment?' India had dismissed the comment as ridiculous, but now she wasn't so sure.

When India had eventually fallen asleep, the familiar dream had come back to haunt her. The theme was always the same: she was searching for something elusive, something she could never find. Finally, she woke up in a cold sweat, her head thumping, and her limbs feeling as heavy as lead.

Now, India quickly got up to answer the door, dislodging Beans, who displayed his displeasure by meowing loudly and arching his back at her. Ignoring her feline friend's protests, she quickly negotiated her way around the unpacked cases and boxes strewn across the room.

A woman stood in the doorway in a polo shirt with 'Carlisle Landscaping' emblazoned on it, and wearing Dr Marten boots. India recognised her as Jez Carlisle's colleague.

'Hi there,' said the woman. 'I'm Teagan, and I live in the cottage next door.' She was holding a large, round cake tin, and had a warm smile on her face. 'I baked you a cake as a moving-in present,' she said, leaning forwards and regarding India. 'I 'ope you like cake,' she added.

India's head felt muzzy from her nap and inwardly she cursed Teagan for disturbing her peace. But outwardly she returned her neighbour's smile.

'Hello, Teagan, pleased to meet you,' she said with as much enthusiasm as she could muster.

The girl grinned widely, immediately transforming her masculine features, giving her a kindly look and softening her square jaw.

'That's very nice of you,' India went on. 'Would you like a cup of tea to go with the cake?'

Teagan nodded eagerly, and wasted no time in stepping into the hallway.

'Err, excuse the mess.' India was suddenly aware of the unpacked boxes everywhere, as they walked through to the kitchen. 'My friends helped me move the rest of my things in today,' she explained, while trying to dislodge the woolliness the nap had left in her head.

Despite her bad night, the day had started out well, with Dimitri collecting the rest of her belongings in his van and delivering them safely to Ruby's house. At Izzy's insistence, she hadn't even needed to go to the flat herself.

Teagan made herself comfortable on a kitchen chair and placed the cake tin on the table. 'Nice friends you 'ave,' she said, while glancing around the room. 'What'd you think of the 'ouse then? I've always thought it's got a strange name.'

India leaned on the worktop and regarded her visitor, who seemed to be bombarding her with questions all at once. 'The house will be much better once the renovations are done,' she said. 'Apparently *Taabeez* means amulet in Hindi.'

Teagan shrugged as if this didn't explain anything about the odd name, which India supposed it didn't.

As she waited for the kettle to boil, and located cups, India couldn't help reflecting that she would never have asked a stranger, neighbour or not, into her house for tea back in London. But then she'd rarely seen her neighbours in Hackney, despite living in her ground floor flat for five whole years.

As she poured the tea, she became aware that Teagan had gone very quiet. She placed the cups and cake on the table, and looked up at her neighbour, who was studying the portrait of Ruby as a young woman, hanging on the wall.

India had liked the painting as soon as she saw it. It was soft around the edges and there was a kind of a luminous glow to it, as if the artist had been deeply in love with their subject.

'She was a beauty, wasn't she?' India said to her visitor, who seemed lost in thought.

Teagan looked back at India, and her face broke into a grin. 'Yeah, she sure was a lovely lady,' she said, before biting into her cake and taking a large slurp of tea.

'So… how long have you lived in Isfield, Teagan?' India sat down at the table. 'Did you know Ruby very well?'

'Oh yeah, I knew her,' Teagan rolled her eyes skywards, then looked back at India. 'I've lived 'ere a whole year now.'

India longed to ask Teagan questions about Ruby, now that it was established she knew her grandmother. 'Do you have family in Isfield?' she asked.

'Only my sister Skye, who lives over on the council estate,' Teagan stared back with a sad look on her face. 'She's why I came to live 'ere. Skye was recently diagnosed with a rare form of cancer.'

'Oh dear, that's awful,' India sympathised. 'I'm sorry to hear that. How is Skye getting on?'

Teagan pulled her lips together and frowned. 'She's doing alright, to be honest. She's 'ad all the treatment available and is slowly getting better.'

India tried to think of something comforting to say to Teagan, who was looking quite downcast. 'I'm sure she'll be fine with you helping out,' she said, knowing she would be devastated if Izzy – the closest she had to a sister –were going through something similar. 'Skye is very lucky to have a sister like you,' she added, leaning towards the girl, and placing a hand gently on her arm.

'Thanks, that's kind of you to say so.' Teagan dipped her head and sniffed, then pulled out a tissue from her pocket and dabbed at her eyes. 'I hope you don't mind me asking, but I'd rather you didn't tell anyone about Skye and her illness,' she said, lifting her head and giving India a watery smile. 'I don't normally talk about her to anyone. It's just too hard.'

India was quickly warming to her new neighbour. 'I don't mind at all, and I can understand that completely. But if there's anything I can do, let me know.'

Teagan thanked her for the offer and, as she stood up to go, hesitated by the door. 'Is Carlisle Landscaping doing the garden work for you?' she asked, looking back at India. 'There sure is a mountain of work to do out there,' she added.

'Yeah, if the quote is right, I'll be happy to go with them. I've got Jez coming around to have a look tomorrow afternoon,' she said, trying to ignore the racing of her heart at the mention of the handsome gardener.

'Great news. I 'ope we can help you,' she said. Suddenly Teagan's expression changed, and she looked as if she had the weight of the world on her shoulders again.

'What is it?' India frowned as she watched Teagan biting on a short fingernail and looking a bit uneasy.

The girl sighed heavily. 'I probably shouldn't be telling you this,' she said, 'but Carlisle Landscaping is struggling a bit at the moment, so any work that comes our way is badly needed. Not that I want to influence your decision in any way.'

'Oh dear, that's not good.' India immediately thought about Skye and how hard it might be for them if Teagan lost her job. And as she saw her neighbour out, she vowed to give the garden work to Carlisle Landscaping whatever the price.

Chapter Eight

It was the first day of 1941, and the mood amongst the students that morning was sombre. The talk had focussed on the terrible bombing raids on the city of London three days earlier.

There had been an unofficial two-day lull on the night raids, but when the bombing resumed, it was dubbed the second great fire of London. On the twenty-ninth of December 1940, over three hundred incendiaries were dropped around St Paul's Cathedral, described in the newspapers as 'like apples falling from a tree'.

On arrival in Ambleside, Ruby had been made welcome by Jude's artist friends, and had been told that all the students were housed in two hotels: The Salutation for the women; and The Queen's for the men. Luckily, there were a few spare rooms in The Salutation, enabling Ruby to rent somewhere for the duration of her stay.

The Queen's Hotel had plenty of rooms free, due to many of the young men from the college joining up by their nineteenth year. Jude had explained to Ruby how heart-breaking it had been to see the men leaving their art behind to face an uncertain future. And if word came back that one of them had died, bleakness descended on the group for weeks on end.

This morning, the art students were working

inside a barn in the grounds of Ambleside Manor. It was a freezing cold morning, with the only warmth coming from a small paraffin heater in the corner of the shed. Fascinated by their talent, Ruby had watched their pictures develop under the watchful eye of the tutors.

Now, they all looked up as the door opened and Reilly walked in, his cheerful face immediately brightening up the atmosphere in the barn. 'All right, everyone?' he greeted them all, his generous mouth curved into a wide smile.

Ruby's heart skipped a beat as she took in his tall, broad frame, which seemed to fill the tiny space. She tried hard to hide how she was feeling but it wasn't proving easy. Her fingers tingled remembering the vivid dream she'd had the night before, which featured Reilly, bringing a flush to her skin as he glanced in her direction.

Shifting to a more comfortable position on the bale of hay, Ruby sat beside Jude who was working on her half-filled canvas. For once, Jude's constant chatter was silenced by the concentration needed to portray in oils, the portly man dressed in a Home Guard uniform, who was standing in the middle of the barn.

The two young women had quickly become friends since Ruby's arrival in Ambleside, and it hadn't taken Jude long to notice the spark between Ruby and Reilly.

'Reilly's never far away from the artists,' she had told Ruby, even though Ruby hadn't asked after Jude's handsome friend. 'Whenever he's not working, he usually finds the time to visit us in the barn, or most evenings he's to be found in the local pub, The Golden Rule. He's not courting anyone,' she'd added with a knowing look.

And although Ruby had tried to deny any interest in Reilly, Jude had just cocked her head and laughed.

'Reilly works the land and looks after the livestock for Lord Henry Fairfield, the owner of the Manor,' Jude had explained when Ruby asked what he did for a living. 'It was Reilly who persuaded Lord Henry to allow the art students to use the redundant barn for their painting studies.'

Ruby couldn't deny the attraction burning in the depths of Reilly's dark limpid eyes whenever he glanced her way. But she held back, waiting for him to confirm her suspicions, afraid she had been mistaken somehow. The sound of Jude's voice addressing Reilly jolted her out of her daydream.

'You should have a go at painting,' she remarked to Reilly, who was studying a portrait in progress. And then addressing Ruby, Jude added, 'Reilly is a good artist, you know.'

Reilly straightened his back and looked across at Jude. 'What! I'm not a good artist. Even if I were, some of us 'ave to earn a living,' he said good-humouredly.

Ruby caught his eye and nodded her understanding. How she envied these young people, who were carefree and enjoying their craft without the burden of having to work.

Here in Ambleside, it seemed they were protected from the war, with no visible sign of it here in this idyllic place. For a moment Ruby and Reilly gazed across the room at each other, then she remembered herself and dropped her gaze. She could drown in those beautiful, brown eyes.

***

Whenever she was nearby, Reilly could feel himself being drawn to Ruby like a moth to a flame, and trying not to stare at her often proved fruitless.

As she chatted amicably with Jude, he took a moment to study her profile, taking in the aquiline nose and full red lips. He could hardly fail to notice the way Ruby looked at him since she had arrived in Ambleside. The soft pool of desire was evident in her brown eyes, but part of him drew back, unsure she would have time for the likes of him.

He'd heard from Jude what had happened to her in Brighton, and his heart went out to her. Losing her friend in the explosion must have been devastating, and it was obvious she was putting a brave face on things. However, he could see the pain in those intense dark eyes.

Now, as he approached the two women, Reilly was bolstered by the welcoming expression on Ruby's face. He was feeling nervous about speaking to her but determined to overcome this obstacle today.

'Alright, Ruby? How's Ambleside been for you so far?' he asked. 'Not missing yer home too much?'

Ruby turned to look at him. 'Good so far, thank you, Reilly,' she said. 'My room at the hotel is perfect, and I've found everyone very friendly.'

He nodded, feeling strangely tongue-tied. The conversation buzzed around them, about clothes rationing, and how British and Australian troops had captured Tobruk, while he racked his brains for something to say.

'Is our friend Jude expecting you to take part in this class as well?' he asked, pointing to the canvas and the piece of charcoal Ruby was holding in her hand.

Ruby smiled and looked at Jude. 'Oh yes, she likes

everyone to have a go,' she replied jovially. 'Not that I can draw or paint anything; you can blame it on my sore right arm.'

Reilly returned her smile then glanced quickly at his watch. 'I have a few minutes to spare and could show you how, if you like?' he offered, ignoring his racing heart and the warning in his head that he should be back to work by now.

Ruby looked a bit taken aback but her eyes shone. 'That would be nice, thank you,' she told him.

Taking the canvas from Ruby's hand, Reilly sat self-consciously down beside her, striving to ignore her intoxicating scent. Then, steadying his hand, he began to draw her beautiful face with the charcoal.

Despite being in such close proximity to Ruby, Reilly worked quickly, and soon became absorbed in his work. After a while, having finished the basic outline, he stopped working and once again glanced down at his watch.

'I really have to go now,' he said, showing her the sketch. 'It's not very good, but I would love to finish yer portrait another time,' he added enthusiastically.

Ruby studied the half-finished drawing. 'Not very good? I think you're being very modest, and Jude was right, you're very talented, Reilly.' She looked up and held his gaze, and he saw that she meant what she said.

She was looking at him so intently that Reilly's cheeks flushed. 'Thanks,' he murmured, and the look that passed between them told him all he needed to know. Ruby Summers felt the attraction between them, exactly the same way he did.

Retrieving the canvas from Ruby, Reilly tucked it under his arm, then he leant towards her, feeling his heart miss a beat.

'Hopefully we'll see each other tonight in The Golden Rule?' he said, lowering his voice, and his reward for this brave invitation was an alluring smile from his heart's desire.

Chapter Nine

The next day Jez Carlisle appeared on India's doorstep, and she felt her pulse quicken at the sight of him.

'Good morning, India,' he said, regarding her with that turquoise gaze. 'How're you doing today?'

'Morning, Jez,' she said as cheerfully as possible. 'I'm fine, thanks,' she returned, but in truth India was feeling a little bit off-balance.

The postman had just delivered her a small parcel – a jiffy bag with her name and address written in her mother's spidery writing. When she heard the doorbell, India had quickly stuffed the bag away in a drawer, unable to face the thought of reading her father's long-lost letters.

'Shall we crack on then?' Jez said as she hesitated on the doorstep, before turning around and heading into the garden, clipboard in hand.

India pushed the letters out of her mind and caught up with him on the pathway, where he was staring at the long grass.

'Right, let's see,' he said. 'This'll all look fine once we've tidied things up a bit.' He scribbled something on his notepad and looked over his shoulder. 'Front gate is good and only needs a little repair here and there.'

India squinted into the bright sunlight of the

morning, still feeling a bit odd. 'Okay,' she said, trying to look everywhere but at Jez's tight t-shirt, which was stretched across his arm muscles, and doing a good job of taking her mind off her father's letters.

A short while later, Jez had highlighted a tree that needed cutting down, as it was currently blocking light into the house, and an overgrown hedge to the left of the house, which needed pruning. And that was just the front garden!

India felt exhausted just thinking about all the work involved, and dreaded what the quote would be. But she knew the garden needed to be sorted before she could think about selling the house on. Leading Jez through the side gate into the equally overgrown back garden, India was still acutely aware of his close proximity.

The grass here was even longer as she waded through the undergrowth. Suddenly she tripped over a hidden tree root, and before she knew what was happening, she was lying in a heap on the ground, flat on her back.

'Bloody hell!' India said, embarrassed at how she must look with her arms and legs everywhere in amongst the weeds. Struggling to stand up in a dignified manner, she watched Jez hold out his hand to help her up.

'Oh dear, are you alright?' His wide brow wrinkled in concern as his large body towered over her.

'I'll survive,' she said, trying to salvage her pride. Taking hold of his outstretched hand, she felt a shiver run up her arm, but he quickly propelled her upright, as if she weighed nothing more than a bag of sugar.

Feeling hot and bothered – and not just from the fall – India brushed herself down. She could feel his eyes on her again and she looked up to see him smiling kindly. Then as if he realised he was staring openly at her, Jez quickly dropped his gaze and turned back to the task in hand.

'Probably best to cut the grass down first, then draw up a plan of how you want the garden after that,' he told her formally.

'Sounds like a good idea,' India agreed, and couldn't help thinking she'd never been quite so attracted to a man in this way before.

'I'd suggest decking near the back door for a seated area in the summer,' Jez continued. 'Maybe some borders running around the outside of the garden, too.' He glanced across at the right-hand corner of the garden. 'Do you want that arbour left?'

India stared at the dilapidated seat of the arbour and the roof where the wooden slats were hanging off. 'I think so. Is it salvageable?'

'I'd need to have a closer look at it, but from here it looks sturdy enough, just a case of repairing the structure,' he said thoughtfully.

India felt as if she needed to defend Ruby for letting the garden get into such a poor state, but decided not to mention her after remembering the look Jez had given her last time she made a remark about her grandmother.

She waited patiently for Jez to look up from his scribbling. The sun was burning hot on her head, and she wondered about offering him a cold drink. He surprised her, however, with his next question.

'So, where've you moved from, India?' Jez offered her a questioning gaze as he widened his eyes at her.

His words seemed at odds with the expression on his face, which seemed to tell her he was feeling the spark between them just as she was. But she felt there was something else; something he wasn't saying. 'Hackney,' she replied, when she found her voice.

Jez hesitated for a moment as if her answer had caught him off-guard, and then he nodded thoughtfully. 'You'll find it very different here then,' he observed. And again, she had the feeling he was saying one thing and meaning another.

'Well, I'm very adaptable,' she told him a little defensively, and even though she had no need to, she added, 'My stay in Isfield will only be until the renovations on Ruby's house are complete.'

Jez nodded at her and then straightened his shoulders. 'I'll get a quote out for you in the next couple of days, and I'm sure we'll be able to slot you in very soon if you want to go ahead.'

I'm sure you could, thought India, *after what Teagan had revealed*. However, she just nodded and watched as Jez drove off into the distance with a wave of his hand.

India walked back indoors to resume her unpacking and make a much needed iced-tea, feeling thoroughly unsettled by Jez Carlisle.

Chapter Ten

January 1941

The upbeat sound of Glenn Miller's *Chattanooga Choo Choo* rang through the air as Reilly pushed open the double doors of the village hall. He was a little later than he had intended, as he'd been sprucing himself up for Ruby, putting on his one good suit and slicking his hair with Brylcreem.

Stepping into the hall, Reilly stopped to soak up the carefree atmosphere. The lights were dimmed and people were gathered on the dance floor, dancing to the four-piece band.

As the song came to an end and everyone drifted back to their seats, he scanned the room for Ruby. In the low light, it was hard to see exactly where she was. However, he soon spotted Jude in a small crowd on the edge of the dance floor, and tapped her lightly on the shoulder.

'Reilly!' she said, turning towards him. Taking him by the shoulders, she looked him up and down. 'My, you do look nice. Come and join us, you know everyone here.'

The band started playing again and Reilly wanted to ask where Ruby was, but the music was so loud that he gave up trying to make himself heard as he stepped in amongst the huddle of people.

Jude noticed him glancing around and she indicated towards the ladies' room. He thanked her and attempted to make conversation with someone next to him, but a moment later he could smell a familiar scent nearby and knew whose it was.

He turned to see Ruby standing next to him, looking splendid. She was wearing an emerald green dress studded with beads, which hugged her hourglass figure, and a stunning purple necklace. Reilly's pulse raced at the sight of her.

'Good evening, Reilly,' she greeted him, a smile twitching at the corner of her lips.

Reilly was finding it hard to tear his gaze away from her face, and a strange feeling stirred in his chest. 'All right, Ruby?' he managed. In that moment, he knew this woman was special, and Reilly wanted her more than anything else in the whole world.

Ruby's cheeks were flushed and her eyes bright. And, Lord, the sight of her was making his knees go weak. He leaned forward and whispered in her ear, 'You're looking gorgeous tonight,' and was rewarded with a dazzling smile.

As *The Way You Look Tonight* began playing, Reilly held out his hand to her. Then Ruby was in his arms and they were swaying to the music, which seemed to be playing just for them. The feel of her warm body in such close proximity to his, along with her exotic scent, was making desire race through his veins.

It was as if everything was simple while he was around this woman, and the world was in its rightful place. It was quite a heady feeling, and one that Reilly had never experienced before.

As the dance finally came to an end, Reilly was reluctant to let Ruby go, so they danced on. Eventually the band stopped playing and went for a break, which forced them to release each other.

Ruby sat down with the others while Reilly headed towards the bar. But on the way there, he trod on something hard on the floor. Bending down to locate the offending object, he saw it was Ruby's necklace; it must have fallen off while they were dancing.

Without waiting to be served, he walked back to where she was sitting. 'I think this is yours,' he said, holding out the necklace. 'Sorry. I really hope I haven't damaged it. I trod on it on the dance floor, you see,' he told her apologetically.

Ruby looked startled and her hand flew to her bare neck. 'Oh dear, thank you so much, that necklace is very precious to me,' she said, as she inspected it. 'It's fine. It's not damaged,' she told him after a moment, and smiled up at him.

Reilly offered to do up the clasp for her, and as she turned around for him to do this, he couldn't help wondering who had given her such a beautiful piece of jewellery.

Ruby seemed to read his thoughts. 'A dear friend of mine gave me this necklace,' she said, lifting her brows. 'Her name's Scarlett.'

Feelings of recklessness ran through Reilly's body. 'Ruby… would you… I mean, do you want to go for a walk? Get a bit o' fresh air?' he asked. He desperately wanted to get to know her better, but knew it would be impossible to talk properly inside the dance hall.

Ruby's eyes were shining as she nodded at him, and Reilly tried to ignore the excitement mounting inside him.

With this beautiful woman by his side, he felt happy and could ignore everything else happening in the world. *This was the here and now,* he told himself, *what lay ahead would have to take care of itself.* His heart raced as Ruby slipped her arm through his, and together they made their way to the door and stepped out into the cold starlit night.

Chapter Eleven

India stopped work and straightened her back. With great satisfaction, she glanced up at the newly stripped wall and the redundant coving lying on the floor of the drawing room. In the background, Take That blared out from her iPod – a sound which never failed to spur her on in her work.

She had slept well the night before and, despite it only being nine o'clock, she had already done a good few hours' work. Jez Carlisle was due to start work on the garden today, after she'd accepted what she felt was a very reasonable quote.

Thinking about the garden and how much work needed doing, had made her want to buy some flowers to add colour to the house. As soon as they were open, she had gone along to the Isfield Farm shop just up the road, and purchased a beautiful bunch of flowers, full of orange and red dahlias, dotted with a few large sunflowers. They were still sitting in the sink, ready to go into the crystal vase, as soon as she finished working on the wall.

She was just about to make a cup of tea when the doorbell rang.

'Good morning,' she said to Jez, who was standing on her doorstep looking as gorgeous as ever.

He returned her greeting then, glancing around

the garden, went on, 'Before we begin, I was going to suggest we repair the arbour first, then there'll be somewhere nice to sit even when the rest of the garden is in disarray.'

'Good plan,' she agreed, berating herself for noticing his attractiveness again.

'I think that's everything I need to tell you,' he said. 'Teagan will be arriving this morning to begin cutting down the long grass, then she'll do the arbour. And I'm off to another job today.' Jez placed a pencil behind his ear and bid her goodbye.

Soon after Jez had gone, Teagan appeared at the door, looking in much better spirits than the last time India had seen her. She declined the offer of a cup of tea and made her way to the back garden, tools in hand, while India went back to work removing the old skirting board from the drawing room wall.

By early afternoon India needed a break. Before making a drink and a sandwich, she remembered the flowers still waiting to be put in water. But when she went to the kitchen cupboard where she'd placed the vase on the day she'd arrived in Ruby's house, she was surprised to find it wasn't there.

A thorough search of the house ensued, and India eventually found the vase in the front parlour in a small sideboard. It was a mystery how it ended up there, as she was sure she'd put it in the kitchen cupboard on that first day.

Putting it down to absentmindedness, India placed the flowers in the vase, admiring the splash of colour they brought, then went out into the garden to get some fresh air.

'Are you sure you wouldn't like a cold drink now?' she called to Teagan, who was busily hacking away at the long grass.

The girl stopped and leaned on her scythe. 'Orange squash would be cool, India, thanks,' she said. 'What do you think of your arbour now?' She pointed to the newly repaired garden bench with a grin.

'It looks great, Teagan. You've done a good job, and the roof looks much better. I'll give it a go in a minute.'

When India returned with tea for her and orange squash for Teagan, she handed out the drinks then sat down on the arbour. 'Feels sturdy enough,' she said, moving up and down on the wooden slats. 'There's a nice bit of shade under that roof now, too.'

Teagan gulped her orange squash thirstily. 'How're you getting on with the house today?' she asked, wiping the back of her hand across her mouth.

India explained what she'd been doing in the drawing room, then asked after Skye's wellbeing, but immediately Teagan's expression changed and her good mood vanished.

'She's okay, thanks,' Teagan replied morosely, her gaze straying in the direction of the council estate down the road.

India was immediately sorry for her insensitivity, although she wasn't sure what she'd said wrong. 'Maybe it would do her good to get out of the house occasionally?' she suggested.

Teagan gazed at India and nodded, but looked uncertain. 'Skye is not really well enough for that yet,' she replied. 'But thanks for the suggestion.'

India watched Teagan put down her empty glass. Her shoulders were slumped and it was obvious that she didn't want to discuss her sister any further.

'Did you see much of my grandmother before she died?' India asked, eager to change the conversation to safer ground.

Teagan looked up from where she'd been staring at the long grass. 'Yep, I did see her here and there. She was such a nice ol' lady. A bit lonely at times, though.'

India was pleased to see Teagan's mood had improved, but the comment about Ruby being lonely made her feel uncomfortable. 'I would've visited her if she had wanted me to,' she said wistfully, a picture of her grandmother spending her final days alone in this big house spinning in her head.

'Yeah, shame she didn't have no visitors.' Teagan cocked her head to one side and then added, 'Except her son who came occasionally.'

India's heart lurched at the thought of her father being in this house. 'That would have been my dad. When did he last visit Ruby, do you know?' The realisation that Teagan had seen her father coming and going, made her feel a mixture of excitement and dread.

Teagan squinted in the sunlight and thought for a moment. 'I saw him… let's see, it's July now, I reckon it was the end of last year. That's right, it must 'ave been December, 'cause he bought Ruby a Christmas present.'

India tried to still her racing heart at the thought that only seven months ago her father had been right here in this house. 'Teagan… I know this may seem like a strange question, but… what did he look like?' She held her breath and waited for the girl's reply.

When Teagan gave her a questioning gaze, India felt she had to explain the reason for her question. But she couldn't keep the sadness from her voice as she felt her throat tighten. 'It's been such a long time since I've seen him, you see. Thirty years.' It was strange how her feelings were changing; at first, she hadn't wanted anything to do with Noah, but now she was desperate to know anything about him.

'Oh, I see what you mean.' Teagan shrugged, and looked as if she were thinking hard. 'I'd say, just a regular old guy, with lines and grey hair. You know what I mean?'

India looked down at her teacup and mulled over Teagan's words. Grey hair? Teagan said her father now had grey hair. Of course, he would have, but all India's memories of him were of a tall, good-looking, black-haired man. She swallowed and took in a long slow breath, aware of Teagan's eyes on her.

'It must be hard for you,' Teagan said, giving her an understanding nod. 'Ruby used to confide in me sometimes,' she added. 'She told me lots of stuff you probably don't know.'

While there were many things India would like to know – some of which Teagan might be able to tell her – she suddenly felt vulnerable and a tiny bit tearful, and longed to retreat indoors and focus on the renovations. She rubbed at her forehead where she had the beginnings of a headache.

'India, what's up? You feeling okay?' Teagan's voice was full of concern.

The sympathetic look on the girl's face pushed India's reservations to one side, and she began explaining the situation with her father. She told Teagan that Noah had left when she was small, how her mother had told her he was dead, and that she'd had no knowledge of her grandmother's existence until recently.

'The thing is, I don't really understand why my grandmother didn't leave the house to my father, now I know he's alive,' she admitted.

Teagan gave an understanding nod. 'That part is really weird, I know, but it's because he didn't want it, leastways that's what Ruby told me.'

'I wonder why not, though,' India said, trying to get her head around this new piece of information.

Teagan shrugged in a resigned way. 'Dunno, but Ruby said Noah had shunned all material possessions once 'e was living in a commune.'

'You don't happen to know where this commune is, do you?' India felt herself trembling with anticipation. Might Teagan have the information she needed that would lead her to her father?

The girl shook her head vigorously. 'Nope, really sorry, but I don't have a clue about that one.'

India pulled a tissue out of her sleeve and blew her nose, again feeling the tears not far away. Teagan only seemed to have snippets of information and nothing solid to go on.

'Anytime you wanna talk about it, though, is good with me,' Teagan told her, leaning towards India and touching her arm. 'I must get on now as I have loads to do, otherwise that boss of mine will be sacking me.'

She laughed heartily at her own comment, but instead of resuming her work, she leaned on her scythe, put a hand on her hip, and regarded India closely. 'Talking of Jez…' she said, lowering her voice, 'he had his heart broken once, you know. His childhood sweetheart, it was.'

When India didn't comment on this piece of information, Teagan carried on, warming to her subject now. 'He got married really young, he did,' she continued as if in her own little world. 'Course, he still holds a flame for Annie, I'm sure of it.' She put a finger to the side of her nose as if this was a huge secret between them.

India didn't want to indulge in gossip about Jez with Teagan, and began to wish she hadn't told the girl so much about her own family.

'There's something else you might like to know, too,' Teagan insisted, as India turned to walk away. 'Jez knows more about your family than either one of us, and is quite knowledgeable on the subject of your grandmother.'

India tried to hide her annoyance at Teagan, but despite herself, she found her curiosity had been piqued. 'Did he know Ruby then?' she asked, stopping to look back at Teagan.

The girl widened her stance dramatically and lifted one eyebrow at India. 'Know her! He was practically related to her himself, as I'm sure you'll find out soon. His grandmother was Ruby's best friend.'

Chapter Twelve

After escaping the noisy dance hall, Reilly and Ruby walked along the darkened streets in silence, each lost in their own thoughts.

Ruby started to say something to him just as he stopped and turned towards her. 'Sorry... I mean, shall we have a cup of tea back at the hotel?' she asked him, her eyes shining with hope.

'That's a sound idea and just what I were thinking. But would it be all right to do that, do you think?'

Ruby thought about the communal lounge the students used in the hotel. 'I'm sure it will be fine,' she said, excited at the thought of being alone with Reilly.

As they fell into step beside each other, Reilly took Ruby's hand; it was strong and warm in hers. Keeping her eyes ahead as she walked, Ruby could feel an invisible pull towards him – a feeling that was strange and something new for her. She hardly knew Reilly, but she did know that whatever was between them was going to prove hard to resist.

Walking up the steps into the hotel, Ruby unlocked the communal door and then led Reilly towards the lounge. Inside was dark, but Ruby knew her way around, so she opened the lounge door and quickly flicked on the light switch.

The sparsely furnished room was flooded with

light, revealing a large sofa, two armchairs, and a coffee table, with a couple of magazines littering the top. 'Sit down wherever you like,' she told Reilly, who was looking at her uneasily.

Ruby became aware of her own heartbeat thumping loudly in her ears, as he sat down on the settee, his eyes never leaving her face. 'I'll just go and make the tea,' she said all in a rush, trying not to notice how he was gazing adoringly at her.

'Ruby, please don't go. Come and sit down 'ere,' he said, patting the seat next to him encouragingly.

She nodded, knowing that neither of them wanted or needed a cup of tea. As she sat down beside Reilly, he looked longingly into her eyes, then he took her hand in his own.

'There's so much I want to know about you, Ruby Summers,' he said. 'Tell me all about yourself.'

Reilly said the words so tenderly that it pulled at Ruby's heartstrings. She looked into those ebony eyes and struggled to speak. 'I'm not sure where to start, Reilly...' she stammered, unsure of what he wanted to know.

He smiled in that slow, beautiful way, and sat back against the seat, still holding her hand. 'Start at the beginning, o' course, where else? What's your home town? Where did you grow up? All that stuff.'

Ruby followed his lead and relaxed a little. 'Alright, I was an only child born and brought up in Lewes, a little town near to Brighton in Sussex. My parents were, and still are, deeply religious, meaning I had a strict upbringing and very little freedom.'

She swallowed, remembering how trapped she used to feel, and how they had constantly tried to force religion on her. When Ruby was little, she'd had no choice in the matter, but as she grew up, she realised there had to be more to life than their narrow existence.

Taking a deep breath, she gazed at Reilly. 'There were many rules to abide by in our house,' she told him. 'Colour was frowned on and was the work of the devil.' Now she'd started, Ruby was finding it hard to stop. 'Everything had to be greys and browns, and I always longed for bright shades on the walls to escape the dismalness of everything, and to wear clothes which brightened my personality.'

Reilly squeezed her hand and gave her a sympathetic look. 'That's a shame. Surely they loved you, though, and there must have been some good times?' he encouraged.

Ruby stared across the room at a painting one of the artists had done recently –a landscape full of beautiful autumnal shades – then turned back to Reilly. 'I suppose they did love me in their own way, but I don't remember any good times. Once I grew up, I only wanted to escape them,' she said, remembering that sad time in her life.

'You did escape them, though, didn't you?' Reilly lifted one eyebrow. 'I heard you worked in Hanningtons store in Brighton, and lived away from home in a lodging house.'

Ruby couldn't help laughing at this. 'Golly, you seem to know a lot about me,' she said. 'Was it Jude who told you all this?'

'Don't be annoyed at Jude, Ruby. I were asking her questions about you, is all,' he admitted, looking a little ashamed. 'I was made up to hear all about you, and I hope you don't mind.'

'I don't mind, honestly, and I'm not annoyed at Jude. She's already a good friend, even though I haven't known her long.'

Reilly gave her a slow smile and shuffled closer to Ruby on the settee. 'I'm glad you got away from yer parents,' he told her. 'That couldn't have been easy.'

Ruby felt heat flood her body, suddenly aware of being in close proximity to Reilly, but unable to move away from him. 'I was twenty-one when I left home to live in the lodging house in Brighton,' she explained. 'My friend Scarlett helped me find my way. As I told you before, she gave me the necklace.' Ruby indicated the amethyst stone on a chain around her neck.

'Scarlett sounds like a good friend to have,' Reilly said thoughtfully.

'Oh, she is a good friend. Scarlett had her own worries about me moving to Brighton, due to past events in her own life, but she put those aside to help me.' Ruby felt a pang of regret at how much she missed her friend.

'You've been lucky to have her in your life then, by the sounds of it,' Reilly told her without taking his eyes from her face.

She put her hand on her heart. 'I thank God every day for Scarlett,' she said. 'But that's enough about me, Reilly Brownlow, what about you?'

He leaned forwards on the sofa. 'Not much to tell really, Ruby. I grew up in Toxteth, me ma's white and my da is black.' He looked at Ruby with pain in his eyes. 'Their love was forbidden and frowned upon, especially by my middle-class English grandparents,' he said. 'But they ignored all the prejudice and got wed anyway.'

'That must have been hard, not just for them, but as you grew up?' Ruby had heard about areas such as Toxteth, and read reports that the area was rife with crime and how discrimination was commonplace there.

He nodded sadly. 'Me ma's parents cut her off; they couldn't accept their daughter marrying a black man.' Sitting up, he squared his shoulders. 'We lived in a mixed-race community and it were alright most of the time. There were people from different backgrounds there, but we mostly got on really well.

'O' course, sometimes our families came up against prejudice. Ma was labelled as lower class and lacking in morals, and us, their children, were called social outcasts.'

Ruby's heart ached for the young Reilly, growing up being pointed at and judged in this way. 'I'm sorry to hear that,' she said quietly. 'How many siblings did you have?'

'Like you, no siblings. With the difficulties as they were, they decided not to have any more children.' Reilly lifted his chin and stared into the middle distance. 'Me ma taught me to be strong, and told me to ignore the accusations and labels, and get on with me life.'

'How did you end up here in Ambleside then, miles away from Toxteth?' Ruby was interested in how Reilly, like her, had escaped from such a different life.

He looked down at his hands thoughtfully. 'Me da spent his life inside a factory, and I knew I didn't want that. I wanted to work outside in the fresh air.' He looked up at Ruby with a pensive expression. 'Unfortunately, when I left school, he found me a job in the factory where 'e worked, and at first, I didn't know how to escape this fate. Or how to tell him I just couldn't do it.'

Reilly leaned back on the settee and let out a long

sigh. 'Thankfully, me ma saw how it was with me. She took me aside, on the quiet like, gave me enough money to live on for a few months, and told me to go in search of outside work.'

'What a lovely person she was,' Ruby said, thinking how very different their mothers were.

He gave a slow nod. 'I found out later she 'ad been putting money aside for years to help me when I left school. Even then, it weren't easy, though. I travelled around asking about jobs, with no luck for months. O' course, I knew that there *were* jobs, but the colour of my skin prevented me getting them.'

'Gosh, that must have been awful. How did you get the job at Ambleside Manor?' Ruby was interested in how he had overcome these difficult hurdles and stayed strong.

'I'd nearly run out o' money when I found myself in Ambleside,' he said, his expression brightening. 'I were having a drink in The Golden Rule when I overheard a conversation about Lord Fairfield looking for a farmhand. I asked who this man was and where he lived, but was only met with blank stares. But I didn't give up, and I located Ambleside Manor and approached Lord Fairfield 'bout the job.'

Ruby held her breath, wondering how Reilly would have got on approaching someone like Lord Fairfield about employment at the manor.

Reilly's eyes sparkled with enthusiasm. 'I were in luck. Lord Henry Fairfield was like his namesake, a fair man. It were like he didn't even notice the colour of me skin, and he gave me the job straight away. I was made up and couldn't believe my luck.'

Ruby smiled. 'That's wonderful. And has Lord Henry lived up to his name since then, and proved to be a fair employer for you?'

Reilly nodded happily. 'He has, and I've been very fortunate. Like Scarlett helping you, I'm not sure where I would be without his faith in me.' Reilly shrugged his shoulders. 'Probably working in that factory in Toxteth. Looks like we both been lucky to have people helping us find our way, haven't we?'

As Ruby wholeheartedly agreed with him, she became aware that the atmosphere in the room had changed. Reilly was gazing at her in that intense way again, and she couldn't help staring right back at him. His eyes were shining with desire as he moved towards her. She really should stop him coming any closer, but she couldn't seem to move.

'Reilly...' she whispered, but he appeared not to hear. And suddenly she didn't care, because she wanted to be in his arms, and to feel those full lips on hers. Her body was flooded with warmth and every nerve in her body was tingling.

Ruby's eyelids closed as his lips came down on hers, soft at first then harder as she responded to his passion. The room disappeared around them, as an invisible thread pulled them together, making the two of them feel like one.

The sound of voices outside in the street jolted Ruby back to the present, and she wrenched herself reluctantly out of his arms. Standing up abruptly, she brushed a crease from her dress, feeling slightly dazed.

'I think you'd better go now, Reilly,' she said huskily.

He gazed at her with desire still evident in his dark eyes, then he stood up and shook his head. 'O' course...' he said, taking a step towards her. 'Sorry, Ruby, I didn't mean to take advantage of you.'

'You didn't take advantage,' she told him, knowing she had wanted that kiss as much as he had. 'But I really think you need to go now,' she said, feeling her skin cooling and her common sense returning. 'I'm sure the students will be back soon.'

Reilly nodded and began walking towards the door. Ruby followed him out of the hotel in silence, and as he hovered on the top step, he once again pulled her in his arms. This time, the kiss was shorter but no less passionate. Then he leant towards her, whispered in her ear that he would see her tomorrow, and then he was gone.

As she closed the door on him, her legs felt weak and her pulse was still racing, but Ruby was smiling. That night, alone in her bed, she relived their kiss over and over again, and when she did eventually sleep, it was Reilly's face she saw in her dreams.

Chapter Thirteen

India put down her tools and turned on the radio, then walked across the room and opened the window. She breathed in the fresh air and stared over at Jez, who had almost finished removing the dead maple tree.

She watched him walk towards the far end of the garden carrying the tree and roots, and couldn't help admiring his muscular physique. As he headed back in the direction of the house, he glanced over and caught her eye, making her flush with embarrassment at being discovered.

Remembering Teagan's words, India longed to go outside and ask Jez about his grandmother, but she didn't know him well enough to begin firing questions at him. She also wanted to know why he had said he hadn't known Ruby, when it seemed he had known her well.

Turning from the window, she went back to work on removing the mantelpiece, but by two o'clock her stomach was growling. As she was waiting for a heating engineer to call her back about the gas fire, she decided she'd stop for lunch.

Whilst tidying her materials away, she wondered if the local pub, The Laughing Fish, was open. She really fancied a nice cold beer along with something to eat right now.

Only one way to find out, she thought, slipping off her overalls. As she let herself out of the house, she saw Jez leaning on his spade, admiring his handiwork.

'Do you know if the pub's open?' India asked him, feeling a flutter in her chest at the sight of him.

'The Laughing Fish is always open,' Jez replied, before taking a glug of water from his bottle and regarding her with that penetrating gaze of his.

India thanked him and walked down the pathway, pleased to see the sun was out after an overcast morning. A few minutes later, she became aware she was being followed and, glancing back, saw Jez heading towards her.

'I always have my lunch in the pub on Fridays,' he explained in response to her quizzical look. 'Do you mind if I join you?'

India nodded and kept walking in the direction of the pub, trying not to think of his close proximity. When they reached the big white building, he held the door open for her to go inside. The shaded interior of the pub was a stark contrast to the bright sunshine of outside, and India's eyes took a moment to adjust.

'I'm sure Henry will be in here somewhere,' Jez said as he approached the small bar area, picked up a bell, and shook it vigorously.

The bell's tinkling sound echoed around the room and immediately a head popped up from behind the counter. 'Can I help you?' said the head, as two large hazel eyes stared at them.

A young man with heavily lacquered hair and a layer of pink gloss on his thin lips straightened up. 'Sorry, love. I was just doing some tidying you know how it is, don't you?' he said. And without waiting for an answer, he went on, 'What can I get you? Oh, hello there, Jez, how're you doing?'

Jez returned Henry's greeting, then they both ordered a drink.

'Coming right up, my lovelies,' Henry trilled. 'Just go and sit down. There's no shortage of seats today, as you can see.' He indicated the empty pub.

India took in her surroundings now her eyes had adapted to the change in light. The cosy interior was done out in red tones, and had seating with small nooks in which to hide away. As she sat down at a table by the window, she noticed the walls were covered in vintage photographs of Isfield as it had been many years before.

She watched Jez sit down opposite her, but before they could speak, Henry appeared. He put their drinks and a menu on the table then, producing a damp cloth, began scrubbing furiously at non-existent marks.

'There! That's better, isn't it?' he said, admiring the immaculately clean table. 'How's your business doing?' he asked, looking across at Jez.

'Business is very good, thank you,' Jez answered. 'Henry, this is India McCarthy, Ruby's granddaughter, and your new neighbour.'

'Pleased to meet you, Henry,' she said, holding out her hand to the barman. 'How's the fence holding up?'

Henry put his heavily ringed hand into hers. 'Welcome to Isfield, India, I hope you enjoy living here. The fence is pretty good, thanks, as Jez here did a great job on it.' Then he looked over at the bar, where a customer had appeared. 'Enjoy your drinks now,' he told them, then walked quickly off.

India couldn't help laughing. 'He's a bit of a character,' she commented to Jez, and as their eyes made contact across the table, her heart flipped over.

'He certainly is, but Henry has OCD quite badly, as you can see. At least it means the pub's always clean, though.' Jez glanced at the barman, who had served the customer and was now frantically polishing the bar. 'Seriously, though, be careful what you say to Henry, as he's even worse than Teagan for gossip.'

India had only just met the likeable Henry, but could see that he probably knew everyone's business in Isfield. Jez's reference to Teagan annoyed her a little, though. She admired what the girl was doing for her sister, and she seemed very kind despite her gossipy ways.

'The old photos are a nice touch,' India commented, keen to change the subject. 'I'm quite interested in the history of Isfield,' she added thoughtfully.

Jez looked up from where he was studying the menu. 'Isfield is steeped in history,' he told her, 'especially the pub during the war years.'

India leaned her elbows on the table. 'I'd love to hear all about that,' she said.

She remembered driving into Isfield for the first time just a few weeks ago. After the long, dark days of winter, driving through tree-lined roads with the sun dappling through their branches, had cheered her as she'd approached the pretty little village. On both sides of the road were lush green fields and vast areas of greenery, with the odd house here and there. The air seemed fresh and clean – a vast change from the polluted atmosphere of busy, overcrowded Hackney.

'Are you still with us?' Jez interrupted her reverie.

'Yeah, sorry. I was just comparing Isfield with Hackney,' she told him. 'I think I'm beginning to like the countryside,' she added truthfully.

Jez gave an understanding nod. 'I love it, and

wouldn't want to live anywhere else,' he told her. 'As to the pub history, it's all on the website, but in 1939, it had just been taken over by a new landlord and was struggling. Then three-and-a-half thousand Canadian troops were billeted nearby, and the rest, as they say, is history.'

'So, the Canadian army saved the pub,' she said, leaning back in her chair.

'Yeah, that seems to be about the measure of it,' Jez said, lowering his gaze to the menu.

As India focussed on deciding what to choose for lunch, she wondered whether now was the right time to ask Jez about his family history. Taking a deep breath, she said, 'Teagan was telling me that our grandmothers knew each other, is that right? If so, that's an interesting bit of history.'

He gave her a quizzical look. 'Has Teagan been gossiping again?' he asked sharply.

India had the feeling that she was on dodgy ground and felt uncomfortable with Jez's tone. She also had a feeling of unease when Ruby's name was mentioned, and knew she needed to get to the bottom of it.

'Look, Jez, there seems to be a problem between us when I mention Ruby. And another thing, why did you tell me you hadn't known her?' she said, shifting in her chair.

For a moment he said nothing, then he sighed and pushed a lock of thick golden hair away from his forehead. 'I'm not sure what you mean, India,' he replied.

'I'm sorry, but I think you do know, Jez. Teagan wasn't gossiping, she was making a comment, that's all.' She looked down at her hands, feeling confused. 'Not being in touch with my father, there's no-one else to ask...' She hardly knew this man sitting in front of her, but at the moment he was her only link to her grandmother.

When Jez still said nothing, she started to explain. 'There's a lot I don't know about Ruby, and so many lost years,' she said, looking up at him. 'It would be nice to know something about her... anything really.' India knew her words were sounding jumbled and coming out in a rush, but she couldn't help it.

'What do you mean "lost years"?' Jez said, placing his drink on the table and regarding India with a furrowed brow.

'Well, obviously, while growing up I would've liked Ruby to have been part of my life,' she went on, more hopeful of a breakthrough. 'And now living in her house, I feel compelled to find out more about her and her life.'

Jez was studying her intently, taking in everything she was saying. She watched his expression change from puzzled to something unidentifiable.

'What is it?' India asked. She couldn't understand why he was looking at her like that?

Jez sat rigid in his chair, and looked slightly uncomfortable. 'The thing is, India, you not being in touch with either Ruby or Noah for so long, it's no wonder there are lost years.' He lifted his eyebrows and shook his head slightly. 'I think I may have misunderstood the situation.'

'What do you mean misunderstood?' She watched him let out a long breath. *Was that relief she saw on his face?* she wondered. It made India feel strange, as if there was a crossed wire here somewhere.

Jez paused and took a swallow of beer then, as if he were choosing his words carefully, said, 'Ruby

McCarthy was a lovely old lady with so much in her past to make her sad, but she was very lonely in her final years, especially since my grandmother Scarlett died.'

Jez was looking a bit shamefaced, and India was trying her best to understand. 'And your point is?' she said, feeling the breath catch in her throat.

'Ruby often talked of how she longed to see you and, like you've just said, how she was missing out by not seeing her only granddaughter.' Jez leaned his elbows on the table and looked into her face. 'I assumed you didn't want to bother with an old lady like her, but I may have been wrong.'

'Wrong! I think that's quite a fair assumption.' Sitting up straighter, India glared at Jez and began to wonder what she had found attractive in this arrogant individual.

'I thought you had only come to Isfield after she left you the house, ignoring your grandmother and your father for all those years….' His words trailed off as he stared blankly at her.

Anger tore through India at this injustice, especially as Jez had no words of regret at his misjudgement, but was sitting there looking mutely at her, the expression in those turquoise eyes unreadable.

'I didn't visit her because I didn't know her,' India said through gritted teeth and as calmly as she could. Then she stood up, turned on her heel, and walked out of the pub door without a backward glance.

Chapter Fourteen

February 1941

The last few weeks had passed in a haze of happiness. Ruby spent her days relaxing with Jude and her friends, and her evenings and weekends with Reilly. They took long walks together in the beautiful countryside and spent time in the pub with the others.

Ambleside had worked its magic for Ruby and she was feeling back to her old self again. The terrible dreams where she re-lived Harriet's demise had gone, along with the dark clawing guilt, leaving behind good memories of her vivacious friend.

A letter had arrived just a few days ago from Gerald, the landlord, at The Fortune of War pub, asking when she would be returning to Brighton. 'The punters are missing your pretty face,' he'd written, and updated her on how the war was treating Brighton. She read with dread how the bombing raids were increasing in the seaside town, and that schoolchildren were being evacuated to Yorkshire.

Ruby took the letter and hid it in her underwear drawer, unable to face leaving Reilly behind or to think about going back to her normal life in Brighton. Instead, she wanted to remain in Ambleside forever and ignore the problem of her dwindling savings.

It was Saturday evening, and today had been Reilly's day off from Ambleside Manor. They had spent the time in each other's company, walking miles together across stunning countryside, exploring woods and lakes.

This evening they were sitting on a bench watching the sun sinking lower in the sky, bathing Windermere Lake in a velvet glow. Ruby listened to the soft sound of the water lapping against the jetty. Suddenly her heart was pounding, and she fought against the feeling that soon her idyllic life here in Ambleside would be over.

'Ruby, my darling, what's the matter?' Reilly said, squeezing her arm.

His voice cut through her thoughts, and the warmth of his hand on her arm coursed through her body, lifting her out of her sudden gloom. She turned her face towards him and forced a smile on her face.

'How could I not be alright with you beside me, my love?' she said, feeling the finger of dread up her spine.

Reilly nodded and she had the feeling he was about to tell her something. There was a look in those beautiful ebony eyes, suggesting he was holding something back. Whatever it was, Ruby decided, she would rather not hear it.

As he opened his mouth to speak, she quickly stood up from the bench. 'Shall we go and find the others?' she said. 'I'm sure they'll all be in the pub by now.' She watched the uncertainty drain from his eyes and knew that for now at least, she had a reprieve.

Reilly stood up and took Ruby in his arms, where he kissed her passionately. Maybe she was imagining it, but there seemed to be desperation in that kiss.

Was Reilly feeling it, too? Was he also mirroring the alarming feeling that their time together would soon be at an end? Ruby dare not ask him the question; right now, she would rather not know the answer.

As they walked back arm-in-arm towards the pub, Ruby wrapped her happiness around her like a blanket, clinging to it like a drowning man to a lifeboat. She glanced up at Reilly in the fading light, and saw he looked deep in thought, with his face creased in a deep frown.

Normally she would say, 'A penny for your thoughts.' But tonight, she dare not ask that dangerous question.

Chapter Fifteen

India hurried out into the sunshine and almost ran back towards Ruby's house, glad to be away from Jez and the accusing way he had been looking at her.

It hurt that he thought of her as nothing but a gold-digger. And even though she still hadn't had anything eat, she simply couldn't stay in his company one more moment. She would raid the fridge and make do with a sandwich for lunch when she got home.

When Ruby's house came into view, India's heart missed a beat as she recognised the red sports car parked up outside. She hesitated on the pavement for a moment wondering whether to run back the way she'd come.

Forcing her legs to move, she walked past the car and through the gate. She paused on the pathway and stared at the blond-haired man, dressed from head to toe in denim.

'What are you doing here?' she said as loudly as her shaky voice would allow.

Turning quickly, with his finger still poised on the doorbell, he regarded her with those wide, blue eyes that had once drawn her into their liquid depths.

'India, my love!' he said, swiftly moving towards her. 'I've missed you so much, my darling.'

India involuntarily stepped backwards and

shuddered. 'What do you want, Archie?' she said.

He threw his arms wide and shrugged his shoulders. 'I want to make amends, babe,' he said huskily, looking down his fair eyelashes at her. 'When you took off like that, you didn't give me a chance to explain, did you?'

India lifted her chin, pushed past him roughly, and unlocked the front door. 'Explain what, you sleeping with another woman?' she replied scathingly, as he followed her into the hallway. 'Get out, Archie!' she told him angrily. How dare he try and make excuses after she'd seen him in bed with that other woman.

Archie stopped inside the hallway and regarded her with that beseeching look she was so familiar with, then he reached out his arms towards her.

India dodged out of his way and walked through to the kitchen, aware he was still following her. 'How did you know where to find me?' she asked, as she began filling up the kettle for tea, at the same time wondering how to get rid of him.

Archie leant on the kitchen top as if he were making himself right at home, which annoyed her even more.

'There was a copy of the deeds to this place in a drawer,' he shrugged, as if this was of no consequence. 'You know you want to make it up with me, India,' he said confidently. 'I'll promise to behave in the future.'

India was beyond angry at Archie's arrogance, and turned from the sink to face him. 'Please leave now. I do not want to make it up with you, now or ever,' she retorted, lifting her hand and pointing to the door. 'We are finished, so get out of my house now!' she told him with as much force as she could muster.

As she stared at Archie, waiting for him to move, she reflected on how much her feelings had changed. When she'd found out about his infidelity, she had been upset, but since the break-up she had seen their relationship in a different light.

He was a talented musician, there was no doubt about that (she had heard him play at one of his many gigs), and she had always hoped he would make it big. But as time passed, despite constant gigs in pubs around London, Archie and his fellow band members had failed to get important bookings.

When two of the band members left and the local gigs began easing off, Archie still wouldn't give up on the dream, which India didn't have a problem with, but he made no effort to earn money in any other capacity, preferring to let India pay all the bills.

Just then there was a tap on the kitchen window, and she looked up to see Jez peering in.

Despite still being annoyed at him, she couldn't help thinking he had chosen just the right moment to appear. Archie was also staring at Jez, and his smirk had now been replaced with a frown.

India quickly opened the back door and smiled. 'Hi there, Jez, please come in. Archie's just leaving, aren't you?' she said, looking pointedly at Archie.

Jez looked slightly confused but stepped into the kitchen, his large frame filling the doorway.

'Archie, this is my boyfriend Jez,' she said, trying hard to keep a straight face while he eyed her gardener warily.

Archie glared from her to Jez and found his voice. 'Found someone else already then, India? And after what you said about me. You bloody tart!' he snapped angrily.

Jez took a deep breath and stepped towards Archie. 'Don't you dare talk to India that way!' he said firmly, towering over him. 'Now, you heard what the lady said. Get out. You're no longer required!'

Archie stared at Jez for a moment and then, with fists clenched, turned on his heel and rushed through the hall. They both burst out laughing as the sound of his sports car roared into life.

***

'What was all that about?' Jez turned to India once they'd finished laughing at Archie's hasty retreat.

He had a warm feeling in his chest at India describing him as her boyfriend, which was a warning he was getting too close to her, but he knew he'd have the devil's job denying that now.

'Oh, it's a long story,' she said, making a funny face. 'I kicked him into touch before leaving Hackney, and I can tell you it was long overdue. Thanks for getting rid of him for me,' she added, tilting her head from side to side.

Jez knew he owed India an apology; he still didn't know what had come over him in the pub. 'India... look, I really didn't mean to upset you earlier.' He took hold of her gently by the shoulders, and gazed into those beautiful dark eyes of hers.

'It's not for me to judge what you've chosen to do over the years. And to be honest, I think it's a real shame Ruby didn't get in touch with you before she died.'

India looked at him sadly, all laughter at Archie's expense gone now. 'It did hurt that you drew conclusions about me, which just weren't true,' she admitted, dropping her gaze.

Jez put one finger under her chin and lifted her face up. 'I'm sorry, really I am. It's just that Noah mentioned his family had cut him and Ruby off over the years.'

He longed for her to forgive him and for the two of them to get back on good terms again. He couldn't think about anything that might happen after that, and knew his heart was ruling his head right now.

Jez leaned in closer and brushed his lips against hers. Her mouth felt moist, and a shiver of desire ran through his body at her closeness.

However, she pulled out of his arms abruptly and shook her head in a confused way. 'Noah… you've just said you know my father,' India said urgently. Standing back to look at Jez, she added, 'I remember now that you mentioned him earlier, but it went right over my head.'

Jez immediately regretted mentioning Noah's name, but it was too late now, and India's obvious delight at his words made his heart quicken. 'Yeah I do, although I haven't seen him since Ruby's funeral,' he admitted sombrely.

India smiled at him. 'But where is he now?' she said excitedly.

'Well, he lives in Brighton,' Jez replied tentatively, knowing he had no choice now but to tell her where Noah lived. Although he couldn't help wondering what path lay ahead.

'Your father has his own photographic studio, but he also works in a place called the Brighton Flea Market, in Kemptown.' He ran a hand through his hair and thought how utterly gorgeous she looked, and how much he longed to take her in his arms and kiss her properly.

India looked a bit dazed and lifted a hand to touch her head as if she felt dizzy, as they gazed at one another for a moment. 'Right, thank you. I must get on with some work now,' she said in clipped tones, changing the subject and looking at him directly.

'However, before I do that, I want to tell you something,' she said, lifting her chin. 'While I was growing up, and up until a few months ago… I thought my father had died when I was little,' she told him with a hitch in her voice.

Jez's mouth fell open at this shocking revelation. 'Oh, my God, India, that's awful, but why, what on earth happened to make you think that?'

India dipped her head and sighed, then after a moment she looked up at Jez and explained how her mother had lied to her. 'I suppose she had her reasons, and it's taking me a while to forgive her, but obviously I missed out on so much.'

Jez let out a deep sigh and dug deep into his trouser pocket. 'This was my grandmother,' he said, holding out an old, crumpled photo. He'd intended to show India the picture when she first asked about Ruby, but hadn't found the right moment.

She took the photograph and stared intently at the image, before looking back up at him. 'What a striking-looking woman she was,' she said, holding his gaze. 'You have the same turquoise eyes as her.'

Jez nodded, appreciating India's compliment; his grandmother had been beautiful, and even in old age she had been a striking looking woman. 'Keep the picture for now,' he said impulsively. More than anything he wanted to help in her quest to find her father, despite what the outcome might be.

'There isn't much to tell about our grandmothers, really, India,' he went on. 'Just two old ladies who were best friends. My grandmother died in 2005. She was ninety-six, and up until then, they were still very close.'

India listened intently as he ploughed on. 'They were always there for each other, so my mother always said, and she used to visit them frequently.' Jez dipped his head and swallowed, feeling a cloud hanging over him at the mention of his mother.

'Is your mother no longer with us, Jez?' India said softly, leaning towards him.

'My mum is still alive,' he replied uneasily. 'Unfortunately, she's suffering from dementia, and living in a nursing home in Hove.'

'I'm so sorry to hear that,' India said, squeezing his arm and tilting her head to one side. 'It must be hard for you.'

Jez shrugged and exhaled deeply. 'Yep, it sucks. Mum's had the disease for years now,' he said looking at her intently. 'Sometimes her memory's good, though, so it might be worth you asking her about Ruby,' he added thoughtfully.

India looked a bit uncertain at this suggestion. 'I don't know, Jez. She won't know who I am, will she?' Then she seemed to change her mind, and looked up at him with a determined frown. 'Tell you what, give me her details and I'll pop along and see her when I get time. You never know, she might remember something.'

Jez gave her the details of his mother's nursing home and, with mixed feelings, watched her put it in her phone.

Chapter Sixteen

Reilly wanted to take Ruby in his arms and comfort her, as she stood beside him at the bar. Already he could feel her melancholy mood tonight, and he yearned to soothe that worried look from her face.

However, he couldn't do that, because he knew what was about to happen would change everything for them both. Taking a deep breath, Reilly glanced across the crowded pub to see Jude and the others sitting in the far corner, deep in conversation. She noticed them and immediately raised a hand to wave enthusiastically.

'I'll go and sit with them while you get the drinks,' Ruby told him, waving back at Jude and trying to smile, and she turned and strolled towards them.

As Reilly waited at the bar, his gaze was drawn back to Ruby surrounded by their friends. She was deep in conversation with Jude, with their heads bent close together; Jude's fair hair and Ruby's glossy black curls made a striking combination.

A wave of love swept over Reilly for his beloved Ruby, and it broke his heart to see her putting on a brave face this way. Considering he hadn't actually told her his news yet, he wondered at her perception in knowing their lives were about to drastically change.

The answer to that must surely lay in the intense

closeness they shared; despite only knowing each other a short time, they often sensed how the other one was feeling.

There had been many times over the past weeks when they had come close to making love, and their feelings for each other were becoming more intense every day. But Ruby had remained resolutely strong, telling him there would be time enough for lovemaking in the future. Reilly, though, knew that wasn't true. Time was running out.

Chapter Seventeen

Jez concentrated on the road ahead as he sped towards Brooklands Museum on Daisy-Duke. Sleep had eluded him far into the night, and he knew he had to fight his tiredness and watch his speed on his precious bike.

Today he had to have his wits about him, while still keeping up with the other members of the Brighton-Dukes. Most of them were much further along the road, but today wasn't a day for hurrying, so Jez was taking his time.

Jez loved spending his spare time riding with the Brighton-Dukes. He always referred to his Ducati bike as 'her', and had christened her Daisy-Duke after a character in the American TV series *Dukes of Hazard* in the early eighties.

The bike gave him so much pleasure, with her fire-red colour and a roar like thunder every time he started up the engine, and he loved her with a passion. Jez was content for his life to stay the way it was, with no complicated relationships to negotiate, and riding Daisy-Duke as much he pleased.

Immediately, India came into his thoughts, and he knew that in a way her loss had been his gain over the years, which made him feel uncomfortable.

It had been wrong of him to point her in Annika's direction, because it was nothing but a red herring. He hadn't meant to suggest a visit to his mother, but once the subject came up, one thing had led to another, and it was all he could think of to say.

Usually, when he was out riding his beautiful bike, he was free of all life's problems and nothing bothered him. But today, India's face and those exotic good looks swirled around in Jez's mind. There was no doubt that since she'd begun living in Ruby's house, his life had been turned upside down.

From the moment he had set eyes on India, the attraction registered deep within his core, catching him completely unawares, and he had very come close to kissing her several times. At first, he was able to deny how he felt, believing her to be selfish and uncaring, particularly after the way Noah had described her mother.

But now things had shifted. Knowing that what had happened over the years hadn't been India's fault, somehow changed everything.

Jez had to find a way to stop India digging into the past, though. The past held dark secrets which could never be revealed. In a way, he wished he wasn't so attracted to her, because it was a burden keeping Noah's counsel, and now he was trying to save India heartache at the same time.

As Brooklands came into view, Jez put all thoughts of India out of his mind and followed the other members of the Brighton-Dukes towards the entrance. For once, he'd be glad to get off Daisy Duke and stretch his legs; India and her search for answers would have to wait another day.

***

India approached the nursing home with trepidation. The three-storey Victorian house towered above her and was only a stone's throw from the beach.

Her mind was running in circles and she wasn't really sure why she was visiting Jez's mother. She probably wouldn't be well enough to tell her anything about Ruby McCarthy, and no doubt it would be a complete waste of time.

Attempting to still her racing heart, she rang the bell of the nursing home and waited for someone to answer. After a moment or two of no response, she rang it again. Eventually, the tinny sound of a woman's voice addressed her through the intercom, which was located next to the doorbell.

'I'm here to see Mrs Carlisle,' India said, then heard the answering sound of the door buzzing. Pushing it open, she found herself in a long, dimly lit hallway with a doorway at the end. A woman appeared dressed in a white tunic and dark coloured trousers.

'Good morning,' the woman said cheerily. 'Please come this way.'

India signed in as she was asked and followed the woman through the door into a smaller hallway, with several doors leading off in different directions. She was then ushered towards a staircase.

'It's at the top of the stairs, first room on the right, and don't forget to sign yourself out later,' the woman told her.

India felt nervous as she climbed the steep stairs, and told herself she need only stay a few minutes if Annika was in a bad way. When she arrived at the top, there was a corridor of rooms to her right. To the left of the landing was a glass doorway, through which India could see a lounge, where several of the residents sat in armchairs.

After finding the room marked 'Mrs Carlisle', India saw the door was ajar and knocked tentatively. When there was no answer, she pushed it open wider. As she walked into the room, she saw it was light and spacious, with a wide window, and a single bed pushed up against the wall.

At the opposite end of the room was an elderly lady sitting in a rather comfy-looking armchair facing a large television set. The woman had her head bent low and was studying the buttons on a TV remote control.

India hovered in the doorway and then coughed, feeling like she was intruding on the woman's privacy. 'Hello, Annika,' she said, trying not to startle the woman.

When Annika looked up at the sound of India's voice and stared across the room at her, India was immediately struck by how young the woman's face actually was. With her head bent low, she looked eighty years old or more, but now that India saw her properly, she could tell she was much younger than that. And her shoulder-length grey hair was streaked with the same golden colour as her son's.

'Who are you?' Annika fixed India with an intense gaze, then narrowed her eyes at her.

'I'm sorry to disturb you...' India said, stepping into the room, 'but Jez suggested I visit you.'

Annika's eyes began darting about the room in confusion.

'Please... don't be frightened, I know you don't know me, but I'm Ruby's granddaughter.' India looked behind her, thinking she might have to retreat back into the corridor.

However, mentioning Ruby immediately caused

Annika's face to clear, and she smiled sweetly at India, reminding her of Jez's dazzling good looks. Taking advantage of the woman's change of mood, she quickly stepped into the room and sat down on the bed.

'I heard you used to know my grandmother, Annika. Can you tell me anything about her?' she said gently, trying not to frighten the woman.

Annika's face lit up. 'That's an easy one,' she replied. 'What do you want to know about Ruby?'

India wondered where to start when she noticed Annika gazing intently at the amethyst necklace around her neck. 'What is it?' she asked the older woman.

Annika's blue eyes widened as she studied the amethyst. 'I know that necklace,' she said. 'My mother told me once how she gave it to Ruby when World War Two broke out.' She held out her hand towards India, as if she wanted a closer look at it.

India took the necklace from around her neck and handed it over, watching as Annika ran her fingers over the contours of the purple stone. She seemed to be in her own world and lost in another time as she stared at the necklace in the palm of her hand.

Leaning forwards, India thought she heard Annika mutter something like 'nothing but bad luck' under her breath. As the moments passed, she began to worry that she might not be able to retrieve the necklace.

'It's beautiful, isn't it?' she said, hoping to jolt Annika back to the present, and when the old lady didn't respond, she tried again. 'Ruby left it to me after she died, along with a letter.'

At the mention of Ruby's name, again Annika glanced up, and India watched the necklace slip from her fingers onto the carpeted floor. She quickly retrieved it and slipped it into her pocket.

'What don't you understand?' Annika asked, giving India a quizzical look. Then, before India could reply, she added, 'He didn't do it, of course... I mean, he was such a nice man and so very much in love with her.'

India sat up straighter on the bed and cocked her head to one side. 'Who didn't do what?' she asked patiently, hoping Annika would elaborate.

'Oh, I forget his name now,' she said. 'But you must know who I mean, dear. By the way, who's Jez?' she said lifting her eyebrows, before adding, 'Has anyone ever told you how much you look like Ruby?' Annika was studying India's face almost as much as she had done the necklace.

India felt uneasy. Annika seemed to be jumping from subject to subject now, but she decided to play along, hoping that things would become clearer. 'Not exactly, but I can see a resemblance from the photo of Ruby,' she said, smiling encouragingly.

Annika sat back in her armchair, folded her arms, and gazed at India with clear eyes. 'She was very beautiful, you know.' When India nodded in agreement Annika continued, 'So was my mother, of course. They were two very attractive young women.' She stared down at her hands. 'It was so unlucky, and when that awful thing happened...' She shook her head sadly.

Gazing towards the window now, Annika's mind seemed far away. 'I was very young when it all happened, but my mother told me all about it many years later,' she murmured.

India wanted Annika to explain a bit more, but it seemed she was only giving her snippets of information. 'Can you tell me a bit more about all this?' she asked, just as they were interrupted by a stout lady bearing a tray full of teacups and biscuits.

'Hello, my dears,' she greeted them. 'I heard Annika had a visitor, and as its tea-time thought you might like a cuppa?' she looked pointedly at India.

'Thanks, that's very kind,' India said, glancing regretfully at Annika, who now appeared to be dozing off with her head laid back on the back of the chair.

The tea-lady deposited the cups and biscuits on the table next to Annika. 'She tires easily these days and often falls asleep,' she said almost to herself. 'It won't be long before she's awake again, though, so I'll leave her cup here.' Turning to India, she added. 'I'm sure if you come back another day, she'll be more than pleased to see you.'

India thanked the woman and watched Annika for a moment, serene in her slumber. Then, gathering up her handbag and jacket, she leaned towards her. 'Goodbye for now, Annika,' she whispered softly.

As she made her way downstairs, she reflected on how Annika had begun opening up about Ruby, even though her comments had been quite muddled. Maybe another visit would be in order soon, when she hoped Jez's mother could tell her a little more about her grandmother.

Chapter Eighteen

The cold finger of dread worked its way slowly up Ruby's spine as Reilly put his hands on her shoulders and looked into her eyes. She had the unreasonable urge to run, in a bid to escape what he was about to tell her.

'I'm sorry, my love,' he said. 'I received my call-up papers this morning.'

Ruby felt as if her heart were being ripped from her body at Reilly's words. Her dream of staying here in Ambleside, cocooned from the outside world and its terrifying events, was now at an end.

She dropped her gaze. They were sitting in a corner booth in The Golden Rule and the pub was buzzing from the conversations around them. She'd thought she could be brave when this day came, but it was so hard to let go of this beautiful man. How could she lose him now when they had only just found each other?

Ruby looked up into his eyes and saw Reilly was waiting patiently for her reaction, and she searched her mind for the right words. 'How long have we got before you have to leave?' she whispered. The moment she had dreaded was here and there was no more hiding from the truth.

'Only two weeks, I'm afraid,' Reilly told her quietly. 'I'll 'ave to leave in fourteen days' time,' he clarified, sighing deeply.

Ruby tried to hide her alarm. She had thought she would have months left with Reilly before this happened, but to have such a short time left together was truly unbearable.

'Listen to me, please, Ruby, everything's sound and I'll be home on leave afore you know it.' Leaning forwards, he took her hands in his, running his fingers over her ring finger, and Ruby saw his eyes full of hope. 'I want to marry you,' he said softly. 'Will you marry me, Ruby?' he repeated, and then added, 'One day soon, when this war is over?'

Ruby's heart leapt. 'Oh, Reilly, yes I'll marry you!'

He smiled radiantly at her and she fought against a multitude of emotions. *When could they get married? Would this happen before he left?* Her mind was running in circles, making her head spin.

Then she thought about Brighton and how she would have to leave Ambleside soon. 'I won't be here when you're home on leave, though, will I?' she told him, fighting against the hot tears. 'How will I see you?'

'I'll come and visit you in Brighton, Ruby,' he told her. 'And we'll arrange the wedding for when I'm home on leave,' he added, taking her into his arms and holding her tightly.

Ruby pressed her face against his shirt. With the frightening prospect of Reilly in combat and the heady euphoria of his proposal, she let the tears fall, unable to hold them back a moment longer. The warmth of his body beneath her cheek made desire flame within her, as his familiar scent filled her nostrils.

She lifted her face to his with hope springing in her chest. 'Surely, my love, you are exempt from service?'

She knew she was clutching at straws, but she had to do something to quell this desperate feeling of panic tearing at her insides.

Reilly lifted her face towards his and kissed her lightly on the lips, forcing her to look into his eyes. 'It's true I could be classed as exempt from service, because I work on the farm. But me job can be done by the land-girls, and this country needs all its men to fight wherever possible.'

He was pleading with her to understand. 'Besides, I want ta go now that I'm nineteen. It's the right time for me.'

Ruby remembered back to the week before when they'd celebrated his birthday, and she had ignored the warning bells in her head. In truth, she had ignored the signs for weeks now.

'God forbid, nothing bad will happen to me, Ruby,' he reassured her. 'And I promise you now that when I get back, we'll get wed.' Reilly's voice cut through her thoughts, and somehow she managed a smile, trying to ignore the images in her head of him lying mortally wounded on the battleground.

'Do you understand why I want ta go? Do you believe that we'll get married, Ruby?'

She nodded, realising that for Reilly's sake she had to accept what lay ahead. 'I'm sorry to be so upset,' she told him, searching for something to help Reilly's words come true, and instantly she knew what to do.

Taking the amethyst necklace from around her neck, Ruby held it out to him. 'You must take this with you,' she said firmly, and Reilly's eyes widened in surprise.

'Ruby, I-I can't do that,' he began falteringly. 'It's far too precious, and I might lose it.'

Determined to ignore his protests, Ruby ploughed

on. 'Scarlett told me once that this is a good luck charm, and supposed to have powers of protection,' she told him, knowing that until now she had never really believed this to be true. But right now, and at this moment in time, she believed it with all her heart.

Reilly looked taken aback and shook his head. 'Ruby, I'm not sure,' he said. Then, seeing the look on her face, he nodded in a resigned fashion, and took the necklace from her hand. 'I promise you'll have it back soon then,' he said, placing it in his pocket.

With a sigh of relief, Ruby kissed Reilly passionately on the lips, pushing away all thoughts about the dangers he might face in combat, and putting all her faith in the amethyst necklace.

Chapter Nineteen

The views across the Sussex countryside were beautiful as India walked through a gap in the low wall into the graveyard. It didn't take long to locate Ruby's gravestone. Being only a short time since her grandmother's death, the headstone still looked clean and new, and sadness filled India as she read the inscription:

> *Ruby McCarthy*
> *Born 10th September, 1918*
> *Died 1st August, 2017 Aged 99 years*
> *Rest in Peace*

Sitting down on a nearby bench, her eyes fell on a much older grave next to Ruby's, and her heart missed a beat as the words danced in front of her eyes.

> *Reilly Brownlow*
> *Born 20th June, 1919*
> *Died…*
> *Rest in Peace, my Love*

Reilly's gravestone was much older than Ruby's, but there was no way of knowing when he'd died as there was a large gouge in the stone where the date should have been. India was sure it had been vandalised, and wondered why anyone would bother doing that to a gravestone.

Having replayed the conversation with Annika over and over in her head, the questions without answers had plagued her during the night. So, that morning, she'd decided to take a break from the renovations, wanting to make progress on finding out about Ruby.

She'd taken the opportunity to ask a local person where the churchyard was and been directed opposite the old mill, up a narrow country lane, which was only just wide enough for her little car. At the top of the hill, India found a picturesque church straight out of a children's storybook.

St Margaret's, the local churchyard, was the obvious place for Ruby to be buried, having lived in the village most of her life. And it hadn't taken India long to find her gravestone here.

But finding the gravestone had thrown up even more questions. If Ruby had been married to someone called McCarthy, why did she have a photograph of Reilly Brownlow with a declaration of love on it?

And to make it even more confusing, her grandmother was buried here next to Reilly in St. Margaret's churchyard. India supposed that could be put down to coincidence, but she didn't think that was the case.

The mystery surrounding her grandmother and Reilly Brownlow wasn't the only thing causing India to have sleepless nights. Since Jez had revealed where she could find her father, conflicting thoughts had spun in her head day and night.

The sound of a vehicle arriving in the lane and then a moment later her name being called across the churchyard, jolted India out of her reverie. She blinked into the sunlight looking for the source of the sound.

'Hello, India,' Teagan said, appearing in front of her. 'Were you asleep on that bench?' She put her palms together against the side of her head to indicate slumber.

India laughed. 'No, I wasn't asleep. Just looking at where Ruby's buried,' she looked up at Teagan, 'and trying to make sense of things.'

Teagan leaned on a garden rake she'd been carrying over her shoulder and gazed over at Ruby's grave. 'Oh yeah, this is a lovely spot for her,' she observed, and for a moment seemed lost in thought herself.

India cleared her throat and stood up. It was obvious to her that Teagan had been fond of Ruby.

'Who is Reilly Brownlow that's what I'd like to know,' she said, taking a step towards the two graves. 'And who on earth vandalised his grave?'

'He was a murderer, that's who he was, what died in prison,' Teagan said abruptly from behind her back.

India spun around to face her. 'What?' she said, and her stomach turned over as she remembered Annika's words of 'he didn't do it'.

Teagan's face looked flushed and the redness was spreading to her neck. 'Oh yeah, it's true. Ruby told me he was an evil man.' She was still staring at Reilly's grave, and the look on her face was making India feel uncomfortable.

Ruby's photo of Reilly came to mind and India felt as if there had to be another explanation. 'Teagan, how do you know all this about Reilly?' she probed.

Teagan moved away from the graves and sat on the bench India had just vacated. 'It was Ruby what told me,' she said.

India sat down heavily next to her. 'Can you tell me anything else about Ruby and Reilly then?' She was relieved to see the intense look had gone from Teagan's face. 'I mean, I know you haven't lived in Isfield long, but it seems Ruby confided in you.'

'Yeah, sure, I've got half an hour before I start work on the graveyard,' Teagan replied, indicating the lawnmower on the church path. 'I'm here to do some grass cutting, and as you can see it desperately needs doing.'

India nodded at the overgrown grass, and noticed that Teagan was looking pensive again, as if she was thinking of the best way to tell India what she knew

'It ain't a pretty story, India. Your grandmother had a hard time of it,' Teagan said at last, studying her fingernails intently.

'It's okay. I'm ready to hear it,' India reassured her, pushing her shoulders back and bracing herself for what was to come. It was nice of Teagan to worry about her welfare in all this, and be concerned for her.

Teagan leaned forwards and rested her elbows on her knees. 'The first thing she told me was that she was with Reilly, only after she thought her true love had been killed in action during WW2.'

India nodded, not liking where this was going already. 'Right, so what was the name of the man she truly loved then?'

'His name was Dick McCarthy – your grandfather o' course. He was a naval man and she adored him. She married him then he went off to fight, and a few months later she heard he'd been killed.' Teagan was staring into the distance now, lost in her thoughts.

India still couldn't get the picture out of her head of Ruby's beloved photo of Reilly Brownlow. 'So, where

117

does Reilly come into all this then?'

Teagan lifted her eyebrows and regarded India. 'When Dick eventually returned years later, Reilly attacked him, even though it should 'ave been the other way around, as he had taken Dick's wife,' she said.

India stood up and walked over to the graves again. 'Are you telling me that Reilly killed Dick?' she said, feeling her chest heavy at the thought of how appalling this was for Ruby.

Teagan sauntered over to stand next to India. 'Oh yeah, it were jealousy fair and square, leastways that's what Ruby told me,' she explained. 'Awful, ain't it?' she added, pursing her lips.

India turned to face Teagan. 'But I found a photo of Reilly in Ruby's house, and on the back she had written how much she loved him, or someone had written that on the back.' She waited for Teagan to explain this away.

'I saw that photo once, too,' Teagan reflected, still looking at the grave. 'Ruby told me it belonged to Scarlett who was Ruby's best friend, as you know.'

'Scarlett was in love with Reilly, too?' India was totally confused now, and couldn't believe what she was hearing. Surely Teagan had got it wrong?

'Yeah, apparently Reilly was a right cad and afore he went off to war, he was having an affair with Scarlett, hence the photo.

'Course by the time he came back, Scarlett had seen the light and married someone else,' Teagan explained airily, running her fingers through her spiky hair, making it stand up on end.

'It's all very confusing,' India said. 'I can't help wondering why Ruby had the photo of Reilly if it was

Scarlett's all along?'

Teagan shrugged and looked blankly at India. 'Not sure about that one. I expect Ruby was given it after Scarlett died, because they were such good friends over the years. There is other stuff in the house which belonged to Scarlett,' she added knowledgably.

India rubbed her fingers over the amethyst necklace around her neck, knowing that it used to belong to Scarlett. But she didn't know what to think about the rest of it. 'It's like a tragic love triangle,' she reflected sadly.

'And another thing,' Teagan said, next to India. 'Ruby told me that Reilly is still getting revenge from beyond the grave.'

'What on earth do you mean by that?' India felt a cold shiver run up her spine at Teagan's words, and almost didn't want to know what explanation she would offer this time.

'Ruby's house is haunted by Reilly Brownlow, that's what she said. 'Course I never believed that,' Teagan said, tilting her head to one side. 'Things were disappearing or being moved from their normal place, without rational explanation, apparently.'

India looked at her askance. 'Don't be silly, Teagan,' she said, attempting to laugh but remembering how the crystal vase had moved when she was sure she hadn't touched it. 'Of course it's not haunted,' she said. She'd been living there a few weeks already so was sure she would know if there were a ghost in Ruby's house.

Teagan threw back her head and laughed. 'Yeah, that bit's probably not true, Ruby was old, don't forget, and were more than likely going senile.'

India didn't like Teagan talking about Ruby that way, but she let it go. As she drove back to Taabeez, she was pleased her neighbour had told her what she knew about Ruby – apart from the bit about Reilly getting revenge. That was spooky, and made her feel a bit uneasy.

Chapter Twenty

March 1941

'It's a beautiful night,' Ruby remarked, staring up at the clear inky sky. 'Look at all those stars.' Feeling Reilly's eyes on her, Ruby turned to see a look of such longing and desire on his face that she caught her breath.

With only a week left before Reilly was to leave, they had escaped the noisy pub in a bid to find some time alone. But alarm bells were ringing in Ruby's head.

'Reilly, I…' But before she could move, his lips were on hers, first soft then hardening as he deepened the kiss. As Reilly began exploring Ruby's mouth with his tongue, she moaned with pleasure, her body responding to his.

Suddenly a passer-by rudely brushed past them on the pavement, bringing Ruby back to the present with a start. Disentangling herself from Reilly, she found herself whispering, 'Let's go inside.' And, taking hold of his hand, she pulled him towards The Salutation Hotel.

'Are you sure?' Reilly asked, concern furrowing his brow, which was completely at odds with the passion still evident in his ebony eyes.

Ruby looked up into his eyes. 'You're leaving

in a few days' time and we don't know when you'll be back,' she told him firmly. She didn't feel sure of anything, except that whatever happened between them, they needed to make the most of every single minute.

She often told herself she hardly knew Reilly Brownlow, but that wasn't true. In the weeks she'd been in Ambleside, Reilly had become like her soul mate. And with him leaving for the war shortly, her time with him was precious. The 'live for today' philosophy she'd adopted since Harriet's death, was at the forefront of her mind tonight. Ignoring the doubts crowding her head, Ruby ushered Reilly towards the building.

He followed her up the hotel steps towards the lobby. Quickly walking ahead of him, she led him upstairs to her room, where she pulled the curtains across the French windows to shut out the world.

Switching on the standard lamp, Ruby glanced around the room with her heart racing. Thankfully, she'd made the single bed and straightened the candlewick bedspread before she went out that evening.

Reilly took a step towards Ruby, his eyes lingering on her face, and held out his arms. Heat flooded her body as she moved into his embrace, causing a shiver of anticipation to flutter in her stomach and an aching need deep within her core.

As Reilly's lips came down on hers, she gave herself up to him unconditionally. When he began pulling the zip down at the back of her dress and gently pushing her towards the bed, she let out a soft moan of pleasure.

A little voice inside Ruby's head told her she was on dangerous ground, especially when she felt Reilly removing her underclothes and stockings. But she was powerless to stop, barely aware of anything except Reilly's musky scent, her own throbbing heartbeat, and her bare skin tingling beneath his soft touch.

Desperately now, she needed to feel his naked flesh against hers. Her hands seemed to have a mind of their own as she tore at his shirt and began pulling him closer towards her.

Gasping with need, Ruby shivered and felt cold air on her bare skin as Reilly abruptly pulled away from her. Her half-closed eyes fluttered open and, feeling slightly drugged, she watched him hurriedly discarding his shirt and trousers.

The amethyst necklace hung around his neck, glinting in the half-light, and Ruby felt comforted that he would be taking it into battle with him. As Reilly stood before her in his pants, her gaze strayed to the tip of his arousal, straining against the undergarment, and she caught her breath.

Reilly's lips parted then his eyes locked onto hers as he slowly removed his underpants. She drank in his beautiful, honey-coloured body, her eyes running over his broad, muscular shoulders and smooth skin. Seeing him exposed this way caused an avalanche of lust to burn in the deepest recesses of her body.

Ruby might not have been with a man before, but in this pivotal moment she was totally unafraid of what was to come, completely putting her trust in Reilly.

'Ruby...' Reilly's tone sounded husky and urgent as he came towards her. 'Are you sure, my love?' he asked again, his voice low and hoarse with desire.

Ruby nodded silently. Holding out her arms, she let out a sigh of pleasure as his body covered hers, answering his need with her own. Tentatively she began sliding her hands slowly over his bare chest, closing her eyes and revelling in the feel of his warm flesh.

As Reilly touched one of her breasts, he began circling the nipple, sending spirals of heat through Ruby's body. She threw back her head in wanton abandon as he moved to the other one, and felt her head spinning with the pleasure, rippling and nipping at her senses. Hunger gnawed at her and she arched her back, moving towards him, urging him again and again to answer the aching need between her legs.

'Not yet, my love... not yet,' Reilly murmured, stroking the inside of her thighs.

'Please... oh please, Reilly...' Ruby moaned, her body screaming and aching for his touch in her most intimate of places. She was ready for him and feeling gloriously exposed as she pushed herself further towards him.

While she writhed in wild anticipation, she was vaguely aware that Reilly was holding back. He lowered himself towards her, then he spread her legs either side of his strong hips and guided himself between her thighs.

As he began thrusting inside her, slowly at first then faster, Ruby had a feeling that at any moment she might explode into a million pieces.

Then he quickened the pace, and she was gasping and trembling as small flames of fire spread from her loins, completely consuming her, until she could bear it no longer. 'Please! Oh my God. Reilly... please,' she screamed out, writhing in ecstasy.

Then it happened. Reilly let out a low animal-like moan and thrust so deep into Ruby that she cried out at the quick sharp pain that tore through her body.

Losing all sense of the world and sanity, she was drowning in a haze of lust as the red-hot flames finally exploded into a firestorm.

Lying with limbs entwined and bodies hot with passion, Ruby felt Reilly's shallow breathing against her ear. Tears, hot and fierce, poured down her cheeks as Reilly hoisted himself up on his elbows and stared tenderly down at her face.

Lifting a hand to gently wipe away her tears, Reilly let out a long sigh. His eyes were soft with love and tenderness. 'Ruby, my love, why are you crying? Are you all right?' he frowned, his dark eyes full of concern.

Aware that he must be referring to her lost virginity, Ruby wanted to reassure him that she had chosen this path. 'I'm fine, absolutely fine,' she said, running her fingers through his thick, dark hair. 'Reilly, I hope you understand I wouldn't normally do this kind of thing?'

Reilly caught hold of her hand. 'I know that, and I'm sorry if I hurt you,' he said, looking down at the small crimson stain slowly spreading on the sheet beneath them.

'You didn't… not really,' she said, her eyes shining. 'It was what I wanted.' He took hold of Ruby's face and looked deep into her eyes. 'I love you, Ruby,' he said intensely.

Ruby saw the truth in his words and the love reflected deep in Reilly's ebony eyes, and she was flooded with an intense, all-encompassing feeling of wellbeing. She returned his gaze and knew deep in her heart that he was her destiny, her one true love.

She also knew that she would never in a thousand years have enough of this beautiful man and his lovemaking. Never tire of the feel of his smooth, honey coloured skin beneath her touch, or the feel of his warm lips on hers. 'I love you, too, Reilly,' she said, and then watched as his generous mouth curved in a beatific smile.

Chapter Twenty-One

The loud ding-dong of the doorbell woke India with a start, and her eyes flew open. Sitting up shakily, she forced herself to take a long shuddering breath, then squinting into the half-darkness, she lifted her hand to find her cheeks wet with tears.

She'd had a dream where a young woman had been sobbing uncontrollably and clutching at her swollen stomach as she stared out to sea. Around her, a storm was brewing, the skies were darkening, and there was a strong wind howling as it rained heavily.

Endeavouring to shake off the effects of the dream, India glanced down at her phone to see it was already nine o'clock. Quickly, swinging her legs out of bed, she rushed downstairs to answer the door.

India was dismayed to find Jez standing on the doorstep, amusement etched on his face as he glanced down at her night vest, pyjama shorts, and bare feet. She smiled back at him.

'Good morning, Jez,' she said, feeling self conscious under his gaze and very aware she was standing in front of him in her skimpy nightwear.

'Morning to you,' Jez offered. 'Sorry to disturb you, India. Just wanted to let you know we're starting work on the decking this morning.'

India nodded and couldn't take her eyes off his

handsome face. She shifted on her feet and began closing the door, eager to go and get dressed. 'Thanks for letting me know,' she said, her words coming out in a rush.

'No problem,' he replied hesitantly, putting one foot in the doorway. 'Do you fancy a bite to eat in the pub tonight?' he asked, looking a bit uncertain and running his fingers through his hair.

'That would be lovely,' India said, her heart beating faster at the thought of seeing him later. 'We could sit outside if it's still nice,' she added, remembering how she'd seen The Laughing Fish had seating set up in the pub garden.

'Yeah, that would be cool,' Jez responded, giving her a beaming smile before disappearing around the back of the garden.

Rushing back upstairs, India ran a brush through her hair, pulled on jeans and a t-shirt, and went in search of much-needed caffeine. While the kettle was boiling, she watched out of the window as Jez unloaded equipment from his truck, and cursed under her breath that he had seen her look such a state.

As he disappeared round the side of the house, India noticed the photo he'd given her of Scarlett. She picked it up from its place on the windowsill, and looked again at the fine-looking woman gazing into the camera lens.

She longed to discuss with Jez what Teagan had said about Reilly and her grandmother. And as he was the only one in the world she could talk to about her father, she picked up the photo he'd left behind and hurried out of the back door.

'Jez,' she began, trying not to notice his tight combat style shorts as he laid down the plank of wood he'd been positioning and turned towards her.

'Hmmm?' he said distractedly.

'Here's your photograph back, thanks for showing it to me,' she said, holding it out to him. 'Your grandmother was very beautiful, wasn't she?'

'Yeah, she was that. No problem, glad to help,' he said, placing the photo in his pocket and turning away again to resume work.

Determined to try again, she hesitated while Jez began working, seemingly oblivious to her unease. Shuffling on her feet, India wondered how to approach the subject, and eventually Jez stopped work and turned to her.

'Are you still here? Haven't you got anything to do, India?' he said with a good-humoured chuckle. When she didn't reply, he downed tools and perched on the grass in front of her. 'Alright, India, what is it? You might as well tell me, or I'll never get anything done.'

India knew it was now or never. 'Just a few questions about my father,' she ventured. For so long India had believed her father to be dead, always wishing things had been different, that he had lived and been part of her life.

Now that she knew he was alive, so many jumbled doubts were buzzing around in her head, making her feel confused and unhappy. *What if he preferred her not to contact him?* After all, he had always known where she was, but he'd never attempted to get in touch. Now that Jez had given her the key to unlock the mystery of Noah, she needed to seek him out, but she was paralysed with fear.

'Sure. What do you want to know?' Jez looked relaxed on the grass, leaning back on his elbows with his long brown legs stretched out in front of him

India bit down on her lower lip. *What did she want to know?* The list was endless, but where to start was hard.

Jez frowned then lifted one hand to shield his face from the sun. 'Have you been to the Brighton Flea Market yet? As I said before, he's often found there.'

'Not yet,' she said, sitting down beside him and staring down at the grass. *Why*, she asked herself, *couldn't she go to the flea market and confront Noah?* A little voice in her head kept telling her that's what she must do, but somehow her courage kept deserting her.

Jez gave an understanding nod and began telling her about Noah, how he had his own flat and photographic studio in Brighton, how he'd struggled for years in his career, but was now a successful photographer and a collector of all things quirky.

India listened with interest. It was odd to hear about what Noah had been doing all these years, and as Jez talked, India couldn't help noticing his expression. 'It seems like you're fond of him,' she observed, a strange feeling growing inside her.

Jez's look suddenly became guarded. 'I've known him a long time,' was all he said. 'And of course, his mother and my grandmother were very close.' Jez looked as if he were holding something back, his smile wavering a little.

As the conversation came to an end and they both stood up, India felt the atmosphere between them change. Jez was staring at her tenderly, his eyes shining with desire. Suddenly they were dangerously close to each other, merely inches apart, and as Jez leaned in even closer, India was forced to look into that startling turquoise-coloured gaze.

With her senses on high alert, she became acutely

aware of Jez's bodily scent, which was a mixture of newly-mown grass and sandalwood. With his lips hovering over hers, she felt her eyelids grow heavy with desire and his breath soft against her cheek.

As his lips met hers, moist and soft, he deepened the kiss and she felt herself willingly respond to him. Feeling only a strong awareness of her own heartbeat and of her body being flooded with warmth, the world fell away as she lost herself in Jez's strong embrace.

Chapter Twenty-Two

Ruby was filled with happiness. It was Sunday, the day after her night with Reilly, and her mind constantly drifted back to their lovemaking, leaving her unable to keep the smile from her face. She was getting ready to go out and meet him when there was a gentle knocking on her door.

'Ruby, it's me,' said a familiar voice, and she opened the door to find Jude standing in the doorway looking excited.

The two women hugged and then Jude stood back and smiled broadly. 'Good morning, Ruby, and how are you this morning?' she tilted her head from side to side knowingly.

'Shush! Come in, Jude.' Ruby felt herself blushing and pulled Jude quickly inside the door. She was acutely aware that everyone had seen her and Reilly leave the pub together the night before.

'Don't be a silly goose, Ruby. We're all rooting for you both. You make such a lovely couple,' Jude replied.

'I'm sure I don't know what you mean.' Ruby raised her eyes and did a mock swoon and they both laughed. 'If you really want to know, I'm getting ready to meet him now,' she said, trying not to think of the future and a time when Reilly would no longer be here.

'Good for you. I hope you have a wonderful time

together. He's a very handsome man.' Jude looked genuinely pleased for them. Then she dug in her coat pocket and produced a letter addressed to Ruby. 'I picked this up in the hallway for you,' she said, holding the letter out to her.

Ruby took the letter and recognised the handwriting on the envelope. 'Thanks, Jude,' she said. 'It's from Scarlett'

Jude smiled as she walked towards the door. 'Have a good time today with lover-boy,' she laughed with a sparkle in her eye. 'See you both later in the pub.'

Ruby bid Jude goodbye and, glancing at the clock, realised she just had time to read Scarlett's letter before she went out. She sat down on her bed, quickly opened the envelope, and began to read.

Dearest Ruby,

It's been some months since writing to you, and so much has happened in that time.

Did you hear about the King and Queens's visit to Plymouth, after there were thirteen raids on the port? Hopefully, their visit boosted morale, at least for a short time.

I have some news of my own to tell you. Eric's son Frankie called on me again after I thought I'd seen the last of him. At least he wasn't angry this time, and because I felt I owed him an explanation, I invited him in. I thought if I got to know him a bit, he would see I wasn't the harlot he thought I was.

We sat down with a cup of tea and he told me about himself. He said he worked at the shipyard with his father normally, but had joined the RAF and was waiting for his papers to arrive.

Looking at Frankie properly for the first time, I

realised how very handsome he was (he has Eric's hazel eyes and thick dark hair, but is taller than his dad and has the most beautiful smile). I was curious about him, and although at that point I had no feelings for him, looking back I think that's where it all started.

On his second visit to me, he told how he'd got his papers and would be reporting for duty. As he stood on the doorstep in his RAF uniform, looking at me with those hazel eyes, something stirred deep inside me. And I knew he needed to leave, but he didn't. Instead, he stepped inside the hallway and took me in his arms.

Before I knew what was happening, his lips were on mine, and he was kissing me as if his life depended on it. And then we ended up in the back parlour, and things went a little further, and I feel like the hussy Frankie first thought I was. But the truth of it is, Ruby, that now I know I loved this man from the very first minute I laid eyes on him.

As we kissed goodbye on the doorstep, however, I heard Eric calling my name. Pulling away from Frankie, I turned to see him standing with a large bunch of flowers in his hand and a shocked look on his face.

Oh Ruby, I felt terrible for Eric. He turned on his heel and was gone, and I haven't seen either of them since. I received a letter from Eric a few weeks later, telling me he had also joined up. He said it had been his plan all along, after a request from the war office to build field guns to help the war effort now his shipbuilding was no longer needed.

'You know, Scarlett, how my passion is in building ships,' he said to me. 'Recently I have lost my passion. So, I have put my foreman in charge, and joined the

army.' He said nothing in the letter about the fateful
day he arrived unexpectedly on my doorstep and saw
me in his son's arms.

This house is now feeling more like a prison and
the days stretch ahead of me, dismal and empty. I
begin my training as an ARP warden in two weeks'
time and will be staying at a lodging house near to
yours. While I'm in Brighton, my house in Lewes
will be occupied by the wife of a serving officer, who
has two young children. She needed to move to safety
away from the dreadful bombings in London.

Goodbye for now, Ruby. I think of you constantly,
Scarlett

Ruby put the letter down, feeling her head in a
whirl. Poor Scarlett, it seemed that meeting Frankie had
caused her to lose Eric, and now she was completely
alone. It was obvious to Ruby it was Frankie she really
loved, but how upsetting it must have been for Eric to
have seen them together before going off to war.

The thought of having Scarlett living nearby her
own lodgings in Brighton was heartening, but Ruby
couldn't think about her return to the seaside town
right now. She wanted time to stand still and to remain
with Reilly in Ambleside in this bubble of happiness
forever.

Suddenly she couldn't wait to tell Scarlett the
wonderful news that she was in love with a special
man, too. She vowed, on her return to her room later,
she would sit down and write a long letter back to her
friend. But for now, she laid Scarlett's letter carefully
on the bedside table, took one last glance in the mirror,
and walked out to meet Reilly.

Chapter Twenty-Three

India leaned contentedly back in her chair, letting the evening sunshine warm her bare arms. They were sitting outside The Laughing Fish pub, and she watched Jez walk towards her, drinks in hand.

'Gin and tonic for the lady,' he said with a slow smile, placing both of their drinks on the table between them, before perching on the seat opposite her. 'Cheers, India love,' he said softly.

India couldn't remember feeling this happy for a long time, and knew deep down she had never felt like this about a man before. She pushed away the many doubts about embarking on another relationship.

'Cheers, Jez,' she returned, feeling her face flush as she looked across the table at him, thinking how boyishly handsome he looked today.

After a moment's silence when they were both lost in their own thoughts, Jez laid his hands on the table and grinned. 'Maybe we should spend some time getting to know each other a bit better,' he said with a warm smile, then sipped at his pint. 'You go first,' he added.

Just then, Henry came up to take their order.

'How are you, Henry?' India asked. 'That's a lovely colour,' she commented, gazing at his cerise pink shirt.

Henry paused, pen in hand, and grinned. 'Thanks,

love,' he said. 'I'm good, thanks. Bit busier than last time you were here.' He glanced around him at the seats now all taken, then looked back at them both. 'What can I get you?'

'Fish and chips for me, please,' India said, looking across at Jez, who said he'd like the same.

When Henry went back inside the pub, she became aware that Jez was studying her, still waiting for an answer to his question. India fiddled with her Pandora bracelet, feeling a bit at odds with herself.

'I'm not sure where to start, Jez,' she said. 'I'm an only child, and as you know, I grew up without a father. My mother worked hard, and as a single parent that wasn't easy.' She paused briefly, wondering how to explain where it had all gone wrong.

Jez gave her an understanding nod. 'Were you close to your mum while growing up?' he asked thoughtfully.

'We were very close. There was only the two of us while I was young, but it all changed when she met my stepfather.'

Jez lifted his brows quizzically. 'What happened? Didn't you get on with him?'

India thought about that for a moment. 'Now I'm grown up, I can see what happened a bit more clearly,' she explained. 'I was fourteen, and at a difficult age when he came along. I resented his intrusion in our lives, and now I think about it, I made my mother's life hell.'

'Right, well, maybe you need to cut yourself some slack there. When you're a teenager, things get jumbled up, hormones are rife, and nothing makes sense,' Jez said sombrely.

India swallowed, then looked up and stared into

the middle distance. 'The trouble was, she was so in love with him that I felt pushed out.' Jez was listening so intently, and seemed to understand, so she was encouraged to go on.

'I've tried, in the intervening years, to get our relationship back on an even keel. But since I've found out Mum hid Noah's letters from me, it's kind of scuppered that idea.' India shook her head sadly. 'Your turn now,' she suggested light-heartedly.

Jez drained his glass and ordered more drinks as their fish and chips were delivered. 'I have one brother called Pete, who was the clever one out of the two of us.' Jez lifted his eyebrows. 'I always felt a bit stupid next to him, as he was very academic.'

'I'm sure that wasn't true,' India said, knowing that his business might be struggling but it had been successful in the past.

'Like you, it's only now I'm older that I can see Pete isn't so much cleverer than me, just very different.' Jez dropped his gaze. 'My father died of cancer when I was fifteen... which was hard.'

India leaned across and touched Jez's arm. 'I'm sorry to hear that,' she said tenderly. 'So, we both grew up without a father?'

Jez nodded. 'Mum was a strong woman and kept us under control, although...' he paused, as if trying to find the right words before going on, 'I hit a rough patch in my teenage years.'

India again had the sense that Jez was holding something back. 'How did you get through that?' she asked. The guarded look was back on his face, and India wanted to ask what was wrong, but then suddenly it was gone as quickly as it appeared.

'When I found I loved gardening, I also found my

niche, which helped,' he continued cheerfully, taking a large gulp of beer.

'Jez, I'm so sorry about your mum.' India felt the need to offer him sympathy as she thought about Annika. The look in his eyes tore at her heartstrings, and she could see it was very painful for him to talk about his mother.

Jez's brows wrinkled in a deep frown. 'Thanks. It's a horrible disease,' he said with such sadness that India's heart turned over. 'I should probably mention that I was married briefly. To a girl called Annie. We grew up together and, to be honest, we got married too young, so it all ended very badly.' He looked across at India enquiringly. 'You ever been married?' he asked.

India thought about all her relationships that had ended badly. 'Nope, never,' she said, taking a sip of her drink before looking up at Jez mischievously. 'The right person hasn't come along.'

As soon as the words were out of her mouth, she felt embarrassed, but Jez seemed unfazed and leant back on his chair regarding her intently, as if weighing up her comment.

'Okay, changing the subject, what things do you enjoy doing in life apart from work? I love riding my bike, Daisy Duke,' he told her. 'Have you ever been on a motorbike?'

India thought about it and then laughed. 'I had a boyfriend once who had a bike, but he went far too fast and it used to frighten me to death,' she told him honestly.' I like the name, though. Daisy Duke,' she added, tilting her head to one side.

Jez smiled. 'Daisy Duke was a character in the *Dukes of Hazard*, which was an eighties TV series. Obviously, before our time, but I call her that name because she's big, fiery, and red!'

India laughed. 'My job doing interior design is a passion, and I love putting it into practice in my home, too,' she went on. 'I also love a bit of history, which has come into its own since living here in Isfield.'

She looked across at the railway line, which was situated behind the pub. 'The Lavender Line looks interesting,' she said, watching an old steam train pull into the station. 'Perhaps I should have a look around it soon.'

Jez sat up and leaned closer to India. 'We can do better than that. How about tomorrow we take a ride on one of the steam trains together?' he said enthusiastically.

'I'd love that', she replied, her heart leaping at the prospect of spending more time with him.

When they'd finished their meal, Jez insisted on paying the bill, and she felt a warm glow as she watched him go into the pub to settle up.

'Thanks, Jez, but you didn't need to do that,' she said as he emerged. She stood up and retrieved her cardigan from the back of the chair, before waving goodbye to Henry through the pub window.

'It was my pleasure,' he said, falling into step beside her and looking at her with that beautiful smile. 'I'll walk you home, if you like,' he added lifting his eyebrows.

India stopped. 'Do you know, I haven't asked you where you live yet?' she said, surprised that this hadn't come up in conversation.

Jez pointed in the direction of Ruby's house. 'I have a little bungalow in Station Road, not far from you,' he explained, then he hesitated and looked at her sadly. 'It was my mum's place,' he explained.

India gave him a sympathetic look and Jez caught her hand as they began walking in the direction of Taabeez. She felt a shiver of pleasure run up her arm at his touch, and when they reached her gate, she was reluctant to let such a perfect evening end.

'India…' Jez said, as he turned towards her.

Then she was in his arms and his lips were on hers. Once again, she found herself lost in the sensation of being flooded with warmth, and every nerve ending in her body shivering with pleasure.

As the kiss came to an end, India became aware they were standing outside Ruby's gate locked in a passionate embrace, and in full view of passers-by. She pulled herself out of his arms and gazed up into Jez's flushed face.

'Would you like to come in for coffee?' she asked breathlessly, despite the warnings in her head. Tonight, she was ignoring them, because her heart was winning that particular battle.

'That would be very nice,' Jez replied huskily, before following her up the path.

As India approached the front door, something made her look up, and she caught sight of Teagan standing in her bedroom window next door. She lifted her hand to wave at the girl, but she quickly disappeared.

Once they got into the hallway, and Jez took India in his arms, all thoughts of her neighbour were immediately forgotten.

As Jez began murmuring in her ear, India managed to tear herself away from his solid chest and whispered that they should move out of the hallway.

Jez nodded at her slowly without taking his eyes off her face, and to her surprise, he lifted her clean off her feet and began climbing the stairs. India giggled as she indicated which bedroom, and was heady with excitement as he set her down on her feet inside the door.

Jez took her in his strong arms and nibbled at her earlobes, then began dropping light kisses on her neck and face. Shivers of excitement darted through her as he began removing her clothes, while she pulled at his shirt impatiently.

Eventually, standing naked before each other, her gaze roamed his beautiful body. His smooth chest and rippling muscles were utterly delicious, and her hands itched to touch every part of him, as a groan of pleasure escaped her lips.

As their bodies came together, they found their way onto the bed, with Jez covering her body with passionate kisses, sending darts of pleasure soaring through her whole being.

India threw her head back and gasped as he touched her most intimate of places, his hands now exploring and probing, causing shivers of delight to rush through her body time and time again.

As their lovemaking intensified, India lost herself in a swirl of pleasure. Soon she was unable to tell where Jez began and she ended. And as their two bodies merged into one, she knew with absolute certainty, that this was where she belonged.

Chapter Twenty-Four

Ruby's fingers were shaking as she attempted to do up the tiny mother of pearl buttons on her ivory blouse. Taking a deep breath, she pulled it off impatiently and chose a red polka dot dress to wear instead.

She had woken this morning with a thumping headache and feeling nauseous, having hardly slept for thinking about Reilly and what today would bring. The last seven days had passed so quickly that Ruby couldn't believe their time together was over. Today they would say their goodbyes, not knowing when or if they would see each other again.

Glancing across at her little green clock, Ruby realised it was almost time to leave for the pub and Reilly's goodbye drinks. Shutting her mind off to what this meant, she finished brushing her victory rolls into place, applied her red lipstick, and hurried out the door to meet Jude.

The Golden Rule was packed to the rafters when they walked in, and Ruby's senses were on high alert as she searched for Reilly among the crowded pub.

'Jude, I'm feeling a bit claustrophobic,' she said, her heart racing out of control as she fought the urge to escape the pressing crowd.

Jude's pretty features creased into a frown. 'Don't worry, Ruby, you sit down over there, and I'll bring the drinks to you,' she said, pointing to an empty booth in the corner of the pub, before turning to fight her way to the bar.

When Ruby eventually reached the empty seats, she sat down and sunk her head in her hands. Taking deep breaths, she tried to alleviate the feeling that air was being sucked from her body. Her heart sank as she felt someone leaning over her.

'Ruby, are you alright, my love?'

Her heart jolted at the familiar voice, and she looked up through half closed lids to see a worried Reilly staring down at her. As Ruby's gaze ran over his regulation army uniform, she thought how handsome he looked in his khaki jacket, with its shiny brass buttons. An unexpected feeling of pride rose in her chest, and for a moment she couldn't speak as the words dried in her throat.

Reilly sat down next to her and pulled her into his strong arms, and for a moment the two of them stayed that way, locked in mutual pain, while the pub carried on around them. Suddenly a loud voice interrupted their reverie.

'Reilly, old chap, come over to the bar. Yer mates are waiting for you.'

They pulled apart quickly as the young man, who had a shock of red hair and was also wearing army uniform, shrugged and then disappeared back into the melee.

Reilly sighed and slowly let go of Ruby, just as Jude reached their table with a tray of drinks. 'That was me friend Pete,' he said to them both awkwardly.

Ruby lifted her chin and gathered her courage. 'That's alright. You go and join them, darling, I'll see you later.' She was trying to smile, knowing that he would be leaving soon and she had to find the determination to set him free.

Reilly nodded at her with his eyes fixed on her face, then he put his lips to hers. The kiss sent thrills of desire surging through her, and she never wanted it to end. A moment later, she watched him disappear back into the gathering of men, with a lump in her throat.

Jude had been watching them from the other side of the table. 'Here you go, Ruby, this'll help you feel better,' she said, placing their drinks on the table between them.

'Thanks, Jude,' she managed, before taking a small sip of her drink. She felt as though her heart was breaking into hundreds of pieces.

'Ruby, I'm really sorry you're feeling so bad,' Jude said. 'But you knew this was going to happen,' she added softly and placed a hand on Ruby's arm.

Ruby nodded sadly and thought about the previous night, which had been spent in a haze of passion. They'd known their time to say goodbye was really then; not tonight, in this over-crowded, noisy pub.

But all Ruby wanted to do now was cling desperately to Reilly and beg him not to leave. She brushed away her tears, feeling Jude's gaze still on her. 'I don't know how I'm going to bear it,' she admitted miserably.

Jude leaned back in her chair and looked at her intently. 'You're a strong lady, Ruby. It will be hard, but he'll come back to you,' she reassured. 'Hold onto that thought, and just get through tonight somehow.'

Ruby knew her friend was talking sense, and she needed to put a brave face on things for Reilly's sake. He'd told her only yesterday how hard it had been to say goodbye to his parents, who had travelled down from Toxteth to see their son.

'Ma tried to be heroic,' he'd told her with a frown, 'but she ended up crying, and Da just shook my hand proudly.'

Ruby set her jaw and smiled across at Jude. 'You're right, of course he'll come back,' she said, thinking of the necklace underneath his uniform, and praying that Scarlett was right about it being a good luck charm.

As the hours slipped by, Ruby made an effort to socialise with Reilly's friends. Her smile was set on her face, but it was a smile nonetheless. Jude stayed by her side, giving her encouraging sideways looks, which helped her find the strength she needed to get through the evening.

Finally, it was time for Reilly to leave. And as the whole pub lined up to say their goodbyes, Ruby watched him hugging them all in turn. She waited patiently for him to approach her, and willed herself to stay strong.

At last it was her turn, and in front of everyone, he took her in his arms as if he never wanted to let her go. Their kiss drew a raucous round of applause from the whole pub, but Ruby could not have cared less. This kiss had to last them both a long time.

As they drew apart, Reilly whispered into her ear, 'I love you, Ruby, never forget that. I'll be back 'afore you know it, and then we'll be man and wife.'

Unable to answer him, Ruby could only manage a whispered, 'I love you, too,' and watch as he turned from her and walked towards the waiting car.

As he gave her one last lingering look, Ruby lifted her hand and waved. Then the vehicle sped away and Reilly was lost from view.

Chapter Twenty-Five

'Well, what do you fancy then?' Jez asked, proffering the menu and gazing across at India like a love-struck teenager.

It was Sunday morning, and they were sitting in the Cinders Café at the Lavender Line, about to order brunch. India was opposite him, looking absolutely ravishing, with that dark hair framing her heart-shaped face, her eyes positively shining.

She had on a red dress today, which clung in all the right places, making Jez want to pull her into his arms again and make love in this most public of places.

They had just spent a night of passion in Ruby's house; a night Jez was going to remember for the rest of his life. He knew now that he had fallen in love with India and realised he had never loved anyone in this way before. He had no idea where this would lead when certain things came to light, but right now he was going to enjoy being with the gorgeous woman in front of him.

Only hunger had driven them both from India's bed, at ten o'clock this morning. And he could not deny that despite not touching a drop of alcohol yet today, he felt completely and utterly drunk on love.

India offered him a slow, sexy smile. 'I'm absolutely starving,' she declared, holding his gaze. 'It's the full

English breakfast for me,' she said, looking at him seductively from under her long dark, lashes.

Jez's heart beat faster as his eyes raked over her face, and for a moment he couldn't answer, memories of last night's passion bringing a flush to his cheeks.

India glanced around the café. 'I love the ambience of this place,' she said, looking across at the old, restored fireplace and the railway memorabilia adorning the walls.

Jez laughed. 'It's not exactly luxury, and a bit basic, but a great place for breakfast,' he replied, indicating the red checked tablecloths and the wooden chairs they were sitting on. 'This would have been the railway waiting room years ago.'

India leaned on her elbows and studied him. 'You know, Jez, I'm beginning to like Isfield very much indeed. I mean, at first the slower place of life was hard after London, but...' She looked down at her hands lying flat on the table, and a frown was etched on her forehead.

Jez placed his hand on hers. 'What is it, India?' he asked, desperately wanting her to say she would stay in Isfield, and racking his brains as to how to voice how much he wanted that to happen.

She looked up at him, her dark eyes clouded, but then their breakfast arrived and the moment had passed. He couldn't help wondering what she had been about to say.

A while later, they walked through the double doors out onto the historic platform, where a few other people were gathered. 'It's like going back in time,' India told him. 'I love the old signs.' She pointed to one with *R. White's Lemonade* emblazoned across it.

'Yeah, there's a great atmosphere of the past here,'

Jez replied. 'It's all run by volunteers, too; people who are keen train enthusiasts.' He took hold of her hand, and it felt like the most natural thing in the world, as if they'd been together for years.

'I bet there's some stories to tell here,' she said, looking up at the signal box standing proudly at the front of the station.

Jez gave an understanding nod. 'The signal box is a Grade Two listed building, and was one of the first things to be restored in the 1980s,' he told her. 'The men operating it would have seen the secret trains making their way to Newhaven during preparations for D. Day,' he added knowledgably.

'That was in 1944, wasn't it? You obviously know all the history of this place,' India replied, just as their train steamed into the station with a screech of the brakes and a loud panting sound.

They stepped onto the steam train along with the other passengers, and found they had a carriage to themselves. India sat by the window, watching the other passengers banging doors shut before boarding the train.

As Jez leaned towards her, his nostrils were filled with her musky scent, reminding him again of their night of passion. He put his arms around her and nuzzled that soft white neck of hers.

'Not now, Jez,' she said playfully, turning to face him. 'What other stories do you know about the station then?'

Jez sighed contentedly and leaned back on his seat. 'I remember one famous story, it's quite sad, though; I'll warn you now,' he said. 'Do you still want to hear it?'

India nodded enthusiastically.

'Well, I've heard that the station is haunted by the ghost of a young woman. The story goes that she said goodbye to her fiancé on platform two during WW2,' he explained. 'But the young man never returned from the war.'

'Gosh, that is sad,' India said.

They both looked out of the window at the guard about to blow the whistle, for the train to begin its journey.

'Her ghostly figure is often seen wandering the platform, always searching for him, but he never returns.' Jez finished the story and shrugged as he saw a cloud pass over India's face.

'Of course, it's probably not true, but it helps to have a good ghost story to draw the visitors in. Are you enjoying it all so far?' he said, trying to lighten the atmosphere. Then he dropped a kiss on her beautiful lips and was quickly rewarded with a beaming smile.

India looked into his face with a soft expression. 'I'm loving it, Jez. Thanks so much for bringing me here today, and for last night's dinner. It's my turn to pay next time, though,' she said mischievously, her dark eyes sparkling.

Jez felt a warm glow that there would be a next time. 'Fine with me,' he said. 'Let's enjoy every minute of this day together,' he added.

As the whistle blew and the train began chugging out of the station amid the loud whooshing sound of the steam, Jez snuggled up to India and felt himself relax. All his doubts about starting a relationship with her disappeared into the mist of steam enveloping the vintage train station.

Chapter Twenty-Six

Heraklion, Crete

May 1941

All around him the noise was deafening. The artillery fire, which had struck the ship just minutes before, was still going on. Why didn't it stop now? The Germans had hit their target and the ship was drowning along with its evacuated passengers.

The smell of gunfire and shells clung to the water, causing a dense mist to surround him, and he couldn't see more than a few inches in front of his face.

Reilly's whole body screamed at him to stop, to allow his painful muscles respite. But he knew he had to keep swimming for the shoreline with every ounce of energy he had left in his tired, bone-weary body. The waves seemed to be pulling him backwards instead of forwards, but he kept going; behind him was the sinking ship, and there lay certain death.

It seemed like only a moment before that there had been peace on board, then all hell had broken loose. Men like him, who thought they were on the way to Egypt and a safe haven, had been left fighting for their lives instead.

On the journey here, Reilly remembered how they

had all been led to believe this battle was in the bag. They'd been told the British knew of Hitler's plans to invade this Greek island, so they would have plenty of time to prepare for its defence. And in the month since Reilly's arrival on the island, he had seen that everything was going in their favour.

The water muffled some of the sounds echoing through the air now, and Reilly was grateful for that. He couldn't make out the dying men's cries clearly, nor hear the last groaning sounds of the ship breathing her last. His sole focus was on the shore, where he would likely be captured by the German army, but at least he would be alive.

His nostrils and mouth were now full of water, choking him and making it almost impossible to breathe at times. His arms and legs felt numb with cold, but he struggled through the water and fought against the leaden feeling of his sodden fatigues, which were weighing him down and threatening to pull him under.

His darling Ruby came into his mind. Would he survive to see her again? It seemed like years since he had held her in his arms. How he longed to feel her sweet lips on his, to feel the warmth of her body beneath his, and hear her gentle whispers of love.

Every night he dreamed of Ruby, but in his dreams she was walking away from him, bidding him farewell in the far distant landscape. Constant doubts about whether they would be reunited wore him down and made him feel like giving up the fight.

However, he couldn't give up while there was still a glimmer of hope that he would see her again. So, he kept fighting on, his head bent under the water and the shore just out of reach.

Reilly felt his movements slowing. He knew that soon the energy would be gone from his body and he would have to stop battling the water. But suddenly he felt a nudge through the waves, and he turned his painful head towards its source. A fellow soldier swam alongside, pointing ahead of him, offering Reilly a war-weary smile.

When he looked in the direction the soldier was indicating, the smoke and mist slightly cleared and he could just make out the outline of the beach. Thank God! He had almost made it. Just a few more strokes and he would be walking onto the shoreline. Through sheer determination and grit, he had managed to get his body to safety; he would live another day after all.

As Reilly's feet touched solid ground beneath him, he thought again of Ruby and knew without a shadow of a doubt that whatever lay ahead, he would survive, and he would see her again. With renewed energy, he forced himself upright and began wading through the now shallow water, towards dry land.

Chapter Twenty-Seven

India was working hard on the house renovations but couldn't stop daydreaming about Jez. She was hyper-sensitive to everything, and kept thinking of his smooth tanned skin beneath her touch as they made love. Her body yearned for his every minute of the day, making her heart thud and her breath quicken.

When Izzy rang later that day, her friend could tell from India's voice that something had changed so she had no choice but to spill the beans. 'It's early days yet,' she explained, glad Izzy couldn't see the flush creeping over her face as she remembered the look in Jez's eyes as he gazed at her with such adoration.

Izzy sounded cautious on the end of the phone. 'Be careful, India,' she warned. 'I'm pleased for you, but take it slowly,' she added.

How do I take it slowly when Jez has suddenly become my whole world? India wondered, as she went back to work, pushing aside any doubts still lingering in her head.

Trying to focus on the renovations, she stared at the fireplace. The heating engineer had been and disconnected and removed the old gas fire. Then yesterday, the chimney sweep had removed the covering on the fireplace and swept the chimney, which meant that it could be used, once restored.

Now India assessed how to return it to its former glory. With her interior design degree completed some time ago, she'd had to do research online to remind herself what to do next. And the first job was to remove the paint on the detailing around the fireplace. So, she set to work using white spirit, and scraping the paint the white spirit wouldn't budge.

A few hours later, she was ready for a rest and exhausted from her efforts when she saw Teagan arrive in the garden.

'Good afternoon, Teagan,' she greeted her neighbour through the window. 'How are you today?'

Teagan leaned on her spade and regarded India with narrowed eyes. 'Well, don't you look like the cat what's got the cream?' she said. 'Who put that look on yer face?'

India laughed out loud. 'Gosh, there's no hiding anything from you, is there?' she said. When Teagan continued to stare at her, she added, 'Nothing much really,' thinking that was an understatement if ever there was one. 'I had a date with Jez last night.'

She felt her face redden and her heart beating faster at the mention of his name, then remembered how Teagan had been watching them from the window when they came back from the pub.

Teagan, however, didn't mention seeing them, but was quick to burst her bubble of happiness. 'I told you afore, I think Jez is still holding a torch for his ex-wife Annie,' she warned.

India knew there was no love lost between Jez and Teagan. Jez claimed Teagan was a gossip, and Teagan seemed to put him down at every opportunity. But she hadn't expected such a negative reaction.

'Sorry, didn't mean to put a damper on the romance,'

Teagan said, then turned to start digging. 'Don't mind me.'

India returned to the lounge feeling deflated. However, she told herself she would try to take her relationship with Jez slowly, even though she was sure he was different from every other man she'd known and would never hurt her.

***

With the awkward conversation on her mind, India found it hard to settle back to her paint stripping, and decided to unpack a suitcase she'd brought from her flat in Hackney. She hadn't found the time to go through it yet.

Retrieving the case from under her bed, the first thing she saw when she opened it was a small oil painting in a gilt-edged frame. It was rather old-fashioned, but India had loved it as soon as she'd seen in a tourist shop while on holiday with Archie a while ago. It depicted a beautiful woodland scene, and the way the sunlight was bursting through the trees, mixing with the shadows in the forest, made it look magical.

There had never been anywhere to hang the painting in the flat, and she'd always been aware that Archie hated it, calling it rubbish and out-dated. Perhaps it was, but she liked it anyway, and had tucked it away out of sight for several years.

Now, however, she was determined to hang it where she could see it while she worked on the house, knowing it was the kind of picture which lifted her spirits.

Leaving it lying on the kitchen table, India went

in search of picture hooks, and was frustrated to find she had left them at the flat. Knowing she couldn't settle to any more work today, she decided on a trip to Homebase on the industrial estate in Lewes.

She locked up the house and called to Teagan that she would be gone about half an hour. In reply, the girl said she would be leaving to do another job shortly

It didn't take India long to reach the DIY store and she enjoyed taking her time to browse the aisles for anything else she needed. On her return to Taabeez, however, she found Teagan was running late and still hadn't moved onto her second job.

India went into the kitchen, humming happily to herself, and flicked on the kettle switch before placing the picture hooks on the table next to where she'd left the painting.

Except that it wasn't there any more. Feeling confused, she stared at the empty table where she'd placed the painting just an hour ago, then quickly rushed outside to see Teagan was about to walk through the back gate.

'Has anyone been in the house while I was at Homebase?' India asked, shading her eyes against the sun with her hand, knowing this sounded like a very silly question.

Teagan stopped and looked at her as if she'd gone mad. 'What? Course not. The house were locked, weren't it?' she said.

'Yeah, but... have you been here the whole time, Teagan?' India felt as if there was something very wrong here. How had the painting disappeared? Perhaps she'd been mistaken and had left it somewhere else in the house, but she distinctly remembered putting it on the kitchen table. 'I think I'm having a funny five minutes,' she told Teagan, forcing herself to smile.

The other girl shrugged as if this were perfectly true. 'Whatever,' she replied with a shrug, then told India to keep out of the sun for the rest of the day.

India went indoors and searched high and low, but still couldn't locate the picture. She couldn't get her head around how Teagan had been here the whole time, the house had been locked up, yet someone had been in the house and moved or stolen the picture while she was out.

Chapter Twenty-Eight

May 1941

Ruby heard the doctor speaking but couldn't seem to understand the words, as if something had happened to her ears. 'I'm sorry...' She moved her head from side to side in an attempt to dislodge whatever was causing her hearing problem. 'Can you repeat that please, Doctor?'

The grey-haired, bespectacled man sighed deeply and, looking thoroughly impatient, leaned towards her. 'I said, young lady, that you're expecting a child.'

Ruby's heart lurched and her face flamed. Her hearing had returned, but she still found it hard to comprehend what the doctor was telling her was true. She had attended this appointment today in a bid to solve the problem of her constant nausea. She'd been sure he could prescribe medication to clear up the stomach influenza, but... pregnant?

It was true she hadn't had her monthlies for a while, but whenever they'd made love Reilly had assured her that he'd been careful not to let her get in the family way. 'Are you sure, Doctor?' she asked again.

The doctor took a deep breath and leaned back in his chair. 'About two months,' he said, making a point of looking down at the ring-less finger on her left hand. 'It's a perfectly natural thing to happen. But I can see it might be difficult for you if you're not yet married. So you need to inform the prospective father of the good news.'

Ruby felt the air being sucked from her lungs; the need to escape from the doctor's consultation room was quite suddenly urgent. She forced herself into a standing position and, on shaky legs, squared her shoulders and lifted her chin.

'Thank you, Doctor. I'm due to get married shortly,' she told him firmly. This was true enough, but when this would happen, with Reilly away fighting, was another matter.

The doctor nodded at her and began studying the notes on his desk. As she reached the door, he lifted his eyes from the paperwork. 'Good to hear you're getting married, Miss Summers. Many young women aren't so lucky.'

Later that day, Ruby stared out of the window of her room at Regency Square and listened to the sound of the waves lapping against the shore, reflecting on how peaceful everything seemed today, despite the dug-out trench and sandbags along the seafront, which gave away the true situation.

Brighton was not a target for the Luftwaffe, and Ruby had heard that some children had been evacuated here from London. However, if there were any bombs left after attacking the capital, then the German pilots often dropped them on Brighton on their way home.

However, the night Harriet was killed when the bomb went off outside Hanningtons, it seemed the two most historic buildings in Brighton had been a target. The Dome and the Royal Pavilion came close to being hit by a German bomb that evening. Ruby shivered as she remembered reports of Hitler intending to make the Royal Pavilion his home after the invasion.

Now, it was almost midday and she'd been gazing out of the window for hours, trying to get used to the idea that she was soon to be a mother. How she longed for her earlier ignorance, but it was too late for that. It was time to face reality.

She knew Reilly would marry her. After all, he had already proposed and they were unofficially engaged. But now she was expecting, she needed to get married quickly before the baby was born. And even though she longed to tell Reilly her news, it was impossible right now.

In the two letters she had received from him since leaving Ambleside, he had told her how much he loved and missed her. In the most recent note, he explained how his training was coming to an end, and that he'd just heard he was being sent into battle on the island of Crete.

Ruby was desperate to confide in someone and Scarlett was the only person she could think of. But on a recent visit, her friend had been groggy from sleep after spending the night doing ARP duties.

Reaching for her coat, Ruby decided to call on Scarlett again. Hopefully, this time she would be up and about, and Ruby could tell her the news. The thought of having Reilly's baby filled Ruby with joy, but the situation she found herself in was difficult, and she could only hope they would be able to get married on his next leave home.

As she opened her bedroom door, she found Mrs Monday standing on the threshold, holding a letter in her hand.

'Sorry to disturb you, dear,' she said. 'This came for you this morning. I put it in my housecoat pocket and forgot all about it.'

Ruby took the envelope from her landlady, immediately recognising Jude's spidery handwriting. 'Thank you, Mrs Monday. It looks like Jude's updating me on her news from Ambleside,' she said, but immediately she felt a sinking feeling in her stomach.

Jude had only sent her a letter a few days ago, so to receive another one so soon was odd. After closing the door on Mrs Monday, Ruby sat down on the bed and stared at the envelope in her hand. She closed her eyes, as a feeling of dread washed over her.

Reluctant to open the letter, Ruby walked across to the window to see the sun had now gone in and the skies had darkened. Thoughts ran amok in her head as she tried to stem the feeling that the letter contained bad news.

A knock directly below her made Ruby glance towards the front door of the lodging house. To her surprise, she saw Scarlett standing on the doorstep. Relief coursed through her at seeing her friend, and she opened the window.

'Good morning, Scarlett,' she called down to her.

Her friend glanced up at the very same moment Mrs Monday opened the door to let her in, but the look on Scarlett's face sent icy shivers up Ruby's spine.

'Wait there for a moment, Ruby,' Scarlett said urgently. 'I'm coming right up,' she added, before disappearing through the doorway.

Ruby knew that look on Scarlett's face, and was even more frightened now at what might be in Jude's letter. Over the years she had come to know when her friend was about to impart bad news.

Determined to prove Scarlett wrong, Ruby rushed across the room and retrieved the letter, tearing at the envelope with shaking hands. Her amethyst necklace fell onto the floor with a loud clatter, and she stared at it dismally.

'Please no...' she whispered, 'don't let this be bad news.' Forcing her eyes to focus on Jude's sloping handwriting, the first words she read made her blood run cold.

> *Dearest Ruby,*
> *I'm so sorry to be the bearer of bad news, but Reilly is missing presumed dead...*

Unable to read further, Ruby felt oddly giddy. The partially-read letter fell out of her hand and fluttered down to land beside the necklace, and the room began to spin. She felt her limbs weaken, just as Scarlett flew through the door and was in time to prevent her from falling to the floor.

Chapter Twenty-Nine

India stood on shaking legs, staring at the furniture and bric-a-brac in the window of the flea market, hoping her courage wouldn't desert her.

The evening before, while in the pub with Jez, she had suddenly had a revelation that the time had come to find Noah. She didn't want to mention this to Jez, though, in case she changed her mind.

Maybe it was Jez declaring his love for her recently that was making her feel able to face anything, however challenging. But for some reason, she felt strong enough now to face whatever her father had to say.

Despite feeling brave before she left home, now that she was actually here, her heart raced out of control and she had an almost overwhelming urge to turn around and run back the way she'd come. Taking a deep breath to calm her nerves, she pushed open the door to the building and stepped inside.

India looked around the dim interior of the shop, which was crammed with everything from deckchairs to cabinets full of jewellery and other treasures of all descriptions. Every available square inch of space was taken up with an eclectic mix of items, and she stared around in wonder.

'Are you looking for anything in particular?'

The male voice cut into India's thoughts, and she

looked up to see an elderly gentleman peering out from behind a counter, crowded with yet more items for sale. Squinting at the man's face and sparse white hair, she let out a long breath and smiled.

'Um, no. Just browsing, thanks,' she returned, grateful this man wasn't her father and for now she had a reprieve. She hadn't seen Noah since she was a small child, but she knew for certain his eyes were dark brown and certainly not vivid blue like this man's.

'Okay, well, if you need any help, let me know,' said the man, turning his attention back to his paperwork on the countertop.

India wanted to ask the man where her father was, but thought it might sound silly as she wasn't entirely sure Noah did work here. Maybe Jez had got it wrong.

While she was here, she may as well have a look around, she reasoned with herself, as an image of Ruby came into her head. She wandered around, gazing sightlessly at the wares, expecting her father to appear out of one of the nooks and crannies, which made her feel uptight and jumpy.

As India began descending a narrow staircase leading to another floor, she noticed this area was full of paintings and photographs of all descriptions. She began perusing the art collection, when her gaze was drawn to a stack of pictures leaning up against a wall, over in the far corner of the room.

A photograph right at the front of the pile looked somehow familiar, and as she bent down to peer closer, the hairs on the back of her neck stood on end.

The photo depicted a child staring happily into the lens, obviously taken at a birthday party. This was evident because of the large cake, with birthday candles, in the background, and other children in the photo dressed up in party clothes.

The girl had red ribbons in her hair, and her candy pink dress was a beautiful contrast to her raven tresses. Her huge dark eyes, which were filled with childish mischief, gazed in open adoration at the person taking the photo.

India gasped and attempted to straighten, but something had happened to her legs and she felt the energy drain from her body as she struggled not to topple over in a heap.

'Are you alright, Miss?' came the elderly man's voice from behind her.

Before India could answer, she felt a hand beneath her elbow steadying her balance and enabling her to lift herself from the crouching position. She hadn't heard the man follow her downstairs, and as she looked into his concerned face, she couldn't help thinking that for someone so old and on the thin side, he was stronger than he looked.

'I'm fine now… I think. Thank you,' she said, feeling her eyes drawn back towards the photo.

The old man followed her gaze thoughtfully. 'Pretty little thing, isn't she?' he remarked, his gaze darting from her to the photo and back again. 'You had me scared there, Miss. Thought you were going to collapse on me. Maybe we should head back upstairs?'

Still feeling slightly giddy, India tore her gaze away from the picture and followed the man back up the stairs. As he resumed his place behind the counter, she waited for him to sit down, and for the second time that day, she forced herself to be brave.

'That photo I was admiring… do you know whose it is? I mean, who left it here for sale?' she enquired,

166

holding her breath.

The old man squinted back at her. 'Those pictures aren't for sale, Miss. They're waiting to be framed, and that particular photograph belongs to someone who works in this shop.'

India tried to find the hazy memory of the day of her birthday party. Her mother had insisted she wear that uncomfortable dress, which was full of starched, scratchy frills, making four-year old India feel very uncomfortable.

India took a deep breath. 'I might be interested in buying it,' she said, 'when it's been framed, of course,' she told the man. 'Could you pass on my details to the owner, just in case he decides to sell it?' She was surprised at how even her voice sounded despite the pounding of her heartbeat in her ears.

The old man lifted a weathered hand to rub at his forehead. 'Can do, but I don't think he will, my dear,' he said doubtfully.

'Just in case... you never know,' she persisted, holding his gaze.

The old man shrugged, then handed her a pad of paper and a pen and waited while she wrote down her name, email address, and mobile number to give to the owner of the photograph.

India's mind was buzzing with questions as she left the shop, and on the drive home she felt a mixture of excitement and trepidation at what lay ahead. Ruby had told her in the letter that she wanted her to find her father. And although Noah hadn't been at the flea market in person, India had found him in another way.

India couldn't wait to tell Jez that she'd been to the flea market and had left her contact details for her father. What would come of it, she had no idea, but at last she had finally done the one thing she'd been dreading for weeks.

Chapter Thirty

May 1941

Ruby felt nauseous but forced herself to carry on working – anything to take her mind off her predicament and morbid thoughts of Reilly's final moments.

Were his last thoughts of her? And did he suffer, or did he die quickly? A tiny voice inside Ruby's head told her to be grateful she was carrying Reilly's child; at least this way, a part of him would live on. But nothing alleviated the agonising pain she felt at his loss or the grief tearing her up inside.

Tomorrow morning, she vowed, she would go to Scarlett's lodging house to see her. As Scarlett was out working as an ARP warden most nights, she might be sleeping when Ruby arrived. But she felt sure her friend would want to see her in the circumstances.

Scarlett had been there to support Ruby when she'd received Jude's damning letter about Reilly's fate, and claimed that she had seen this was about to happen. But Ruby had been beside herself with grief, and it was only after Scarlett had gone home that she realised she still hadn't told her friend about the baby.

Last night, desperate to speak to Scarlett, Ruby had

used the communal phone in the hallway to phone her, but she'd listened as it rang and rang, and eventually she gave up trying to get hold of her friend.

Arriving for work earlier in the day, Gerald had asked her to step into his office. 'I'm sorry to hear about your young man, Ruby,' he'd said kindly. 'You don't look too chipper, my dear,' he added. 'Do you want me to take you home?'

Gerald's kindness had almost broken down Ruby's barriers, but somehow she managed to control her grief. 'Thank you, but I'll be fine,' she'd replied, lifting her chin and standing up.

'Wait a minute. There's something else I want you to know, Ruby,' he said, shifting in his chair and looking a bit awkward. 'Dick McCarthy's been very interested in where you've been these past weeks,' he went on. 'But you need to be wary of him.'

Ruby felt like laughing at the thought that she'd be attracted to any man other than her wonderful Reilly. 'I have no intention of courting anyone,' she reassured him, thinking about her awful predicament.

She didn't particularly like Dick, either. He was loud and a bit brash, but that didn't warrant the kind of dislike her boss seemed to be displaying.

Gerald sat back in his chair and sighed. 'Dick has a reputation for violence; sorry to be blunt. Did you hear about that soldier who was found dead in the town a few months back?'

When Ruby nodded, Gerald continued. 'Some people think Dick was involved, as the young man who died was courting a girl Dick was interested in,' he said giving a sombre nod.

Ruby was shocked. 'Good God. What happened, Gerald?' she said. 'If he killed someone, why isn't he in prison?' She was alarmed that Dick could get away with something like this.

Gerald shook his head. 'Let's get this straight, it's only a suspicion. There was no evidence to convict him. People said Dick waited until the soldier was drunk and then caught him in a side alley,' he explained with a grave expression.

Ruby remembered the first time Dick and his naval friends had appeared in The Fortune of War, and how all eyes had been upon him. She couldn't deny she had been attracted to him at the time – long before she met Reilly.

Dick was certainly good looking, with hazel eyes, close-cut, army regulation, fair hair, and a well-muscled body. Harriet had giggled and teased her on how his gaze had followed Ruby's every move behind the bar.

Dick had never made any effort at conversation with her, even though Ruby knew he constantly watched her, with an intense look in his eyes. At the time, she'd been flattered by the silent attention he was paying her. But since falling in love with Reilly, she had never given another man any thought. There had only ever been one man for her.

Gerald's warning was unnecessary. And with the posters the government had recently put up saying 'Careless Talk Costs Lives', Ruby felt local people shouldn't be deciding who was guilty and who was innocent, during these troubled times. Dick was away fighting in the war, doing his bit in the Navy, like the other men.

As she stepped out of Gerald's office, she'd nearly bumped into the man himself, hovering outside the doorway. She stopped abruptly but instead of moving out of her way, Dick stayed exactly where he was.

'You all right, Ruby?' he said, placing his hand on her arm.

His eyes were so full of sympathy that Ruby nearly crumpled, but instead she stood up straighter and looked Dick in the eye. 'I'm perfectly fine, thank you,' she said firmly.

Dick shrugged those big shoulders of his and gave her a lingering look. 'If you want some company later, we could meet after ya finish work?' he said, stepping aside to let her go by.

Ruby tried to ignore the intense look in his eyes. 'That's very kind of you, Dick,' she told him, 'but I won't be free to meet later.' And before he could say anything more, she walked quickly back to the bar.

Chapter Thirty-One

India returned to see Jez working in Ruby's front garden. As she walked through the gate, she longed to run up to him and tell him about her visit to the flea market. But he had his back to her, so she paused for a moment watching him effortlessly pulling a dead bush out of the clay soil.

'Hello, India,' Teagan greeted her loudly, appearing from around the side of the house where she had been finishing off the last of the decking.

India smiled and greeted them both, but her heart sank. She wouldn't be able to talk to Jez in front of Teagan, so it would have to wait until later. 'Cup of tea anyone?' she trilled, before making her way indoors.

At last it was five o'clock and she watched Teagan leave and Jez begin tidying the garden tools. She forced herself to be patient as he came up to the back door.

'Hi, darling,' he said tenderly, stepping into the kitchen and taking her into his arms. 'How are you?' he added softly into her hair.

India burrowed into his embrace and sighed with contentment as they kissed passionately. Then he stepped away from her and looked into her face. 'You look happy, India,' he observed. 'Had a good day today?'

India took a deep breath and grinned. 'Yep, you

could say that,' she told him. 'I've been to the flea market,' she added proudly. *Was it her imagination, she wondered, or did Jez's eyes cloud over just for a second?*

'That's great news. You can tell me all about it in the pub,' he said stepping away from her. 'I'm really filthy, so I need to go home to shower and change. I'll see you in The Laughing Fish at seven?'

India got changed into her best linen dress and heeled sandals before making her way to the pub. She felt as if she were walking on air, and that at last everything in her life was coming together.

Maybe once she'd sorted out the house, she would stay in Isfield. She could still sell Ruby's house but move somewhere a bit smaller in the village. *Or move in with Jez perhaps*? Her heart lifted at the thought.

Jez was already waiting for her in the corner booth of the pub, and a tingle of desire shot through India's body when she saw him. He was wearing a dark green shirt and the colour suited his tanned complexion, but as he stood up and kissed her lightly, she noticed a shadow passing across his face again. However, this was soon replaced by a wide beaming smile.

Once they had their drinks and the menus in front of them, India explained to Jez what had happened at the flea market, finishing up by telling him about the photo which had been taken when she was four.

'The old man took my details, so I should be hearing from Noah soon,' she said, feeling a fluttering in her stomach at the thought of being reunited with her father.

Jez, though, didn't look quite so enthralled by her story. 'What's the matter?' she asked him, a shiver of unease creeping down her spine at the expression on his face.

He swallowed and leaned in towards her. 'I'm pleased for you, India,' he said hesitantly. 'I hope Noah gets in touch soon,' he added, frowning.

'What is it, Jez? You don't look happy if you don't mind me saying.'

Jez took a swig of his beer then looked at her intently. 'There's a couple of things you should know before you meet up with Noah,' he said, as if choosing his words wisely. 'One of them, Noah will tell you, and to be honest is not a big deal these days. But the other thing involves me.'

India held her breath, wanting Jez to stop looking at her as if something was very wrong, just when she wanted everything to be right between them. 'Go on then. Tell me. I can take it,' she said bravely.

Jez pushed himself back into his seat and took a deep breath. 'When I was a teenager, your father was very good to me,' he said slowly. 'As you know, my own father died when I was very young.'

India yearned for the old Jez to come back, the one who didn't look so worried. Whatever he was about to tell her would make no difference to how they felt about each other, she reasoned.

'At seventeen, I lost direction and got in with the wrong crowd.' He lifted one hand and ran his fingers through his thick, fair hair. 'You know how youngsters are,' he said attempting a smile.

India nodded, feeling a hard lump forming in her throat at where this conversation may be leading.

'My mother was struggling… with me mostly. You see, I'd lost my way,' he paused and then frowned again, giving a slight shake of his head. 'My grandmother could see what was happening, and asked your dad to help out… you know, be a bit of a father-figure to me?'

Jez suddenly looked even more uncomfortable and stared into his beer before taking another large swig, then he looked up and met her eyes.

'India, I'm only telling you this, because I understand it might be hard for you to hear,' he said uneasily.

As she gazed at him, India felt the lump in her throat turning to unshed tears, which were way too near the surface. It was difficult for her to hear this, but it was obvious Jez was finding it tough, too. Realising that Noah had been there for Jez and not her during her growing years, was like a knife twisting deep inside her heart.

'I'm sorry, India, but that's what happened, and I can't change it now,' he said with a pained expression.

India could see that Jez was desperate for her to understand that whatever happened hadn't been his fault, but she just wanted him to be quiet now. She really didn't need to hear any more, but it seemed he was intent on finishing what he'd started.

'Noah set me on the right track,' he continued, looking pensive now. 'He helped me discover gardening as a career. It all took a while, but we got there in the end, and I owe him an awful lot,' he added reluctantly.

India could see Jez studying her face, perhaps to gauge her reaction to this latest revelation, and she swallowed hard before attempting a shaky smile. 'Thanks, Jez,' she whispered.

Suddenly she had to get away from Jez. The need to escape him was urgent, as she felt her chest growing heavy and her stomach churning.

Standing up abruptly and ignoring the shocked look on his face, India retrieved her handbag from the back of the chair.

'I'm not feeling well, Jez,' she explained. She thought she might be sick at any moment, then she turned and fled from the pub, leaving a stunned Jez staring after her.

Chapter Thirty-Two

Dick was watching Ruby intently from his corner booth and she couldn't help glancing in his direction. When she caught his eye a few times, he nodded in a friendly way and smiled at her. In a strange way, she felt comforted by this and even considered meeting him later.

What harm could it do? She felt so lost, alone, and unable to face the future; maybe it would take away some of her pain for a few hours. She discarded Gerald's warning about Dick as being simply local gossip.

A while later, when the bar had gone quiet, she turned from serving a customer to find him standing in front of her. He still had that intense look levelled at her.

'What would you like, Mr McCarthy?' she said, trying to sound more cheerful than she actually felt inside.

Dick ran his fingers through his cropped fair hair, and leaned casually against the bar. 'You can call me Dick, for starters, honey,' he drawled. 'Then you can come out with me later,' he said, gracing her with a charming smile.

Ruby felt her face go warm under his gaze. 'What do you want to drink, though?' she said, knowing he had deliberately misunderstood her.

'An ale will be fine. But I ain't going ta give up on the other two requests,' he returned, as she reached for a pint glass.

An influx of customers kept her from Dick for the next few hours, but Ruby saw him still hovering nearby. When he disappeared into Gerald's office, she tried to justify to herself why she was so drawn to him. Maybe his relentless attention was helping her forget the ache in her heart, and the tears which were never far away.

As Ruby watched the last few customers leaving the pub, she bid Gerald goodnight and strode quickly out into the cold night air.

Walking along the pitch black, deserted prom towards Regency Square with her tiny torch shining onto the ground, Ruby dreaded going back to her lonely room at the lodging house. She was alone with her grief; maybe Dick's company would have eased that dark, clawing feeling. *No*, she told herself sternly, *Dick might be charming but he was not the answer to her problems right now.*

Ruby paused at the sound of the waves lapping onto the shore, and gazed in the darkness, past the sandbag trench, towards the sea. For a moment she saw herself wading into the freezing water, going deeper until she was completely submerged.

Her heart raced as she leaned against the railings and let the hot tears fall unbidden down her cheeks. Her darling Reilly was dead. Tonight, the agony was so raw, so intense, that all she wanted was to be in his arms again. And in truth, who in this world would miss her if she died? Only Scarlett, and she was a strong young woman who had survived much worse

179

than the untimely death of a friend.

Suddenly Ruby became aware of someone standing next to her in the pitch darkness and her heart lifted. Reilly had come back to be with her again, she had willed it with her thoughts of him, and her eyes flew open expecting to see the ghostly image of her lost lover.

Instead, the dark outline of another man's face appeared, making Ruby gasp with fear. Ice-cold shivers clutched at her heart as she roused herself from her dismal thoughts. Instinct made her lift her torch and start running as fast as she could towards Regency Square and safety.

'Wait! Where you off to, Ruby?'

Ruby had reached the edge of the pavement, where the painted white lines stood out in the darkness, just as the man emerged from the shadows and grabbed hold of her arm. Her side hurt as she stared at him, and through the blackness his face emerged.

'What the hell do you want, Dick?' she said breathlessly, her chest heaving as she took great gulps of air into her lungs. She wasn't sure if she was relieved it was Dick, or frightened because of this man's reputation.

The curfew left the streets of Brighton deserted at this time of night, and only a few people were allowed special permission to be out. Ruby was suddenly acutely aware of how vulnerable she was. She yanked her arm out of his grip and began walking quickly towards the sanctuary of Regency Square, her heart racing.

Dick quickened his pace to keep up with her. 'Listen up, Ruby,' he began. 'I spoke to Gerald today. He told me what 'appened and I'm sorry, really I am.'

Ruby stopped and looked suspiciously towards Dick, who was staring at her with sympathy in those hazel eyes. Suddenly the dam of grief inside her burst and right there on the street, for the second time, she began to sob uncontrollably.

Before she knew what was happening, Dick pulled her into his arms, holding her tightly against him while whispering words of reassurance into her ear. After a few moments, he led her over to a nearby bench.

Unwittingly, she began drawing comfort from his closeness. A tiny slice of the heartache began ebbing away as the words tumbled out of her mouth, and Ruby told Dick all about Harriet, Reilly, and the baby. Clinging to his strong arms, unable to let go, she admitted she didn't know how she'd manage now with the baby coming.

'Ruby, honey, you don't 'ave to worry. I'll look after ya both,' he said. 'I love you,' he crooned, lifting her face to his and kissing her gently on the lips.

Ruby could not profess to feel any passion for Dick McCarthy, but in that brief moment she found a crumb of solace. The thought of someone taking care of her was comforting, and to have shared this terrible burden with another human being was a huge relief.

Chapter Thirty-Three

Jez stopped to survey the work he'd done on India's garden so far as he sat down on the arbour for a well-earned rest. Reaching for his water bottle, he drank quickly to quench his thirst.

He felt restless today, and despite his weary body, he needed to sit for a while as his thoughts went round and round in circles. Minutes later, he was up again, digging the garden for all he was worth.

He glanced towards the house and saw India through the window, moving around the kitchen. After their conversation in the pub last night, the distance between them had widened and stretched so much that they were awkward around each other and barely speaking.

As he sighed and straightened up, she must have sensed him looking her way and met his gaze through the kitchen window. Even from this distance, he could see the expression of hurt on those pretty features.

A strange feeling came over him. He desperately wanted to go into the house, take India in his arms, and reassure her that everything would be fine. *But he couldn't guarantee that everything would be fine, could he?*

He didn't know what would happen when she was re-united with Noah. It was impossible to gauge the outcome, given how her father had acted towards her these past thirty-odd years.

After India had rushed out of the pub, his guilt had been all-consuming and he had decided to phone. 'India needs to see you,' he'd told the older man. 'There are things you need to tell her, Noah,' he'd added firmly.

'Okay, Jez,' Noah had replied, then admitted knowing his daughter had been in the shop looking for him.

Jez had come off the phone feeling frustrated. He doubted whether Noah, who was a man of few words, would do anything to help the situation.

He longed to take that hurt look away from India's face and kiss those full lips, but he very much doubted that was the right thing to do right now. He couldn't stop agonising about how to make amends for being her father's favourite all those years ago.

Suddenly he made a decision. Before he could change his mind, he began striding towards the house, intent on trying to at least make conversation with India. But just then, Teagan walked through the back gate, and he knew he couldn't speak to India with her listening in.

Trying to hide his annoyance at Teagan's appearance, he updated her on what they needed to do to the borders then they both set to work. But he couldn't help noticing that Teagan was unusually quiet today, and kept darting glances towards the house.

'Are you alright, Teagan?' he asked, rubbing a sore spot on his lower back. He hadn't slept well the night before.

She paused in her work and regarded him. 'Yeah, I'm fine, thanks,' she answered. 'But 'ave you seen India yet today?'

Jez looked back towards the house and frowned. 'Only through the window. I think she's busy working on the renovations today. Do you want to see her then?' he asked, lifting his brows at his assistant.

Teagan shook her head as if strenuously denying this. 'Oh no, I just wondered, that's all,' she muttered, as if it didn't matter in the least.

'How're you getting on with finding a lodger? Any luck yet?' he asked, changing the subject as he started digging again. Teagan had told him months ago that she was looking for someone to share the rent for the cottage next door, but hadn't said what the outcome had been.

Teagan glanced anxiously across at India's open kitchen window and bit down on her lower lip. 'Nope, not yet,' she said quietly.

'What's the matter, Teagan?' he asked her bluntly, planting his feet. 'You seem very edgy today.' But she was either ignoring Jez or pretending she hadn't heard him, as she turned her back and carried on working.

***

India knew Jez had followed her from the pub the night before. She hadn't been home long when she could hear him hammering on the front door, and urgently calling her name.

But she'd ignored his pleas to open the door, letting the tears fall silently in the privacy of her bedroom. Then she'd spent a sleepless night tossing and turning in bed, her mind a whirl of conflicting thoughts.

Jez coming clean about his bond with Noah had caused her to lie awake far into the night, with his words echoing through her head. *Why hadn't Noah loved his own daughter that way? What had she done wrong?* Since the moment Jez told her of his closeness with her father, the feeling of rejection had intensified and haunted India.

Over the years and in the course of so many broken relationships, India had learnt to shield herself from the hurt. But this time, there was nothing to help her cope with the pain.

This morning, when she eventually got up, she felt terrible. Her eyes were red and swollen and her chest felt heavy. She'd looked out the window to see Jez in the garden, and as he glanced her way, she tried to smile but it was soon frozen on her face.

When Jez began walking towards her, she could feel her stomach harden and her heart begin to race, but thankfully Teagan had appeared just at the right moment and saved her from having to talk to him.

Taking her cup of tea into the drawing room, India sat down on the old leather settee as her mind went over their conversation in the pub for the hundredth time. Leaning her elbows on her knees, she covered her face with her hands, feeling as if she wanted to lash out at Jez for the way her father had preferred him to her.

Would Noah get in contact with her, now she'd left her details with the man in the flea market? As little tentacles of hope began winding their way into India's heart, she quickly dampened them down. She dare not hope that her father loved her. A little voice inside her head was telling her it was Jez he really loved.

She squeezed her eyes tightly shut as tears burned the back of her eyes. Suddenly the sound of her mobile phone ringing pierced the air. After a moment's hesitation, she pushed the answer button. 'Hi, Izzy,' she said to her best friend.

'India, is that you? I nearly rang off; you took so long to answer!'

'Sorry, Izzy, course it's me,' India said, sitting upright and rubbing at her eyes with her free hand.

'You sounded strange for a moment and not like you at all. You alright, my friend?' Izzy's concern shone through from the other end of the phone.

India attempted to laugh, but it came out sounding slightly strange. 'I'm okay,' she said, aware that Izzy had been her friend for so long she would very quickly know this was untrue.

As they chatted, Izzy's voice was laced with sympathy, and India couldn't help but pour out her torrent of feelings about her father and Jez.

'Okay, well, maybe that's a good thing. After all, Jez knowing your dad the way he does might make it work in your favour. It's never going to be easy, whichever path you choose, and I think there's more to this than meets the eye,' Izzy said diplomatically.

'Course there is,' India agreed. 'Even if Miranda did lead me to believe Noah was dead, that doesn't excuse his behaviour. Also, I'm afraid that when I do meet up with him, I won't be good enough for him, or I won't be the daughter he thought I was.' India couldn't help the hitch in her voice, and swallowed hard to keep the tears at bay.

'Oh, India, don't torture yourself this way.' Izzy soothed. 'None of us know all the answers, but one thing I do know, relationships are complicated and nothing's ever black or white. Keep an open mind until you can ask your father all these questions yourself.'

India assured Izzy she would try to be hopeful that she would be able to get past this difficult time, and that things would become clearer when – if – she did meet up with Noah. Unbeknown to her, she didn't have long to wait.

Chapter Thirty-Four

Ruby was due to meet Dick after work and was walking towards their usual meeting place. As she strode along, a cry for help echoed through the darkness. She stopped and listened, her heart beating fast.

As usual, in the blackout it was hard to see anything, especially as Ruby only had her tiny torch, which she was supposed to keep pointed to the ground. She couldn't tell whether the voice was male or female, then she heard another voice, quite muffled but definitely male. The second voice was bawling loudly at the person to shut up and take what was coming to them.

Ruby gripped her torch, staring in the direction of the noise, concerned for whoever was in trouble. She was only a short distance from the pub and considered going back for help, but it would be empty now, with no-one there to assist her. Realising the noise had stopped, she stood completely still. Then it came again, but the cries for help were becoming feebler.

Afterwards, she was to wonder why she acted the way she did that night, with no thought for her own safety. But she was driven to try and help, hoping to startle the assailant and give the victim time to escape from what sounded like a brutal attack.

As she drew nearer to where the scuffle was taking

place, the outline of a man towering over someone lying on the ground, came into view. The victim was silent now, while the attacker continued to rain blows down onto him.

Red-hot anger filled Ruby at the way this unequal battle was being fought. With her heart racing, she looked around again for help, but as usual the streets were deserted. So she filled her lungs with air and let out a bloodcurdling scream, before running away as fast as her legs would carry her.

In the moment before she fled, Ruby saw the attacker freeze at the sound of her voice. She didn't wait for him to turn on her, afraid for her own life now, but as she ran away she could hear him calling her name. How he knew who she was, was a mystery, because she had kept herself well hidden while he was carrying out his attack.

Feeling sure she had outrun the attacker now, Ruby stopped for a moment and clutched at her side, where a sharp pain threatened to immobilise her. The bench where she usually met Dick was in sight, so she hobbled towards it, hoping he would appear soon. But just as she sat down, someone grabbed her arm roughly.

With her heart in her mouth and gasping for breath, she pulled away and faced the man. 'Good Lord! Oh, I'm glad it's you!' she exclaimed with relief.

Dick's eyes were wide with surprise. 'Ruby, what you doing 'ere?' he said urgently.

'Oh, Dick! Did you see that man, he was…' Her voice trailed off as the light of the moon overhead lit up his face, and seeing Dick's features clearer now, she realised he was the attacker. She stared at him dismally, taking in his fair hair in disarray, his torn clothes, and his fists, which were grazed and bloodied.

Fear coursed through her, mixed with anger. 'What the hell were you doing back there?' she said bravely. 'What had that poor person ever done to you?' Her legs felt weak and shaky, and she fought the urge to flee, knowing he could easily outrun her this time.

Dick's expression changed rapidly from anger to one of resignation, and he slumped down on the bench and sank his head in his hands. 'That low-life 'as done plenty. He raped me sister,' he said morosely.

'Oh my God, Dick. That's awful.' Ruby was feeling sorry now that she'd accused him unjustly. Maybe the man did deserve the beating Dick had been giving him, but taking the law into his own hands wasn't right in her book.

'Surely the police should deal with him, not you?' She sat down next to him. 'If that's what he did, he would soon get what he deserved.'

Dick looked up and gave her a hard stare. 'My sister can't prove nothing, and anyway, with the war on the police ain't got time for local crimes,' he sneered. 'I was only doing what anyone else would do.'

Ruby had no idea what to say to Dick, feeling an uneasy prickling down her spine. He claimed he was looking out for his sister, but beating hell out of that man had been an awful sight.

'It should still be reported,' she told quietly. 'You can't go taking the law into your own hands, you know.'

Dick sat up, pushed his shoulders back, and regarded her. 'Stop worrying about 'im, he's got what 'e deserved now and he won't be bothering her no more.' As he spoke, he suddenly gave Ruby a self-satisfied smile. 'How about a cuddle, my love?' he said, pulling her roughly towards him.

To Ruby's alarm, Dick's black mood had suddenly disappeared and been quickly replaced by something akin to desire in his eyes. She stared at him, puzzled by this sudden change of mood. As she reluctantly went into his arms, she tried to push any doubts about him from her mind.

Chapter Thirty-Five

The next day, India was relieved to see that Teagan was working on the planting and Jez was nowhere in sight. This meant she wouldn't have to think of ways to avoid talking to him, or to look longingly at his beautiful physique while he toiled in the garden.

The weather was cooler today and a bit overcast, and she decided to put all her energies into the renovations. As soon as they were done, she would be selling the house and moving on.

Izzy had suggested India move back to Hackney to be near her and Dimitri, and India admitted the idea appealed to her. It would be nice to be back living nearer to her friend, especially once the baby was born.

Now that some kind of plan for her future was in place, India felt calmer, and she continued working in the front parlour, which was almost finished. With the renovation of the Victorian fireplace complete, she could start on the decoration of the room.

Hours passed as she concentrated on the painting of the new coving and skirting boards, until she realised it was getting dark and she needed the lights on to keep working. Time had gone by so quickly that she realised Teagan had gone home without saying goodbye. Her neighbour had seemed a bit distant recently, but India realised the girl probably had a lot on her mind with her sister's treatment.

Once India had cleared up her decorating equipment and washed her paintbrushes, she went through to the kitchen, opened a tin of soup, and put it on the hob to heat through. While she waited, she looked out of the window and acknowledged the garden was looking very impressive indeed.

Once India had eaten her soup, she felt tired but didn't want to go to bed early. She knew she would struggle to get to sleep, so she switched on her laptop and glanced through her emails.

The sound of the doorbell echoed through the house, and she stood up impatiently and walked quickly through the hallway.

As India opened the door, her heart began racing. Her hand flew to her chest and she stood frozen on the doorstep. The face that stared back at her looked so familiar, the shape so like her own, that her head began to spin.

Somehow, she couldn't make her voice work, as Teagan's words echoed in her head, 'a regular, old guy, with lines and grey hair.'

'Hello, India... can I come in, please?' he said tentatively.

His voice was the same as in her blurred memory. Those large expressive eyes were so like her own, apart from more lines in their creases. The once dark hair was now grey, but still thick and wiry in places, and his olive complexion had the addition of a few age spots. That wide mouth was speaking to her, but India couldn't seem to hear the words.

Later, she would wonder how she got from the front door to the kitchen, because she didn't recall asking Noah into the house. But the kitchen was where

193

they ended up, looking awkwardly at each other until, on autopilot and to bring some movement back into her body, India put the kettle on to boil and began automatically making coffee.

'India,' Noah said with watchful eyes, 'please stop that.'

She turned around and stared at him, this stranger who was her father, standing in her kitchen – or rather, Ruby's kitchen. She struggled to remember Noah as he had been when she had last seen him, a lifetime ago, when he'd been forty-five. Now he was a man in his seventies.

Her eyes were drawn to the camera around his neck, and an image came back into her head with amazing clarity. 'I saw the photograph you took of me, the one waiting to be framed in the flea market,' she said slowly.

Noah took a step towards her and his eyes searched her face. 'I know, Ron told me about your visit. Also Jez mentioned…' Noah's voice trailed off and he shuffled on his feet.

India felt a tentacle of something like anger burning in her head; thoughts jumped about in her mind. *What had Jez told Noah? What had it to do with him?*

Noah sat down at the kitchen table, the coffee now forgotten, and India sat opposite him. They tried to make small talk for a while, and later India could barely remember their conversation. She'd forgotten all those things she wanted to ask him. Instead, she was consumed with a feeling of dread, as if whatever he had to say would only make her feel worse… if that were humanly possible.

Suddenly she couldn't think straight, couldn't make sense of the jumble of thoughts running through her head, making her limbs feel like jelly, and the energy drain from her body. Eventually, taking a deep breath, she looked across at Noah.

'I'm sorry, I'm not feeling too well,' she told him, feeling her stomach churn, and she watched him nod at her knowingly. Then he left, telling her to get some rest.

The next morning as she blearily made her way downstairs, she found a scribbled note through the letterbox from her father.

Darling India,
I know it was a shock seeing me after all these years, but please remember that despite everything, I'm sorry.
Dad xxx

Reading this short note made India think about the letters she had, which were still unopened in the drawer.

Now they had finally met again, even if it had only been briefly, India knew it was time to read the letters her father had written so long ago. She needed to do this so that they could move onto the next stage of their reunion, however painful it would be for her.

Retrieving the jiffy bag from the drawer, she sat down at the kitchen table, setting the stuffed envelope down in front of her. Before she changed her mind, she quickly slit it open and ran her gaze down the contents.

A pile of letters lay in front of her with India's name c/o Miranda McCarthy and their address in London, written in neat sloping writing. They were secured with an elastic band.

She undid the band and looked at the first letter on

the top of the pile. The postmark was May 1985 – two years after her father left, and India had only been six years old.

What surprised her was that the letters were still sealed, which meant her mother hadn't read them. This made her feel slightly better, but she wasn't sure why. Taking a deep breath, she opened the envelope, drew out the white lined paper and began to read.

My darling India,

I've sent this letter care of your mummy, sweetheart, because I want you to know how much I love and miss you. Every day I think about you and long to see you.

Tears blurred India's vision, but she wiped them away, lifted a shaky hand, and forced herself to read on.

I hope you are being a good girl and remembering to work hard at your reading and writing at school, also still practising your drawing, as you are so good at those little faces you do. My address is at the top of the page, so maybe Mummy can help you write a letter back to me? You could do me a drawing, too, which I will frame and put on my wall, as this would constantly remind me of you.

The letter ended quite abruptly with lots of love and kisses at the bottom, and India felt her chest aching. Then suddenly she was sobbing uncontrollably with no way of stopping the sorrow, which was pouring out now.

As the tears coursed down her face, she leant her

arms on the table and buried her head in her hands. She felt as if she were letting go of something, which had been pent-up for such a long time. India was crying for the loss of her father all those years, for the lies her mother had told, and most of all for losing the only man she had ever truly loved.

It was a short while later as the sobs subsided that India became aware of someone standing next to her. Slowly and tentatively, she raised her eyes, and through her blurred vision saw Jez standing by her side, looking down at her with such open love on his face that her painful heart turned over.

He was holding those large arms of his out to her, and for a moment India forgot that she felt betrayed by Jez, that she could no longer love him. And she let him pull her into his comforting embrace.

Chapter Thirty-Six

'I can get a special licence, Ruby.' Dick leaned across the table in the small tearoom and spoke in a hushed tone. 'I 'ave to go back in a few days, so why not? At least then it'll be official.'

Dick's smile didn't quite reach his eyes and warning bells rang in Ruby's head. That morning, she'd woken up in a sweat with her heart racing, after dreaming of Harriet. As she got dressed for work this afternoon, she thought she could feel Harriet's presence in the room.

'Tell me what to do?' she'd pleaded with the empty room in desperation, worried she was losing her mind.

Ruby had to make a decision quickly. Dick was returning to Portsmouth in a few days and was offering her a way out of her predicament. She'd been to see Scarlett the day before as planned, to ask her advice and tell her about the baby.

Upon arrival at Norfolk Square lodging house, Ruby had found Scarlett inconsolable. She'd just had a visit from Frankie, who was in the middle of his RAF training. He had been granted special leave to come home and see his family, after receiving bad news about his father Eric, who had been killed in action at the battle of Tobruk. Scarlett was upset and still feeling guilty when it came to Eric, and Ruby had ended up consoling her, instead of gaining her friend's valuable advice.

Ruby suddenly became aware that Dick was still sitting in front of her, waiting for an answer. 'Give me a bit more time,' she said, remembering his mood swings and how sometimes she just didn't trust him.

Dick's proposal had come just a few days after Ruby had seen him carrying out the attack on the man he'd claimed raped his sister. She still had reservations about whether he was telling the truth that night; she sensed something wasn't right. But she reassured herself that most men would defend the honour of their sister, and she couldn't blame him for teaching the man a lesson.

Dick sat back in his chair and let out a long sigh. 'Well, don't think 'bout it too long,' he drawled. 'Or it might be too late,' he seemed to say.

Despite her reservations about him, Ruby could hardly believe he was willing to take on Reilly's baby as his own. But she knew she needed to tell him about the other thing, which meant he would surely change his mind.

'Dick… there's something else,' she said tentatively, shifting on her seat uneasily.

Dick narrowed his eyes. 'What is it now?' he said impatiently.

Ruby clasped her hands together and took a deep breath. 'Reilly was mixed race,' she said as loudly as she dare, aware of those sitting around them in the tearoom.

Dick continued to stare at her blankly, and now she was the one feeling impatient.

'Do you understand what I'm saying, Dick?' she snapped, wondering whether he was deliberately misunderstanding her. 'It means the baby will almost certainly be black.' She lifted her chin and waited for Dick to say he couldn't marry her.

To her complete surprise, Dick merely shrugged, looking completely unfazed by Ruby's revelation. 'Don't bother me at all, my love,' he said, taking a long drag on his cigarette. 'It's you I'm marrying, not the babe. Just remember that.'

Ruby was shocked. 'What? Are you saying it doesn't matter…?' She couldn't help feeling surprised at his generosity, and guilty at all the doubts she'd had about him, which were now vanishing into thin air.

'I love you, Ruby,' Dick reiterated. 'I told yer before, I've loved you since I first saw you, when you first appeared behind the bar.' He was leaning towards her with that intense look on his face. 'If you don't love me back, then I 'ave enough love for both of us, and the kid.'

Ruby found herself running a hand across her stomach in a gesture of protection. This baby hadn't asked to be brought into the world, and she had to do her best for it.

'Thank you, Dick,' she said. 'I'll give you my answer tonight.' Ruby stood up, postponing the decision until later. 'Now I must go. I told George I wouldn't be out of the pub for long.'

As she walked back to work, her mind was in turmoil. If she married Dick, her baby would at least have a name. Even if he were killed in action, she would be able to bring the child up as a married woman. Questions without answers went round and round in her head as she busied herself behind the bar.

As the first of the evening customers started filtering through the door, Ruby was pouring ale into a customer's glass when a sudden gust of wind blew open the door, making the air icy cold.

'We got company tonight,' joked the man she was serving. 'Spirits of those dead 'uns, jealous of the ale we are supping, who have come back to haunt us.' There was raucous laughter in the bar at this quip.

A shiver ran up Ruby's spine as she remembered Harriet and Reilly. She wondered what each of them would say if they knew she was considering marrying Dick McCarthy.

There was a lull at the bar for a moment, and as Ruby stared sadly into the middle distance, Maude came up behind her. 'You all right, Ruby?' she asked with concern in her blue eyes.

Ruby swiped at her face and then turned to face the other barmaid. 'Can you hold the fort for a minute while I go to the ladies, please?' she said, feeling the need to escape.

In the lavatory, Ruby stared at her reflection in the mirror. Her eyes looked red from lack of sleep, and her victory roll had come loose, causing her hair to hang in a thick blanket around her shoulders. Her eyes strayed to her dark green dress and she saw that her waist still looked trim beneath the narrow belt, with no sign yet of her pregnancy.

She felt sick to her stomach, but decided there and then it was time to make a decision. 'Come along, Ruby,' she told herself, pulling her shoulders back and going over what to do in her head.

Time was short, and Dick was going back in a few days. She didn't love him; she would always be in love with Reilly. Pulling out a small photograph from her pocket, Ruby stared down at her true love's handsome image and her heart lurched.

Reilly had given her the photograph before he went off to war, declaring his undying love, so sure he would be returning to marry her. She had hoped with all her heart that would be the case. Tears pooled in her eyes as she told herself he was gone forever, and she had to accept it and move on with her life.

Ruby would never forget him as long as she lived, but for the sake of her unborn child she had to take a chance on Dick McCarthy, who seemed to love her dearly.

Despite what she'd seen Dick doing to that man, and what some people said about him, he seemed to be a good man. He was offering her the kind of security she needed. Ruby had no way of knowing what to do, but as Dick was acting like a perfect gentleman, she felt sure that both Harriet and Reilly would understand that she had no other choice in the matter.

Chapter Thirty-Seven

India woke the next morning with a thumping headache, but feeling somehow lighter. She had overslept, and looked at her phone to see it was already ten o'clock, so she pulled back the curtains expecting to see Teagan or Jez working in the garden, before remembering it was Sunday.

Part of her yearned to see Jez after he'd appeared in her kitchen yesterday, and another part of her wanted him as far away from her as humanly possible.

When she had at last been able to stop crying, Jez had stepped back from her and regarded her with those turquoise eyes of his, then he'd lifted his hand and smoothed her hair tenderly back from her face.

'I'm here for you, India,' he'd said softly. 'Anytime you want to let off steam or you need a shoulder to cry on.'

Then he was gone, back to the garden alongside Teagan, making India more confused than ever about how she felt about him. The way he'd acted was strange but wonderful in equal measures – not demanding anything from her, but willing to give so much. She had never known a man like him.

For now, though, her relationship with Jez would have to wait. She was too confused to know what she wanted any more, and she was certainly not ready to forgive him for what she saw as his betrayal. There was, however, one thing she was ready for today, and that was to read the rest of Noah's correspondence.

After breakfast, India sat down at the kitchen table and began sifting through the letters, then she picked one up from halfway down the pile. This one was dated 1993, when India was ten years old, and was addressed to her and not care of her mother.

> *Dearest India,*
>
> *How are you, darling? It's been so long since I've seen you, but I think about you every day and miss you so much.*
>
> *I've been living in something called a commune near Brighton, taking lots of photographs with my big camera. People at the commune love my photos and so I've started selling them. This means I've now got my own studio in Brighton.*
>
> *Do you remember I took a photo of you on your fourth birthday party? That photograph is in pride of place in my studio and I look at it every day.*
>
> *I love you so much, India, never forget that. And remember you can write back to me at the address above (I won't mind if there are spelling mistakes, darling,) but if you don't want to, I will understand, too.*
>
> *All my love*
> *Daddy xx*

All the letters were written in the same vein, with her father telling her how much he missed and loved her. India's heart ached, but the thought kept returning: *If Noah missed her so much, why didn't he come and see her at least once in all those years? And why didn't he check she was actually receiving the letters, instead of leaving it to chance?* She couldn't help wishing with all her heart that things had been different.

She was angry with her mother for pretending her father had died and hiding the letters, but also angry with her father. She had grown up missing him, and he had passed those years missing her, too; it was all so futile and unnecessary.

As India put the elastic band back on the letters and replaced them in the drawer, she felt more confused than ever. It seemed both her parents were to blame for her unhappiness during her growing years, and right now she had no desire to see either of them ever again.

Chapter Thirty-Eight

Ruby stared ahead and tried not to feel disappointed. This was not how she had envisaged her wedding day, in this small registry office, wearing a dress from a second-hand shop, with only Gerald and Maude as their witnesses.

She swallowed the lump in her throat and repeated the words the registrar had said, wishing with all her heart that Scarlett was here with her. Gerald's warning echoed in her head as he stood next to her, shuffling uneasily on his feet.

Dick was looking at her with those piercing hazel eyes, waiting for her to say the words that would tie her to him forever.

'I, Ruby Summers, take you, Dick McCarthy, to be my lawful wedded husband...' she began, her voice shaking slightly.

A short while later, the deed was done, and even though she felt like running a mile, Ruby pushed away her doubts and put a smile on her face. She thought of her unborn baby, knowing that Reilly wouldn't have wanted her to bring the baby up on her own. So she was doing the only thing she could in the circumstances. *Why then*, she wondered, *did she feel as if her world was coming to an end?*

As they walked out of the registry office into the

afternoon sunshine, the emptiness inside Ruby refused to go away. It gnawed away at her as Dick held her close with a firm grip, and she tried not to notice the triumphant look on his face.

Gerald approached her as Dick let go of her briefly to chat to Maude, who was standing nearby. 'I hope you'll be very happy, my dear,' Gerald said into her ear. 'At least I'm not losing you just yet. Have a few days holiday with him, and then we'll see you next week in the pub?'

Lifting her chin, she nodded, noticing Gerald's expression when he looked towards Dick. Her boss obviously still didn't like him and she wished things could be different, but for now it couldn't be helped. 'Thank you, Gerald,' she said, meeting his gaze.

Ruby turned back towards Dick as he returned to her side. 'Is your sister here today?' she asked, looking around for a woman who resembled Dick.

He grinned at her in a slow, smug kind of way. 'What sister? I don't know what you are talking about, Ruby. I ain't got no sister,' he said.

Ruby gasped in shock and stared back at Dick. The look on his face once again sent cold shivers up her spine, and it was then she realised what a terrible mistake she had made.

***

'Flaming heck, you've done what?' Scarlett gasped, looking completely taken aback.

'Didn't you hear me, Scarlett? I married Dick McCarthy,' Ruby said. She held a cup of tea in one hand and clutched her dressing gown around her shoulders with the other.

A few minutes ago, the knock on the door had taken her by surprise. It was Mrs Monday explaining she had a visitor downstairs. Having slept until noon due to working late in the pub the night before, she'd asked Mrs Monday to show Scarlett up to her room.

'But why, Ruby? Gerald warned you about him, so why did you marry him? Unless…' Scarlett's face fell as the penny dropped. 'Bloody hell, why didn't you tell me about the baby? Who else knew about this?' she fired questions urgently at Ruby.

Ruby wished Scarlett would stop swearing at her – something she tended to do when she was angry. Scarlett had told Ruby once that she'd had to change her accent in order to work for Madam Sloane, in the posh furrier's shop all those years ago. But Ruby noticed that sometimes her friend's Brightonian accent returned.

'Dick knew about the baby, obviously, but he was the only one,' Ruby sighed heavily. 'And I did tell you. It's just that you were upset about Eric, and you didn't hear me.' Ruby knew Scarlett hadn't taken in a word of the conversation that day when she'd poured out the whole story to her.

'We had to get married quickly before Dick went back,' she explained.

Scarlett dropped her chin and swallowed. 'How could I not have heard you telling me about this?' she murmured, almost to herself, and then she looked up at Ruby with tears in her eyes. 'I'm pregnant, too,' she told her.

'Oh my Lord! We are both in the same boat then!' Ruby put down her teacup and hugged her friend. 'That's unbelievable. Our babies will be born close to each other.'

For a moment, Ruby's heart lifted at this unexpected news, then she remembered that Scarlett would be having her baby alone. 'Did you tell Frankie about the baby?' she said, lifting her eyebrows.

Scarlett shook her head wistfully. 'I couldn't, Ruby, not after hearing about poor Eric,' she said sadly. 'It just didn't seem right.'

'I'm sorry. I can understand how difficult that might have been for you.'

Ruby secretly thought Scarlett should have let Frankie know about the baby, but then her thoughts returned to her own predicament. 'At least I know I've made the right decision marrying Dick,' she said, bravely pushing away the truth.

'Well, that's a bit of good news then,' Scarlett said smiling. 'I hope you'll both be very happy.'

Ruby lifted her hand to show Scarlett the beautiful ring Dick had bought her the day she agreed to marry him. In doing so, the sleeve of her dressing gown rode up, revealing her bare arm. Quickly, she pulled the sleeve down again, averting her eyes from Scarlett's shocked look.

'Ruby! What's that on your arm?' Scarlett stared at her in disbelief.

Ruby's mouth had gone dry and she avoided eye contact with Scarlett. Instead of answering, she strode casually over to the window and began opening the curtains.

Scarlett was suddenly behind her, and before Ruby could stop her, had yanked up the sleeve. 'What are those awful bruises on your arm?' she demanded, taking Ruby by the shoulders and staring hard into her face.

Ruby pulled away from her friend abruptly. 'It's

nothing,' she said, trying to deny what Scarlett had seen as she sat down on the bed.

'Huh! Not from where I'm standing it's not!' Scarlett stood over Ruby with hands on hips, her eyes blazing. 'Did bloody Dick do that to you?'

Ruby suddenly realised she couldn't hide this from the friend she had known for so long, it was too late for that. She looked up at Scarlett and nodded slowly, biting down on her bottom lip.

Scarlett took a sharp intake of breath and sat down next to her. 'Why? Ruby, what's going on here?' she said, softer now. 'I thought you said he was a good man.'

Ruby was sweating and her pulse raced. 'I never said that!' she snapped at Scarlett, then she dropped her gaze. 'I didn't really know him,' she added, trying to calm herself.

'Oh, Ruby. Maybe you should have taken heed of Gerald's warning about him,' Scarlett said, shaking her head.

Ruby began wringing her hands in agitation, needing to explain to Scarlett how it was. 'I thought Gerald was listening to gossip, being overprotective of me. He's a good man, and he looks out for us barmaids and... well...'

How could she tell Scarlett she'd thrown caution to the wind? She didn't really know why she'd done it herself, except that it was for the sake of the child. When Scarlett didn't speak, she added, 'I had the baby to think of, you see. And Reilly is dead, so...'

She looked towards Scarlett and wished with all her heart she had not married Dick. Could she have survived as an unmarried mother, the way Scarlett would have to now? Ruby told herself that Scarlett was much stronger than her, so she had done the right thing for herself and her unborn baby.

'I don't know what to say, Ruby, except I'm sorry I wasn't there for you.' Scarlett looked resigned and then began pacing the room, stopping in front of Ruby. 'You must leave the bugger, you know,' she said. 'Not just for your sake, but the baby's as well.'

'I can't do that, Scarlett,' Ruby said, looking down at the black-and-blue bruises on her arm and reliving the horror of the nights spent with Dick.

Scarlett's eyes were full of sympathy and she looked deep in thought. 'How did he convince you to marry him then?' she asked.

Ruby gazed into the middle distance for a moment. She couldn't tell Scarlett how she had noticed Dick's mood swings before they were married, or about the evening when she had come across him almost killing another man.

'Dick seemed genuine before we were married,' she said. 'He was concerned for me and said he'd loved me for a long time.'

In truth, Ruby had suspected Dick wasn't all he seemed, but she had been torn and in a terrible dilemma. Concern for her unborn baby, Reilly's child, had overridden everything else. Even overridden her common sense, it seemed.

Dick had seemed as if he were offering her the answer to her predicament, and had appeared to genuinely care for her. That's all she had needed, someone to look after her and the baby.

In hindsight, she knew she had convinced herself that marrying Dick was the only option, and closed her eyes to the signs of his violent nature. 'After we were married, the minute we were alone… he said I was his property and would do as I was told.' Heat flooded behind Ruby's eyelids. 'He quickly changed and was like a different person once the ring was on my finger.'

'Oh, Ruby, what happened, you know…when he gave you the bruises?' Scarlett's tone was gentle, her eyes full of understanding.

'Dick called it conjugal rights,' Ruby answered shakily. 'He forced me to… you know, time and time again. In the end, I told him I couldn't do it any more as I was worried for the baby.' Ruby stifled a sob and put her palms over her eyes to shut out the trauma of Dick's actions. 'I hate him, Scarlett!' she wailed.

Scarlett leaned towards Ruby and stroked her arm. 'Thank God, he's gone back to Navy and for now, at least, you're safe,' she soothed.

Chapter Thirty-Nine

India felt muzzy from lack of sleep and here was Noah again, standing on her doorstep waiting to come in.

She had woken suddenly this morning, with a feeling of foreboding after a vivid and harrowing dream. There had been a train crash, with bodies strewn across the track, and people being carried on stretchers towards ambulances. It made India worry that something was very wrong with her to have such morbid dreams.

Noah frowned at her and scrubbed a hand across his face. 'I apologise for the early hour, India,' he said, 'but I hardly slept last night and couldn't wait another moment to see you,' he said anxiously.

India's heart went out to him as she opened the door wider, pulling her dressing gown around her tightly against the early morning chill.

She led him through to the kitchen where the aroma of fresh coffee filled the room. 'Would you like a cup?' she said, pointing to the coffee maker.

Noah nodded and then stood awkwardly in the middle of the room while she poured the coffee. Part of her wanted to send him away, go back to bed, bury her head under the covers, and forget about this whole sorry business.

They both sat down at the kitchen table where an

uneasy silence ensued. Then Noah folded his arms across his chest and regarded her. 'How're you doing, India?' he asked, holding her gaze.

India longed to ask her father what on earth he meant. How she was in the last few days, or the past thirty-odd years? But the words just wouldn't come.

Instead, she broke eye contact with him and stared towards the window, remembering last night's disturbing dream, and how today she had the feeling that Noah would disappear without trace and she'd have to start searching for him all over again.

Her head was thumping when she awoke, making her realise how frightened she was that this man sitting in front of her could hurt her again. Just like he did all those years ago, and just like every other man in India's life had done.

'India?' Noah leaned forward and touched her arm gently. 'Are you okay?' he probed.

Heat flushed through her body as she looked back at him. 'No, I'm not okay,' she said, trying not to lose her temper and feeling her whole body tensing up. Then, knowing there was no way back now, she said what was in her heart.

'Why didn't you come back and see me after you left?' she said, her pulse racing. 'In case it escaped your notice, I was only four years old,' she said, glaring at him. 'Just a baby, really.'

Noah shook his head sadly. 'Firstly, you must understand that it broke my heart to leave you,' he replied, looking at her as if she should know this.

India felt as if he were looking for understanding or sympathy, neither of which she offered as she waited for him to continue.

'My relationship with your mother had become

214

so strained,' he pinched the bridge of his nose and sighed. 'I couldn't live with her any more, India. She… Miranda was hard to get along with,' he explained.

Noah was staring down at his hands, looking quite defeated, and India couldn't help feeling sorry for him.

'I know Mum's not an easy person at times,' she conceded, trying to choose her words wisely, but it was hard to know what to say.

Noah looked up at her with a soft expression. 'Let me explain a few things,' he said, leaning back in his chair and letting out a long exhale. When India nodded, not trusting herself to speak, he continued.

'After I left, I told myself I'd keep in touch whatever happened, but I'm telling you, India, it was nigh on impossible.' He shook his head in a resigned fashion. 'Miranda said it was kinder for you to have a clean break from me, told me you'd already forgotten me.' He stared past India into the middle distance, as if lost in this unhappy memory, and then he looked back at her with a beseeching look.

India was lost for words. She couldn't understand how her mother could use this emotional blackmail against her father, especially knowing how she'd been crying herself to sleep night after night. She had missed him so much after he'd gone.

'I'm sorry, I know you don't want to hear this, but it's the truth,' Noah said, frowning. 'The weeks turned to months,' he continued. 'I was living in a commune and had no money. But I'd become interested in photography and began building up my portfolio in Brighton. I used to travel to London regularly and watch you from afar, coming out of school, and of course I wrote to you.'

India's breath caught in her throat at the mention of

Noah's letters. 'I never got the letters, Dad,' she said, and watched his mouth fall open in surprise. 'Mum made the decision that it was best I didn't read them, and she's only given them to me recently.'

Noah ran his fingers through his hair and widened his eyes. 'Oh my God. I never thought for one moment she would do that,' he said. 'I mean, I knew she'd rather I didn't see you, but...' He shook his head in disbelief.

'She actually led me to believe you had died,' India said quietly, shaking her head. 'I think she thought she was protecting me,' she told him regretfully, 'but obviously that made everything much worse.'

'Good grief, that's unbelievable!' Noah leaned his arms on the table and shot her a sympathetic look. 'I really am sorry to hear that,' he said.

India nodded. 'I know, it's pretty bad, isn't it? But what I can't understand is, even if she did try to keep you away, why didn't you try a bit harder to see me?' She was eager to hear his answer.

Noah paused for a moment as if gathering his thoughts. 'I suppose at first I thought what she'd said made sense; she was your mum and had your best interests at heart.'

'But what about later, Dad, when I was older? Didn't you think I'd want to see you then?' India could feel the anger rising again, making her chest feel tight.

'Miranda said you were happy, and again I believed her. And as the years started slipping by, I convinced myself that you didn't want to see me or need me any more. Then when she met Michael, I felt as if he were taking my place.'

Noah's voice broke on his next words and his eyes filled with tears. 'I hadn't heard from you, and thought you must hate me by then.' He wiped his face with the back of his hand. 'That's when I began taking solace in my photography… which then took me to distant locations. Tell me honestly, India, what did I have to offer you?'

She felt the tears prick the back of her own eyes watching Noah's obvious distress, but she had to tell it how it was. 'What about love, Dad?' she said shakily. 'That was all I ever wanted from you.'

She scrubbed the back of her hand across her cheek and listened as Noah reiterated how sorry he was that they had lost so many years. *But*, she wondered, *was sorry ever going to be enough?* 'I wish you'd never left,' she told him quietly.

Noah stared at her, his dark eyes full of remorse. 'My relationship with Miranda was destroying me, and I had no choice but to leave.'

India couldn't believe it; they were going around in circles. 'It's all her fault again, is it?' She was sick of hearing her father heaping blame onto her mother, even knowing how difficult Miranda could be. *Surely if Noah had really and truly loved her, wouldn't he have found a way to reach her at least once during those lost years?*

He stood up and put his hands flat on the table. 'India, I know it's hard for you to understand,' he said, then slumped back down on the chair. 'But what can I say to make it right?'

She drew in a long steady breath. 'I can't help thinking these are lame excuses for abandoning me the way you did,' she said, feeling relieved to have said the one thing that had been eating away at her from the start of this conversation.

Noah's face drained of colour. 'India, no! That's not the way it was. I left you in good hands and didn't abandon you – at least, I didn't mean to. It may have turned out that way, but… as I saw it, you had everything you needed, a comfortable life…' He shot up out of his seat again and began pacing the floor.

India stood and faced him, her fists clenched by her side. 'Everything I needed?' she said, heat flushing through her. 'It might have looked that way, but the one thing I needed was you.'

She was beginning to feel like a broken record, banging on about being abandoned and the lack of love, but it was so true especially in the light of what Jez had told her about Noah being a father figure to him.

A heavy silence hung in the air as she waited for Noah to deny her accusation. She watched him staring forlornly out of the kitchen window. As he turned back to look back at her, she noticed the dark circles under his eyes and the deep lines etched across his forehead.

'Look, I'm sorry…' she faltered, not really knowing why she was apologising, 'but it's the way I feel about what's happened over the years.'

Noah nodded at her dismally, and India wanted him to leave now. 'Anyway, it's all water under the bridge,' she said resignedly, turning from him to clear away the coffee cups and hoping he would take the hint and go home.

Noah, it seemed, had taken her cue. 'I think I'd better go now,' he said flatly, 'but before I do, is there anything else you want to ask me, India? Anything at all?'

India thought about the long nights when her head had been buzzing with questions, but now they had all but disappeared except for one. 'Yes, there is. Why was I left this house instead of you?'

Noah shrugged as if this was of no consequence. 'It wasn't a difficult decision, as your grandmother always longed for contact with you – as I did, India.' Noah leaned against the kitchen top and regarded her thoughtfully. 'Ruby's lifelong regret was her estrangement from you. So, in the last few years of her life, she told me she wanted you to have the house.'

He glanced around the kitchen then back at India. 'I was making good money by then, and besides, this house has always held bad memories for me.' Noah shook his head with a pained expression. 'I wanted to sell it and buy her something smaller, but she always refused, saying that here she was close to her one true love.'

India nodded, knowing that he was referring to Dick McCarthy. 'Teagan told me all about that,' she explained. 'How Reilly Brownlow killed Dick McCarthy in a fit of jealousy.'

Noah gasped and gave India an incredulous stare. 'What? That's not true, India! That's lies. Believe me, that's not the way it was,' he stared at her, looking shocked. 'You need to know the truth, that's obvious, but I don't know where to start,' he said with a pensive expression.

'At the beginning would be good,' India offered, glad to be talking about something other than her hurt feelings. She was eager to hear what the truth was and if Teagan had been lying, although she couldn't help wondering who to believe.

'Maybe we should talk about that another day,' Noah said, rubbing at his eyes tiredly. As he reached the front door, he turned back towards India. 'Tell me,' he said, 'who is this Teagan?'

'Teagan Hayward, she's Jez's assistant, but maybe

she's got her wires crossed over Reilly,' India told him.

Noah shook his head and then they said an awkward goodbye at the front door. India watched her father walk down the path, turn back to wave to her, and then he was gone.

As soon as he was out of sight, India suddenly remembered she had forgotten to ask him about the 'valuable item' Ruby had mentioned in her letter that Noah was keeping safe for her. That was another question India would have to save for another day.

Chapter Forty

December 1941

The baby's eyes locked onto hers, and Ruby felt her heart contract. Despite all the suffering and hard times brought on by marrying Dick, this bundle in her arms made everything worthwhile.

Over the past few months, Ruby had been frightened for the safety of her unborn child, keeping her head down when Dick was home. But to her relief, he had stopped forcing himself upon her and she had sensed that her growing girth had put him off.

Dick was likely getting his satisfaction elsewhere, which was a relief, but Ruby knew it was short-lived and he would pressure her now the child had been born, bringing with it the accompanying violence.

Her labour had been hard and long, and she'd thought it would never end. Scarlett had held her hand all through it, and she was grateful for that, despite giving birth herself just a month ago. This tiny miracle Ruby was holding close to her breast was her future now.

A new feeling that she must protect this little mite from the world, but most of all from Dick McCarthy, was giving Ruby an acute sense of purpose.

'He's so beautiful.' Scarlett's voice was soft as she gazed at the child. 'Any name for him yet?' she asked, watching him wrap his tiny fist around her finger.

'I like Noah,' Ruby said simply. 'Do you think it suits him?' she asked, smiling at Scarlett, who still had the warm glow of a new mother herself.

'I think it suits him just fine, honey,' she said. 'Noah it is then. I'm sorry, but I'm going to have to dash. Mrs Penny can only look after Annika for a short time today.'

Ruby nodded and the two women hugged. 'Have you written to Frankie yet?' she asked, as she pulled away from her friend.

Scarlett's eyes shone, and Reilly's loss stabbed at Ruby's heart so much that she had to work hard to keep her smile in place

'I wrote to him last week. As far as I know, he's just finished his training, so I'm hoping he'll be home on leave soon, before he gets his posting.' A shadow passed over Scarlett's face. 'Oh, Ruby, I can't tell you how bad I feel about Reilly,' she said sadly.

Ruby's chest ached as she gazed down at Noah. 'Please don't feel sorry for me, Scarlett,' she said. 'And don't forget, this time you must tell Frankie how you feel about him.' When Scarlett had last seen Frankie, he had come bearing bad news about Eric, and Scarlett had hidden her love for him, not even telling him about the baby.

Now her eyes sparkled with love. 'In the letter, I did tell him how I really feel about him, Ruby. And I hope he still feels the same about me.'

Ruby was pleased for her friend; at least one of them would be happy. 'That's wonderful,' she said with a

222

lump in her throat. 'And he wrote back?'

'Not yet, but it's early days yet,' she said with a smile. 'Of course, I still feel bad about Eric, but I knew the moment I laid eyes on Frankie that he was the one I truly loved.'

Ruby's heart turned over. She had never seen Scarlett looking so overjoyed. 'No need to explain anything to me,' she told her. 'I'm pleased for you. We all need to take what happiness we can in this life. And don't you go worrying about me. I have this precious little bundle now,' she said, hugging Noah close.

Chapter Forty-One

India opened her leaden eyes to see the room in half darkness, and the sound of Beans purring loudly in her ear.

With her heart racing and her breathing shallow, she forced herself to sit up in bed and inhale deeply. *Another awful dream*, she thought, shaking her head as if to dislodge the eerie feeling in her bones.

Beans let out a loud meow in her direction and darted over towards the bedroom door. India sighed, picked up her phone, and saw it was only 5am. There was no going back to sleep now, as Beans needed his breakfast.

She fed the cat then let him out into the garden where he bounded away into the distance. As she filled up the kettle then sat down at the kitchen table to wait for it to boil, she tried to remember her dream. It was all rather hazy now.

She remembered the image of Teagan bearing down on her in a threatening way, and shivered. No doubt Noah telling her that Teagan had been lying must have been working its way into India's subconscious. Her emotions were raw at the moment, and this would have contributed to it all.

As the sound of the kettle boiling echoed through the silence, India stared out of the window. Another part of the dream was coming back to her now, and she saw again Teagan's features resembling that of a snarling wolf, complete with big teeth and tawny eyes.

It hadn't been a funny dream at all, and it had scared the living daylights out of her, but in the cold light of day it seemed ridiculous.

After breakfast, India decided to throw herself into the renovations. She was making good progress and was on the last downstairs room, meaning she would soon be ready to begin on the bedrooms.

Upstairs was much less daunting, mainly consisting of painting and decorating. The only room which was the exception was the bathroom, which needed a major overhaul.

At ten o'clock India noticed Teagan arriving in the garden, and a short while later she tapped on the dining room window.

'Morning, India,' she said cheerily.

India returned the greeting, and it was on the tip of her tongue to tell her about the dream, but something made her hesitate. 'How are you today?' she asked.

'I'm alright, but I'll only be 'ere a couple of hours this morning as it's the dentist for me later.' She grinned widely, showing a large gap in her front teeth. 'A crown dropped out in the night,' Teagan explained.

As she opened her mouth to show India the missing tooth, India shivered, seeing again the wolf's wicked grin in Teagan's square-jawed face.

'Someone walk over yer grave?' Teagan asked, leaning on the windowsill and sipping at her water bottle.

India blinked and stared back at her, wondering what on earth was the matter to make her imagine

225

such daft things. 'What do you mean, about the grave thing?'

'Saw yer shiver, that's all. Don't you know it's an old expression?' Teagan grinned.

India laughed then told Teagan she had to crack on. Immersing herself in the renovations might help to alleviate her over-active imagination.

A few hours later, Jez turned up when India was sitting in the arbour eating her lunch. As he walked towards her, her eyes were drawn to his muscular body clad in a tight t-shirt, and India's heart fluttered as she remembered their lovemaking.

She wished herself anywhere but in the garden at that moment, even though she longed to ask him what he'd said to her father. *Had he told Noah to seek her out?*

Jez stopped in front of her and lifted a hand to shield his eyes from the sun. 'Good morning, India,' he said, but his tone was so tender that India felt the words could just as easily have been 'I love you, India'.

She blinked into the sunlight. 'Morning, Jez,' she returned, her pulse racing. Things had felt a bit awkward between them after he'd found her crying in the kitchen and she'd ended up in his arms. The following day, he'd rung to ask her if they could meet up in the pub, but she'd told him she wasn't ready for that yet. In truth, she didn't know if she'd ever be ready to resume their love affair. Right now, she felt embarrassed and confused in equal measures.

'Have you seen Teagan today?' Jez interrupted her thoughts. He was standing upright, blocking out the sun and regarding her with interest.

'Gone to the dentist after a crown dropped out in the night,' India explained, lifting herself up from the arbour.

Jez clenched his jaw. 'What! That was last week. Honestly, she's the limit!' he said angrily, his face reddening.

India was annoyed at his reaction. 'Teagan showed me the missing tooth,' she said in defence of the girl.

'Oh, she's always got one excuse or another,' Jez continued, looking agitated.

'She's got a lot on her mind, Jez,' she said, tilting her head to one side. 'Maybe when she takes Skye for one of her hospital appointments, she'd rather not talk about it.' India was remembering how sensitive Teagan could be about discussing her sister, and the closed look on her face whenever Skye was mentioned.

Jez shot her a confused look. 'What? Who's Skye then?' he asked in a sharp tone. 'Teagan's never mentioned anyone by that name.'

India was baffled. How could he not know who Skye was? 'She's Teagan's sister, you know, the one who has cancer...' her voice trailed off as Jez stared at her with a blank expression.

He shook his head and pursed his lips. 'India, Teagan told me she's an only child, and when she first moved to Isfield she said she was looking for a lodger to share the rent next door with.'

A prickle of unease crept up India's spine as she remembered the snarling wolf that was Teagan in her imagination. *That was just a silly dream*, she told herself. 'Right, that's a bit strange,' she said thoughtfully. 'Why would she tell you one thing and me another?'

'And she told me the other day that she still hasn't found a lodger,' Jez went on. 'Not sure why she would bother lying to you about something like that. What's the point?'

India didn't know why Teagan would lie to her

either, and because her unease was growing where Teagan was concerned, she found herself telling Jez what she had said about his business when India first met her.

His eyes widened. 'Unbelievable! I'll be having words with her about that. The company is not struggling. In fact, I've never had so much work, and to tell that to a potential customer...' he shook his head as he spoke.

India couldn't blame Jez for being annoyed. She, too, felt nettled that Teagan had lied to her about Skye and about the state of Carlisle Landscaping. Then she remembered what Noah had said about Teagan not telling the truth about Ruby, Reilly, and Dick.

It was all very confusing. She needed to ask Teagan about all this later; maybe there would be a perfectly reasonable explanation. She turned to go back indoors, almost bumping into Jez, who was standing so close to her now that she could smell that woody scent of his.

'India, can we meet up later in the pub, or wherever you like really?' he said pleadingly. 'I don't care where me meet. I just need to talk to you, that's all.'

The look in his eyes tore at her heartstrings; they were filled with such longing, and he seemed to be gazing into her very soul.

But India straightened her back and pulled her defences around her before looking up into his handsome face. 'There's nothing to talk about,' she told him, and watched his face fall at her words. Then she strode back into the house on shaky legs.

Chapter Forty-Two

One Saturday morning, Ruby found Scarlett standing on her doorstep, concern in her turquoise eyes and her brow furrowed.

'Hello, what brings you here? Is everything all right with Annika?' she asked, jiggling a fractious Noah on her hip.

Scarlett nodded but walked quickly past Ruby into the small front parlour. 'I've seen something, Ruby. Something that concerns you,' she said urgently.

Ruby remembered how Scarlett had predicted the bomb, which had killed Harriet outside Hanningtons, and how she'd known about Reilly's fate. 'What is it this time?' she asked, bracing herself for bad news. 'It's not Noah, is it?' She glanced down at the baby, who had begun to grizzle now she had stopped moving.

Noah was now three months old, and Dick had been home on leave once since his birth, forcing Ruby to be on tenterhooks the whole time. She had tiptoed around feeding the baby before he was due and attending to his every need, while Dick spent most of his time in The Fortune of War.

To her surprise, her husband was completely uninterested in Noah and hardly glanced in the baby's direction. Even so, Ruby made sure Dick was never alone with the child, knowing Noah's dark eyes and hair would be enough to enrage him. Daily she lived with the worry that when her back was turned, Dick would take out his violent temper on her precious son.

Scarlett must have noticed her distress. 'Flaming heck, Ruby, don't worry. It's nothing to do with the baby, but you'd better sit down for this one.' She stared at Ruby intently. 'It's twofold really, but I'd better tell you the bad news first.'

'The bad news first?' Ruby laid Noah down in his basket in the corner of the room and shivered in anticipation of what Scarlett was about to tell her.

'It's to do with your parents,' she said slowly, as they both perched on the edge of the settee. 'Although, what I'm about to tell you may not happen,' Scarlett swallowed hard. 'I just want to remind you of that.'

Ruby nodded, feeling numb. 'My parents?' When Scarlett hesitated, Ruby became a bit impatient with her friend. 'Can you get to the point?' she pleaded, feeling anxious now as Noah's shrill cry rang out across the room. Ignoring him for a moment, she waited for the bad news.

Scarlett covered her face for a moment as if to shut out the images in her head, then looked directly at Ruby. 'There was a train crash,' she began. 'The two of them boarded the train… and as it gathered speed, it suddenly hurtled out of control and smashed into the back of another train.'

Scarlett blinked at Ruby, as if remembering the terrible scene. 'I know you never got on with them, Ruby, but it was such a horrible death.'

Ruby felt the hairs on the back of her neck prickle with unease, and she lifted a crying Noah from his basket. 'Let's get this straight, shall we?' she said calmly, while rocking him in her arms. 'You're sure it was them you saw get on the train?' She looked towards the wireless sitting silent in the corner of the room. 'There have been no reports of a train crash.' She was hoping that for once Scarlett had got it wrong.

'I didn't mean to upset you, Ruby,' Scarlett said uneasily. 'It's always hard for me to know if I should say anything or not, especially as sometimes I do get it wrong.'

Ruby reassured Scarlett that she wasn't to worry, and began changing Noah, feeling a dark cloud hanging over her. The conversation changed to the effects of rationing in the town, the long queues outside the shops to buy food, and the American GIs arriving in Great Britain.

'That bomb caused a lot of damage at Park Crescent the other day,' Ruby said, shaking her head. 'Those poor people whose houses were bombed out.'

Scarlett nodded solemnly. 'It looks flipping awful down there at the moment,' she reflected. 'Must be terrible to lose your home like that.'

They had all been shocked when, after a quiet few months, the Luftwaffe had dropped a bomb in the Park Crescent area of Brighton, demolishing houses and killing several people.

Ruby straightened up from bending over Noah, suddenly remembering that Scarlett had said her news was twofold. 'What was the other thing you were going to tell me?' she said uneasily.

Her friend took a deep breath. 'Well, yes... now, Ruby, I don't want to get your hopes up. But I have the sense that Reilly may be still alive,' she said tentatively.

'What! Oh Lord, Scarlett. I feel like I can't breathe!' Ruby gasped, feeling shaky on her feet.

Scarlett quickly hurried over to her and pushed her

gently onto the settee. 'Ruby, please calm down,' she cajoled, looking at her with concern.

'Are you saying he isn't dead?' Ruby said slowly, her eyes widening.

Scarlett frowned and tilted her head from side to side. 'Sorry to give you such a shock, Ruby, but I have to be honest here. Again, I'm really not sure. It's only a sense that, somewhere, Reilly is still alive.' She sighed heavily and touched Ruby's arm. 'I had doubts about telling you this, but if there's hope, I think you should know.'

Ruby felt the familiar ache in her chest return, but at least now the air was back in her lungs. 'Oh, Scarlett, if only you're right. If only...' Suddenly all the pent-up emotion over losing Reilly loosened and gave way. She slumped forward and began to sob uncontrollably, great racking sounds shaking her body.

Scarlett's arm went around her in a comforting embrace, until she was able to sit up and dab at her face with a handkerchief. Ruby became aware of the silence in the room and looked across at Noah, who was now staring at his mother with a frightened look on his tiny face.

'Oh, Noah!' Ruby said, standing up and scooping his little body up into her arms. 'Mama didn't mean to frighten you, darling,' she said, cuddling him close as he began to whimper.

Scarlett left an hour later, full of apologies for upsetting her. 'I must go and relieve Mrs Penny of babysitting duties now,' she said, kissing Noah's soft head. 'Please don't worry. I know you will, but you know where I am if you need me.'

As Ruby rocked Noah, she felt a knot in her stomach remembering a recent visit to her parents' house in

Lewes. She'd always had a difficult relationship with them and had grown up desperate to escape their suffocating presence until, at the age of fifteen, Scarlett moved in next door to them.

The two girls had become firm friends, and the day she left home, Ruby had said goodbye to Scarlett with tears in her eyes. 'You've helped me understand my parents' way wasn't mine,' she told her. Scarlett had been like an older sister to Ruby, guiding her and supporting her until she was able to escape.

Ruby had had no desire for a reunion, but with Noah's birth had felt a duty that these two people who had brought her up should meet their first grandchild. However, they might as well have been strangers for all the attention they gave her.

She had sat in their dark front parlour with baby Noah, who was particularly fractious that day, in her arms. She'd expected her mother to show an interest in Noah, but both her parents had been stiff and formal with her.

However, with Scarlett's news came a raw feeling of emptiness that gnawed relentlessly at Ruby. As she settled Noah to sleep, she had a feeling that she wanted to put things right with her parents.

A short while later, she switched on the wireless and immediately an announcement came onto the radio in loud ringing tones. 'This is a news bulletin,' said the announcer in grave tones. 'There has been a train crash on the express train from London to Norwich. So far, we have no further details, except unconfirmed reports there are at least ten people dead.'

Chapter Forty-Three

India tried to not to look at Jez sitting on the arbour in his cut-off denim shorts. She knew he'd been watching her on and off through the kitchen window, darting quick glances at her all morning.

She was aware of the unfinished business between them, things she needed to say to him. Before her courage deserted her, she walked out of the back door towards him and gazed at his long brown legs stretched out in the afternoon sunshine.

India sat down on the newly turfed area in front of him and took a deep breath while he watched her warily. 'Hi, Jez,' she said, and he nodded at her hesitantly. 'I expect you already know,' she began uneasily, 'that Noah has been to see me a couple of times now.'

India pulled her sunglasses down onto her nose and raised her eyebrows, then deciding she needed to get to the point she added, 'Did you push him into getting in touch after my visit to the flea market?'

Jez eyed her over his water bottle, his expression guarded, and sighed. 'I did see him last week,' he replied, then he pulled his fingers through his hair as if deciding how to answer her. 'I asked him whether he was going to meet up with you, but I certainly didn't push him into anything.'

India rested her elbows on her knees. 'Jez, I didn't need you to do that,' she said, feeling her body tense with anger. 'I'd rather Noah had got in touch with me because he wanted to, and hadn't been pressurised into it by you!' she snapped.

Jez folded his arms across his chest and sat up on the arbour. 'Now, hang on a minute, India,' he said with a cold stare. 'Noah told me he was already planning to see you after your visit to the market, so whatever I said made no difference at all.' He hesitated and then blinked at her. 'Let's get this straight. There was nothing like that meant, and I didn't mean to interfere in your business.'

India lifted her chin and hardened her heart to how good Jez looked in his t-shirt, which was pulled tightly across his broad shoulders. She refused to give into these yearnings.

'Did the meetings with Noah go well, then?' he asked.

India shrugged and stared down at the grass. 'Not too bad, but he hasn't told me much yet,' she said. Then she remembered the conflicting information she'd got from Teagan about Reilly and Dick. 'Do you know anything about what happened between Reilly Brownlow and Dick McCarthy all those years ago?' she probed.

He sighed again. 'India,' Jez said slowly, his eyes searching her face, 'you really need to speak to Noah about all that, not me. I'm sorry, it's not for me to tell you the family history.'

India was aware that he knew more than he was letting on, and she felt a lump in her throat, wondering what 'getting things off her chest' had achieved. They were no further forwards, and she still felt resentful about his relationship with Noah.

Jez stood up and stretched out his back, just as India scrambled up off the grass. As she turned to go back indoors, he caught her hand, and pulled her back towards him. Before she knew what was happening, she was in his arms.

The world and its problems fell away as his lips came down on hers, and she was flooded with warmth, her skin shivering with pleasure at his touch. Then into that brief interlude of time, the shrill sound of her doorbell echoed through the garden, penetrating her senses and jolting her harshly back to the present.

Wriggling out of Jez's embrace, she looked up into his face and saw their love for one another reflected in those startling turquoise eyes. India tore her gaze from his and went to answer the door, knowing she wasn't ready to let go of the hurt he'd bestowed on her just yet.

Breathlessly, she took possession of the Amazon parcel and placed it on the kitchen table, before stopping for a moment to catch her breath. As she glanced out of the window, Jez had returned to work and was now digging the garden as if his life depended on it.

Chapter Forty-Four

May 1947

'Come along, Noah.' Ruby ushered her son towards the hallway, while glancing anxiously back towards the clock on the kitchen wall. 'I don't want to be late for work today,' she added firmly. Noah nodded his dark head at her and grinned.

'What time will you be home, Mama?' he said wistfully, lifting his face to hers.

Noah asked this question every time she had to leave him with their neighbour Dora, and even though school had broken up for the Easter holidays, Ruby still had to work. Without the money she earned, she reminded herself, they would not survive.

'Be a good boy today,' she told him as they walked up Dora's front path. When Noah gave her a mischievous look, her heart turned over, making her regret that she couldn't look after him herself.

She'd tried that when they had first moved to Isfield two years ago, but soon found that the only way to survive was to borrow money from Scarlett. That situation could not go on, and Ruby had been forced to find employment.

After the death of her parents in the train crash,

Scarlett's prediction that Reilly might still be alive had given Ruby hope. This optimism was to give her the courage to leave Dick behind, in the belief that one day she and Reilly would be reunited.

Scarlett had urged Ruby to move quickly. This was her opportunity to get away from Dick, she told her, whilst he was away serving in the Navy. At the time it was nearing the end of the war, and Ruby didn't know how much time she'd have left to escape her husband.

Scarlett had been sure it was the right thing to do. 'It may only be a few miles from Brighton,' she told Ruby, 'but Dick will never think of looking for you here. He'll think you've moved to London or somewhere equally far away,' she'd said.

Frankie had been through his own trauma during the war, when he was shot down over France, and Scarlett had gone through many months of worry after finding out he was missing. However, he had been helped to safety by a resistance group called the Comet Line, and they were now happily married and living in nearby Lewes with young Annika.

The house Ruby had chosen in Isfield was situated at the north end of the village, just a few minutes' walk from a working mill, and a ten-minute walk to St Margaret's Church. Just up the road was a post office and shop, and ten minutes south of the village was a pub and railway station. It was an idyllic place to live and to bring up young Noah.

'Good morning, dears,' Dora said now as she stood in her doorway smiling, her arms crossed over her ample bosom.

'Hello, Dora, as always thank you for looking after Noah,' Ruby said, returning Dora's smile and bending to kiss her son's plump round cheeks.

'Oh, you're more than welcome, my dear,' Dora said, ushering Noah into the hallway. 'Say goodbye to Mama, little man. I've got some nice warm, freshly baked biscuits in the kitchen,' she added, giving Ruby a gentle nudge.

Ruby hurried up Dora's path before Noah became upset. At six years old, he was good at being left with her neighbour, but there had been times when he burst into tears and demanded she stay home from work. She tried to tell him she had no choice, but found this was impossible to explain to a small child.

When Ruby had first met Dora, she'd explained she was a war widow, which had been Scarlett's suggestion to stop any wagging tongues in the village. Dora had no children of her own and immediately sympathised with Ruby's predicament, offering to help with Noah if needed.

'I don't need no payment, dear,' Dora had insisted, when Ruby offered her money after securing a position at Isfield Place. 'Not having any kids of me own, I would love to spend time with little Noah.'

Ruby pushed open the large iron gates leading to Isfield Place, and walked up the driveway towards the back entrance of the Elizabethan manor house. She nodded a greeting to the gardener as she passed the beautiful formal gardens, which were full of colour and located to the west and south of the house.

The garden design was stunning here, and she had heard the Art and Crafts movement had influenced it. Ruby read how this was a reaction to the excesses of the Victorian industrialisation, grown from a desire to restore simplicity to buildings, furnishings, and garden design.

To her left, she could see the new tennis courts, which

had recently been built, and to her right, a swimming pool was under construction. It was a beautiful place to work, and her role as housekeeper was hard work. But she didn't mind, because Lady Isabella was a good employer and fair in her treatment of the staff.

With the war over now for two years, life had returned to some kind of normality here though rationing and other restrictions were still in place. As time went on, Ruby's hopes that Reilly had somehow survived the war, began to fade. Noah, however, had grown into an endearing six-year-old child, who looked remarkably like his father.

As Ruby walked through the tradesman's entrance of the house, her thoughts turned to Scarlett, who had married Frankie on his return home from France. Ruby was pleased her friend had found happiness, and grateful to Scarlett for helping her get away from Dick McCarthy and his violent ways.

However, there was always a niggling worry at the back of her mind that Dick would find her one day. In a phone conversation the week before, Scarlett had revealed that Dick was now illegally married again, which meant he was a bigamist as well as a bully. Ruby felt heartily sorry for the woman he married, and thanked her lucky stars she had managed to escape from him.

Chapter Forty-Five

India was continuing her work in the dining room and the morning was flying by, when she was surprised to see Teagan at her front door in floods of tears.

Not knowing what else to do, as her neighbour seemed unable to talk through her sobbing, India took her through to the kitchen and told her to sit down, where she began the process of making tea.

With her mind whirling from the previous day's conversation with Jez, she was determined to ascertain who was lying to her. But Teagan looked very upset.

India put both the steaming teacups down on the kitchen table and waited while Teagan blew her nose and wiped her watery eyes. She had not yet said a coherent word, but instead kept running her agitated fingers through her short, spiky hair.

'What's the matter, Teagan?' India asked. 'Is it Skye?' she said, deliberately mentioning her sister.

A tiny doubt formed in India's mind. Maybe Teagan hadn't deliberately lied to her about Reilly, but had been misinformed by an old, confused Ruby. But that still left the question of why she had made up a story about her sister.

Teagan lifted tear-filled eyes to India. 'I were so angry when I saw Ruby's grave and what they've done to the 'eadstone. Honestly, India, what's the matter

241

with the youth of today?'

India's heart almost stopped. 'What on earth do you mean?' she said, sitting upright. 'What's happened to the headstone?'

Teagan narrowed her eyes at India and crossed her arms. 'It's been vandalised!' she said angrily. 'Don't know who did it, but honestly, India, it broke me heart to see it.'

She was leaning back in her chair now with her lips pursed together, her short, dark hair standing up in untidy clumps. She was holding her coffee cup so tightly that India thought it might shatter at any moment, sending shards of china shooting across the room.

'That does sound awful. I'll get the police onto it and go and inspect the damage,' she said, studying Teagan and wondering if she was lying again. *Had the girl really been friends with Ruby before she died,* India wondered, *or had that been another lie?*

India decided she had to be honest and shook her head at Teagan. 'You told Jez you don't have any siblings,' she began, watching Teagan's shocked expression. 'So, how do you expect me to believe this if you've already lied about Skye?'

There was a long pause as Teagan digested her words. 'Dunno what you mean,' she said, giving an impatient huff and curling her lip. 'It's Jez that's lying, not me.'

India let out a long sigh. 'He also said you've been looking for a lodger since moving next door. Is that true, Teagan? And if it is, why isn't Skye living with you?'

Teagan didn't answer this but muttered something India couldn't hear, then she glared back at her. 'I'm your friend, India. I wouldn't lie to you, not like Jez, who's hiding all sorts of things from you.'

Alarm pulsed through India. 'What are you talking about?' She felt herself faltering under Teagan's scrutiny, and doubts about Jez began crowding her mind.

'I know all about what happened in the old mill,' Teagan said smugly.

India blinked, and despite herself was curious. 'What happened at the old mill?' she said, having no idea what Teagan was talking about. 'Did this involve Reilly and Dick?' Thinking of Reilly made her recall how several items had either gone missing unaccountably, or been moved in the house since she'd moved in.

Teagan shrugged. 'I'll tell you everything Ruby told me if you like, but first I need to get to the graveyard. I've called the police and reported the vandalism, so they're meeting me there.'

'Meeting you there? But why, surely that's my problem not yours?' India was stunned at Teagan taking charge of the vandalism of Ruby's grave, when she was quite capable of dealing with it herself.

'Because I care, India, that's why. And whatever else you think of me, I were fond of your grandmother.' Teagan stood up and headed towards the door.

India was confused. Maybe Teagan was telling the truth this time; she'd certainly looked very upset about Ruby's gravestone. And she still wanted to know what Teagan meant about the old mill.

India quickly decided to check out Teagan's claims about Ruby's gravestone. It would be awful if it had been damaged in the same way Reilly's had. Grabbing her shoes, she called out to Teagan, 'Wait, I'll come with you.'

As she got to the door, her mobile phone began ringing. Stopping to answer it, she heard Izzy's distraught voice. 'Izzy, what on earth's the matter?' India asked, watching Teagan hurriedly climb into her van.

'Oh, Indy, it's the baby… I think I'm losing it!' Izzy sounded beside herself with panic.

'Oh no! How awful. Are you alone right now?' India indicated to Teagan to go on ahead while she focussed on Izzy crying down the phone.

Izzy told her between sobs that Dimitri was driving her to St Ann's Hospital after she'd called the doctor when things just weren't right.

'This doesn't mean you'll lose the baby,' India told her quietly, not really knowing what else to say. 'Stay cool, Izzy. Dimitri's taking care of you at the moment, and I'll be on my way shortly.'

India calculated how long it would take her to get to the hospital; the inspection of Ruby's grave would have to wait until another day.

Shoving her phone quickly into her back pocket, India ran out of the door then stopped just short of her car, taking in deep breaths. In the distance she could see Teagan's van disappearing in a cloud of dust, and she shook her head.

What on earth was the huge rush? Whatever had happened to Ruby's grave wasn't going away, and India was sure Teagan was exaggerating about the police. After all, they hardly responded to burglaries these days, let alone the defacement of a gravestone.

Feeling slighter calmer now, India began the long drive to London. But as she came level with the lane leading up to the churchyard, she slowed the car down.

It would only take a few minutes to investigate Teagan's claim, she reasoned, *and then she could dash off to the hospital to see Izzy.* Making a swift decision, she turned the car left towards the lane and followed Teagan up the narrow road.

Chapter Forty-Six

Ruby and Noah were out walking in the village, heading in the direction of the train station. Noah was train-mad and loved to watch them pull in and out of the station.

The winter had been long and hard. But today they had woken up to what appeared to be a warm summer's day, and as it was Saturday and Noah didn't have school, Ruby had promised him a train ride to the seaside.

The thought of venturing out of the village always filled Ruby with dread; she still lived in fear of coming face-to-face with Dick. But she conceded she couldn't hide herself and Noah away forever, the child needed a change of scenery from time to time. Brighton was to be avoided at all costs, but today she had decided on a visit to the coastal town of Hastings.

Noah enjoyed the hour-long train ride as he always did, and in no time they were stepping off the bus at Rock-a-nore Road. The seafront was buzzing with activity as they walked towards the beach, and they were surrounded by the sound of seagulls and the low murmur of people going about their business.

As they passed a couple of net shops, Noah ran ahead of Ruby on the shingle and pointed to a man seated on a stool painting a picture of some fishing boats.

'Look, Mama,' he said excitedly. 'Can I see what the man is painting?'

Ruby hurried to catch up with her son. His enthusiasm for looking at images, whether it was the painted version or a photograph, had been obvious from a very early age, and Ruby was convinced that one day he would become an artist.

'Noah, wait!' she called to him, worried he would appear rude by interrupting the man's concentration. But Noah was oblivious to her shouts and was already standing next to the artist, chatting amicably.

The man had his back to her when Ruby reached them, but he had stopped working on his canvas and was showing Noah the different colours in his pallet.

As she came abreast of them, Ruby apologised profusely for Noah. 'I'm so sorry. I hope my son hasn't interrupted your concentration...' Suddenly her breath caught in her throat as she stared hard into the man's face.

The man gazed back at her then stood up abruptly, overturning his stool with a clatter as it landed on the pebbles, and taking a faltering step towards Ruby.

His lips were moving up and down with no words coming out as he gaped at her, looking as shocked as she was. Panic filled Ruby, and she grabbed hold of Noah. Tearing her gaze away from the man, she pulled her son quickly back in the direction they had just come.

It couldn't be him, she told herself. *Her mind must have been conjuring up images. Maybe all those years of hoping he was still alive, had resulted in this manifestation of him.*

'Mama, stop!' Noah struggled to free himself from

her iron grip, alarmed at this change of events. But she couldn't stop. She had to get away; her mind was playing cruel tricks on her and she just couldn't bear it.

Once she was a safe distance away from the man, Ruby took a deep breath and leaned down towards Noah. 'It's alright, son,' she said, hugging him tightly to her chest.

As she held Noah close, Ruby became aware that she had been followed across the road. Feeling light-headed, and as if she might faint at any moment, she forced herself to turn around, while still clutching hold of little Noah.

The man was gazing at her in that strange way again, and as their eyes met, adrenaline surged through her body and her mind ran in all directions. He was so thin, whereas Reilly had been muscular, and he had streaks of grey in his hair whereas Reilly's had been jet black.

'Ruby, my love...' the man said, giving her a completely dazed look. 'It's me. Don't you recognise me, my darling?' he said, shaking his head.

He had found his voice, had called her Ruby, and was looking at her through dark, hollow eyes with something like recognition. And his voice sounded just like Reilly's. Her mind continued to whirl as she let go of Noah, while still holding a protective arm around her son.

'Reilly... what happened to you?' The question seemed ridiculous, and her mind struggled to make sense of what she was seeing. She hardly dared hope this man was her one true love.

'Oh, Ruby,' he said, hanging his head as if in agony, while she continued to stare at him. Then he turned those ebony eyes on her. 'It were so awful,' he began.

'I was captured after a long battle in Crete,' he said, his face contorted with pain. 'Twelve days of bloody hell… so many were killed. I were one of the lucky ones, but I spent the whole of the war in a prisoner of war camp.'

Ruby's mouth had gone dry and her muscles felt weak as tears welled at the back of her eyes. This man *was* Reilly, her lost love, the man she had missed every single day of her life since they had parted in Ambleside.

She lifted a hand tentatively to stroke Reilly's cheek, and gazed deep into those dark eyes. In response, Reilly leaned towards her, then she was in his arms and he was holding her so tightly she could barely take a breath.

'Mama, Mama…' Noah cried piteously beside them.

Reilly loosened his grip on her, and for a second his gaze held Ruby's. In his eyes she saw raw hunger and such deep longing that her heart turned painfully over.

Bending slowly towards Noah, who was now clinging to Ruby's legs, Reilly said, 'Don't worry, little chap, I won't hurt your mama.'

Ruby watched Reilly talking to her son, feeling overwhelmed with relief that her lover really was, as Scarlett had predicted, alive and well. It was truly a miracle, and one which she could hardly believe was true.

So many years had passed without seeing him. Yet suddenly, here he was in front of her, talking to Noah, their son, without having any idea that the child was his. For a moment she didn't know what to do, but then as Noah grinned happily back at Reilly, looking slightly more at ease, it became clear.

As Reilly straightened his back, she took a deep

breath and gathered her courage. 'This is Noah,' she said, and before she changed her mind, added, 'He's your son.' The world seemed to stop spinning as the words left her mouth, and all she could hear was the thrashing of her own heartbeat in her ears.

Reilly's eyes darted from Ruby to Noah. 'My son... this is my son? But... I had no idea,' he stammered. Then he stared down at Noah for such a long moment, as if he couldn't believe it, before turning back to Ruby. 'Oh God, Ruby. You must believe that after the war I searched for you, but then I heard about you getting married...' He rubbed a hand anxiously through his greying hair.

She could see he was struggling to find the right words, and she waited, giving him a moment to gather his thoughts.

'Mama?' Noah interrupted, sounding confused. He was staring up at her with concern furrowing his young brow. 'I want to go home,' he whined.

Ruby tore her eyes away from Reilly's face and looked down at her son. 'It's alright, Noah,' she said. 'As this man told you, he won't hurt us and there's nothing to worry about here.' Thinking quickly, she turned back to Reilly and took a deep shuddering breath.

'We need to discuss this another time,' she told him, longing to be back in his arms and feeling her heart lighten at the thought of seeing him again soon. For the child's sake, however, she needed to stay strong. It was enough for the moment to know that Noah, her beautiful son, would now know his father – the man he had never met before today.

Reilly nodded at her without taking his eyes off her face. 'Come and see us at our house later,' she said. 'It's called Taabeez, and it's on Station Road in Isfield.' She was trying to keep her voice firm to reassure Noah, but inside she was shaking like a leaf.

With an iron will, she turned around and walked back the way she'd come with a bewildered Noah in tow, longing for the hours to pass when she would see her precious Reilly again.

Chapter Forty-Seven

Jez parked up outside India's house, surprised to see her car wasn't in its usual place. He'd hoped to tell her face-to-face that Annika had passed away during the night. He knew she'd grown close to the old lady over the last few months.

He was also looking for Teagan; the silly girl hadn't turned up again for work this morning. After yesterday's conversation with India, Jez wanted to know why Teagan had been lying to India and why she'd been bad-mouthing his company. But all that had paled into insignificance when he'd received the call from the care home late last night about his mother.

He felt awful today after a sleepless night. In a sense, Annika's death was a blessing, as she'd hardly known Jez at the end and her life had been all but over for several years now. But the deep sense of loss was still so keen that it was making his chest feel tight and his head thump.

Jez also desperately wanted to break the news to Noah, but so far hadn't been able to get hold of him. A complete technophobe, India's father was notoriously bad at answering his mobile phone, so this was no great surprise.

Jez knocked on India's door, but received no answer, then walked around to the back garden to see if she was there. As she was nowhere to be seen, he headed back towards the gate just as a car drew up alongside his van.

Thinking about Noah, it seemed, had conjured him up, and Jez watched as he stepped out of his car and walked towards Ruby's house. 'Morning, Noah,' he greeted the older man sombrely. 'I've been trying to get hold of you since last night.'

'Oh dear, have you?' Noah dug deep into his pocket and rummaged around but drew out an empty hand, and shook his head. 'Sorry, Jez, not sure where my phone is at the moment. Is everything okay?'

Jez quickly filled Noah in on Annika's passing, and Noah immediately pulled him into a warm fatherly embrace.

'I'm so sorry, Jez,' he said, moving away from the younger man. 'Don't forget, I'm here if you need me.' His dark eyes were full of compassion as he regarded the younger man.

'Thanks, Noah.' Jez stared into the middle distance, feeling his voice choke with tears, still unable to believe his mother was really dead.

'It'll take a while,' Noah said kindly, his expression thoughtful.

Jez looked back at Noah fondly, remembering all the bad times this man had helped him through. 'Yeah, I'm finding it hard at the moment, and keep wishing I'd been there for her when she died,' he said sadly.

Noah shook his head. 'I know, but try not to think that way. She's at peace now,' he said, holding his gaze.

Jez nodded and then looked towards the house. 'If you're looking for India, she seems to be out,' he told Noah.

'I wonder where she is then. More to the point,

where's someone called Teagan Hayward?'

Jez's ears immediately pricked up. 'I don't know where India is, but why're you looking for Teagan?'

Noah narrowed his eyes at Jez. 'Oh yes, that's right, India told me she works for you. Well, the thing is, I need to warn India as I think she may be in danger from the woman.'

Jez felt his anger at Teagan mounting. 'Wait in line then, as I want a few answers from my assistant, too,' he replied. 'What makes you think Teagan's dangerous, though? She's a bit of a gossip and a liar, but I wouldn't have said she's threatening in any way.'

Before Noah had a chance to answer Jez, the sound of a text message reverberated through the air. Puzzled, the two men looked at each other, then glanced around the garden.

Jez watched as Noah's eyes fell on something lying in the grass near to the front door, and when he picked it up, Jez saw it was a mobile phone.

'This must be India's phone…' Noah said anxiously, looking down at the phone, then he gazed up at Jez. 'Listen, I don't want to sound an alarmist but I'm worried. I've found out a few things about Teagan Hayward. Namely that her real surname is McCarthy.'

Jez's scalp prickled with unease, unable to believe what Noah was saying. 'What! How do you know that?'

Noah glanced down at the phone again, where the text was still on the screen. 'I need to stop you there, Jez. We can talk about this later, but I honestly think we need to follow India right now. Look at this message.'

Jez took the phone from Noah's outstretched hand and read the words aloud: *India, where are you? Police are here about Ruby's grave so hurry up.* 'What the hell's going on here, Noah?' he said, concern for India making his heart race.

'I don't know, but if that text is from this Teagan, then there's something very wrong. We need to go to the graveyard now.' Noah placed the phone in his pocket and they both headed towards Jez's van.

Jez climbed into the van and started up the engine. But before he began the short journey to the churchyard, he turned to Noah. 'Are you saying that Teagan is related to Dick McCarthy?'

The cold chill of fear was working its way up his spine. And when Noah nodded in reply, Jez put his foot firmly down and sped towards the churchyard.

Chapter Forty-Eight

Reilly approached Ruby's house with trepidation. His heart was racing and he was feeling slightly disorientated, as if seeing Ruby earlier on Hastings beach had been nothing but a dream.

All the years when he had longed to see her now came back to him. In the prisoner of war camp, all that had kept him going was the thought of being reunited with his darling Ruby.

Now, he could hardly believe he'd found her again, even though it had come too late. Noah might be his child, but Ruby's husband would be bringing him up so there was no place for Reilly here.

Ruby was waiting for him at the front door and he took a sharp intake of breath at the sight of her. The years apart had made no difference; Ruby looked as beautiful as ever. With her red dress showing off her hourglass figure, and her dark hair piled high upon her head, she looked exactly the same as when they had danced the night away in Ambleside.

Reilly yearned to take her in his arms as she moved aside to let him into the hallway. She led him through to the front parlour, and for a moment they stood awkwardly gazing at each other. Then Ruby stepped towards him, wrapped her arms around him in a tight embrace, and rested her lovely head on his shoulders.

With a jolt, he remembered that she was married, and he jumped out of her arms like a scalded cat, glancing around him anxiously.

'What's the matter?' she asked, looking slightly put out, her pretty brows drawn together in a worried frown.

Reilly shifted on his feet nervously. 'Where's your husband?' he asked tentatively.

To Reilly's surprise, Ruby threw back her head and laughed. But when she noticed the stricken look on his face, she stopped and took a step towards him.

'God knows where that blinking blighter is,' she said. 'I hope he's miles away from here and I never ever lay eyes on him again!'

Reilly heaved a sigh of relief. 'You're not married then?' he asked, following Ruby's lead and sitting down on the sofa next to her. When she didn't immediately answer, he took her small white hands in his own. 'What happened, Ruby, you know after I left for the front?' he asked, realising he needed to tread carefully.

Ruby stared into the middle distance and told him what a shock it had been finding out she was pregnant, and at the same time receiving the letter from Jude about Reilly's fate.

'I'm sorry, Reilly,' she said, as her eyes filled with tears. 'I didn't know what to do.'

Reilly could see how devastated and heartbroken she had been, and he pulled her in close to him, desperate to comfort her in her distress. 'It's all right, Ruby, none of this were your fault,' he reassured her.

She took a deep breath and lifted watery eyes to Reilly. 'There was no-one to turn to, you see, and I had to do the best I could for our child, having no means of bringing him up alone.' She told him all this as if trying to convince him. 'Dick McCarthy professed to love me, and proposed to me when I was at my lowest ebb.'

Reilly's heart was aching for his darling Ruby. 'What about your friend Scarlett? Weren't she around to help you at that difficult time?'

Ruby shook her head. 'Scarlett had just heard that someone very dear to her had died, and while she was preoccupied with that awful news... I foolishly accepted Dick's proposal.' Ruby sniffed into a handkerchief. 'I thought he was a kind man, despite being warned to the contrary.'

Reilly had a tight pain in his chest at the thought of his beloved Ruby having to go through such a tough time. Noah was his child, and Dick was obviously not living here, so maybe they could have a future together; he hardly dared to hope this could happen. 'What kind of man was he then?' he asked, holding his breath and dreading the answer.

Ruby's eyes flashed with anger. 'Dick had a violent temper, and after we were married, I was afraid for our safety. I soon realised I had to leave him,' she explained. 'Just before the end of the war, when Dick was still serving in the Navy, both my parents were killed in a train crash. The money from their estate enabled me to move here.'

'Thank God you escaped from him in time,' Reilly said, his fists clenched by his sides at the thought of this bastard Dick McCarthy hurting Ruby and Noah. 'By the way, where's little Noah?' he asked, suddenly realising the child was missing.

'He's with my neighbour Dora for a few hours. She's a lovely lady who spoils him rotten,' Ruby assured him. 'It's your turn to explain what happened to you after we said goodbye in Ambleside,' she added sombrely.

Reilly nodded sadly, thinking of everything he'd been through since the day he had last seen Ruby in 1941. 'Did you receive me letter? The one about me being sent to Crete after my training?' he asked, and when Ruby nodded, he began to explain.

'Crete had become a target after Hitler's occupation of the mainland. And although British troops had been drafted in, our battalion were sent there to add to those already on mainland Greece,' he said shakily, as the memories came flooding back.

Ruby touched his arm softly. 'I think I remember hearing about the German invasion of Crete in May of that year,' she said thoughtfully.

Reilly nodded. 'When I arrived on the island, it were shocking to see the scale of the operation. Thousands of New Zealand and Greek troops were there, along with the British, but they were all poorly equipped for the job. The first German invasion had been unsuccessful, but when they attacked Maleme, it turned events around after the New Zealand infantry defending the area withdrew too early.'

Reilly hung his head and bit down on his lower lip, remembering the carnage of that terrible time. 'Despite suffering appalling casualties, the Germans managed to secure a foothold on the island, eventually gaining the upper hand. In the end, the battle were lost to the Germans after twelve harrowing days.'

He looked up at Ruby, who was gazing at him with sympathy in those beautiful eyes. 'Many men perished, my darling. It were truly horrifying,' he said, shuddering at the memory of the dead and the dying while the battle raged on.

'After it were known the battle were lost, there was mass evacuation, and I was on a ship headed for Egypt and safety, along with hundreds of other men. But the ship was attacked soon after leaving the island, and quickly went down.' Reilly swallowed, remembering how it had all gone horribly wrong.

Ruby gasped and put a hand across her mouth in shock. 'Oh my God, Reilly, how did you survive that? I mean, you must have been so lucky.'

'The ship hadn't travelled far out to sea when it was hit, thankfully, and I were able to swim back to Crete. However, finding myself left behind with thousands of other men, there was no choice but to surrender to the enemy.'

'Was that when you were taken to a prisoner of war camp?'

Reilly nodded solemnly. 'We were first taken to one in Italy, and later moved to a camp in Berlin, where I spent the rest o' the war.' Reilly tried to close his mind to the memories of that awful time, and concentrate on his lovely Ruby sitting in front of him.

She pulled him close and put her arms around him, hugging him to her for several minutes. 'How was it in the camp?' she asked tentatively as they drew apart.

Reilly couldn't speak at first. He shook his head, knowing he could never tell Ruby how terrible it had really been as a prisoner of war in Berlin. The starvation, the rigid rules, which you had to obey or you would be shot with no questions asked. It was truly brutal, but somehow he had got through it.

Instead, he told Ruby about waking up with a feeling of dread every morning, and the terrifying sensation of being trapped which haunted him day after night.

'It were the incarceration, Ruby, that were the worst thing ever. Not having your freedom, which is the most basic of right, taken away from you.' Reilly squeezed his eyes tight shut in an attempt to push away the images threatening to surface.

Ruby gave a heavy nod, and he had the feeling that she understood some of what he had gone through. He remembered back to their time in Ambleside and how they had always known what the other was feeling.

'What kept you going during that difficult time?' she said, squeezing his hand.

Reilly looked lovingly into her eyes. 'The only thing that helped were the thought of being reunited with you,' he whispered, and then he remembered the necklace. 'I'm sorry, Ruby, can you forgive me? I left your necklace with Jude, because I couldn't bear the thought of losing it. I would never have been able to keep it in the camp, because they took everything you owned.'

'It doesn't matter about the necklace now, Reilly. I guessed that's what had happened. Jude sent it back to me, along with the letter telling me you had gone missing,' she told him sadly.

Reilly went on to tell Ruby how after the war, he had been shocked when his search resulted in being told that she was married and had moved away from Brighton. Jude had told him how Ruby believed him to be dead, and how heartbroken she had been when told this news.

'I had to accept you were lost to me, darling,' he told her falteringly.

'Did you go back to Ambleside?' Ruby asked, lifting her eyebrows.

Reilly explained that there was little work for men

like him, who had returned from fighting for their country, and how he had been lost for a while. 'I tried going back to the village, but it didn't work.'

'Were you not happy in Ambleside, working for Lord Henry again?'

'Oh, Ruby. How could I live there without you?' Reilly asked her, and she nodded forlornly. 'Moving back to Ambleside only brought back painful memories of you and the love we shared.'

For a moment they were both silent, lost in their own thoughts of that idyllic time in Ambleside. 'Every time I walked past The Salutation, where we made love in your tiny room, or passed the village hall where I held you in my arms… it hurt too much,' he whispered, blinking away a tear. 'I told myself it were no use trying to find you, Ruby. You were someone else's wife and no longer belonged to me.'

'I'm so sorry, my love.' She stared at him with those big dark eyes. 'I'm sorry for what happened to you,' she added, rubbing at her forehead.

Reilly let out a long exhale. 'It weren't your fault, Ruby. You did what you had to do. Anyway, in time I moved down south, where I looked for some way of earning money in the post-war climate.'

'And you found it in Hastings? I couldn't believe it when I saw you there!'

'I know, Ruby. Me too. I joined the fishing fleet in Hastings, bought one of the net sheds to store me equipment in, and a small boat. It weren't much, but it was a living. And in between fishing, I were painting again. And thank goodness I did, otherwise we would never have found each other,' he said truthfully.

Chapter Forty-Nine

India parked outside the church, but Teagan's works van wasn't there and there was no police car in sight. What was Teagan up to now? She must have driven past the lane, and was obviously making up lies again.

India felt stupid for believing her, but decided to quickly check Ruby's grave, then head off to the hospital. She climbed out of the car, hoping Izzy and the baby would be okay.

Maybe I should call her to let her know I've been delayed for a few minutes, India thought, feeling for her mobile in her back pocket. But it wasn't there, which sent pulses of alarm through her body. She must have dropped it on her way out of the door earlier when she was in such a rush.

India sighed, then strode over to Ruby's grave. It was still intact, and Reilly's still had the date of his death gouged out. As she turned away from the graves, a voice rang out across the churchyard.

'Have you realised yet it's a trap?' came the steely sound.

India swung around to see Teagan leaning on a nearby grave, gazing at her with a weird look in her eyes. 'What's a trap?' she asked, trying not to let her voice portray her nerves, because Teagan was looking a little menacing and was making her feel uneasy.

Teagan pushed herself off the grave and sauntered towards her. It was only then India noticed she had a shotgun in her hands. Fear clutched at her chest as her heart began hammering out of control, and suddenly she knew she shouldn't have come here alone to the graveyard.

'Getting you here, that's what!' Teagan's eyes bulged in their sockets.

'Stop playing games, Teagan,' she said, hoping she would say she was just joking. But Teagan was still looking at her in that odd way, and India was fighting the urge to run.

Slowly she turned her back on Teagan and began walking casually back towards her car, desperate to get away now.

'Oh no you don't!' Teagan shrieked, and she ran in front of India, lifting the gun to take aim.

India froze at the girl's words. 'Okay, Teagan, the joke's over now, you're scaring me. What is it you want?' she said as calmly as her frayed nerves would allow. 'By the way, where's your van?' she ploughed on, attempting to divert Teagan's attention.

Teagan threw back her head and let out a horrible, evil-sounding laugh, sending shivers shooting up India's spine. 'If you care to look properly, India, my van's hidden round the side of the church.' She planted her feet and stared at India, still aiming the gun at her.

'And what do I want? That's funny. I'll tell ya what I want, India McCarthy. For you to listen to the true story of what your grandfather did to Dick McCarthy. When I've told ya all the gory details, I'm going to do the same to you!'

The dark glint of malice shone in Teagan's eyes.

Terrified now, India daren't move. She was trapped here in the graveyard with Teagan, who had clearly gone stark, staring, raving mad.

Chapter Fifty

August 1951

Reilly greeted Ned as he walked past the mill. He was unlocking the side door ready to begin work for the day, and Ned looked around, tipping his cap at Reilly before disappearing inside the mill. A conversation with Ned came to Reilly's mind, when they had been drinking together in The Station Hotel pub a few weeks before.

After moving to Isfield, Reilly had found Ned to be a good sort and easy to talk to. And that particular evening, Reilly had had a bit more to drink than usual, and found himself confiding a little too much over the ale.

Now as he walked towards Isfield Place, Reilly shivered, remembering how he had told Ned that Ruby's ex-husband was a violent, bullying man. He'd added that if Dick McCarthy ever came looking for Ruby, he would make sure he got his just deserts.

Ned had listened with his head cocked thoughtfully to one side while Reilly, his tongue loosened by drink, explained how much he idolised Ruby, and desperately wanted her hand in marriage. At the time, Ned had made no comment at his ramblings, and Reilly had finished the conversation by saying he wished Dick McCarthy were dead.

It was only when he got home that night that Reilly remembered when he'd arrived in Isfield, they'd told the other villagers that he had suffered a bout of amnesia during the war. The amnesia, they claimed, had prevented his earlier reunion with his wife, therefore explaining why he hadn't returned to his family before.

The following day, concerned about how much he'd revealed, Reilly had sought out Ned in the mill and apologised to his friend. Thankfully, Ned had waved away his apology, vowing to keep to himself what Reilly had disclosed that evening in the pub.

Now, as he pushed open the gates and walked through the grounds of Isfield Place towards the potting sheds, Reilly thought how happy he was to be working the land again. His life was settled with Ruby and young Noah, and every day he thanked the Good Lord for his good fortune in finding her again.

Chapter Fifty-One

'The house should have been mine, do you hear?' Teagan clenched her jaw and jabbed the gun towards India.

India's mouth had gone dry and she couldn't form the words that would surely save her life. *What was Teagan talking about?* With her heart racing, she tried breathing slowly and forcing rational thoughts into her head. But images of her dead body, shot by Teagan for no good reason, crowded her head and nothing made any sense.

At last she found her voice, but she dare not move a muscle. 'I don't understand, Teagan,' she said, trying to look as if she was sympathetic and playing for time. 'You really need to explain what you mean about Ruby's house…' But the look in Teagan's eyes halted her words, and she felt like a fly trapped in a spider's web.

Teagan took a step closer, and their faces were merely inches apart when she lowered the gun. 'I don't believe that. Course you bloody understand!' Her finger hovered over the trigger of the gun and her body swayed with the force of her words.

India knew she had to think quickly and try to appear to be on Teagan's side, whatever side that was. 'You can have the house, Teagan, of course you can,' she said, trying to sound convincing. 'If you're the rightful owner, then it should be yours.' Forcing herself to breathe evenly, she held the young girl's gaze and tried to smile.

For a moment, India's words seemed to have the desired effect, and Teagan's expression changed to one of relief. But then her face twisted into an ugly grimace again, and India knew she'd failed to win her over.

'Don't try that one on me, India McCarthy, it's far too late for that!' she said. 'You're sly, like your grandfather, Reilly, who was nothing but a cold-hearted killer.'

India lifted a shaking hand towards Teagan. 'I'm sure that's true, Teagan. Look, I don't know what's happened in the past, but I'm sure we can sort this out,' she said, trying to appeal to the Teagan who had befriended her on her arrival in the village.

But Teagan was having none of it. She advanced on India, once again lifting the shotgun and taking aim. 'Sorry, India, there's no choice. You have to die,' she said coldly. Glancing over her shoulder towards the old mill, she added, 'If it was still a working mill, I would've marched you over there to suffer the same fate as him.

'On the other hand, at least now both Ruby and Reilly will see how their misdeeds have had dire consequences.' Teagan glanced over at the graves then back at India, narrowing her eyes.

India fingered the amulet around her neck, praying that Ruby would help her now in her hour of need. 'Hang on a minute,' she said shakily. 'There's a couple of questions I'd like to ask,' she added bravely, again trying to distract Teagan.

Teagan eyed her with suspicion. 'What questions

are they?' she asked.

'For a start, what was all that about Reilly haunting Ruby's house? There's been a couple of things gone missing or been moved recently,' India said.

Teagan laughed out loud again. 'Course it weren't true. Ruby never told me nothing about Reilly. I knew already. And it was me what moved the vase and took your silly painting,' she said with an ugly grimace on her face.

'But… how did you get into the house?' India was baffled; there had been no sign of a break-in. 'Was it you who damaged Reilly's gravestone?' she asked, feeling like she was playing with fire but unable to help herself.

'Oh, India, you might look intelligent, but you are actually very stupid,' Teagan snarled. 'I stole a key from Ruby while she still lived there. I knew it would come in 'andy one day,' she said, grinning to herself. 'And yep, I did damage Reilly's grave. He deserved it after what he did!'

Just then a rook flew overhead, making a loud squawking noise and coming dangerously close to where they both stood.

Teagan took her eyes off India momentarily and glanced up at the bird. In that split second, India saw her chance and she made a swift lunge for the shotgun. She managed to grab hold of it, then began wrestling Teagan to the ground.

Chapter Fifty-Two

After seeing Reilly off to work, Ruby went to wake nine-year-old Noah for school. Over the last four years, she'd watched a strong bond grow between father and son, as Noah grew to love Reilly as much as she did.

Since their reunion, they'd been living as man and wife, and Ruby was content for the first time in her life. Reilly was working as head gardener at Isfield Place, and life had settled down to a happy, uneventful pace. They were all looking forward to Noah's tenth birthday in a few weeks' time, when a few treats were being planned for his special day.

She was just helping Noah find his schoolbooks when a loud rapping on the door echoed through the house. *Probably the postman*, Ruby told herself, although he didn't usually knock the door down in his haste to give her the day's post.

Leaving Noah to do up his satchel, she went to answer the door. Her heart almost stopped beating... her worst nightmare was standing on the doorstep.

'Hello, Ruby,' Dick sneered, his hazel eyes full of loathing.

Before she could move, he lifted his foot and kicked the door open wider, before placing his hands either side of the doorframe, blocking any chance she had of escape.

Ruby's heart pounded as she glared back at Dick, matching her own look with his. This was no time to show weakness. Safeguarding her son was her first priority and her reaction was swift. Before Dick could move, Ruby yanked the door shut, trapping his fingers between the door and the frame.

Racing back down the hallway towards Noah, Ruby could hear Dick letting out a loud string of expletives. 'Noah! Noah!' she screamed. She ran into the kitchen where she'd left her son, panic rising inside her at the sound of Dick's footsteps behind her.

Noah was frozen and looked terrified as she advanced on him. 'Noah, go now… to your da!' As she wrenched the words from her breathless lips, Noah's eyes fell on the assailant rapidly advancing on his mother.

Dick's appearance seemed to galvanise Noah into action. A slight child, but used to running, he sprinted past the man and disappeared out of the kitchen door into the hallway. Ruby's breath was ragged, and she was struggling to catch her breath. Desperate now to escape from Dick, she was no longer able to hide her fear.

He made no attempt to follow Noah, but only swore again as he turned his evil eyes towards Ruby. With her whole body shaking, Ruby cowered away from him, wedging herself up against the kitchen top, where her eyes darted around the kitchen searching for a means of escape.

Instinctively, her fingers sought the amethyst necklace, and she pulled it out of its hiding place beneath her clothes and clutched at it agitatedly. Glaring back at Dick, she lifted her chin and faced up to him bravely.

'How did you find me, Dick?' she demanded, stalling for time, and surprised at the steadiness of her voice. 'What the hell do you want?'

Dick had watched her take hold of the necklace with an intense fevered stare, and Ruby noticed how much he'd aged since they'd last met. His face was bloated, red, and full of lines, and his body – once lean with toned muscle – was now overweight and flabby. In that brief moment, she felt a smidgen of sympathy for him. He cut a sad figure now, but his next words struck fresh fear into her heart.

'You won't get away from me again, yer bloody bitch!' he roared, letting out a long, cackling laugh. 'You may ask how I found you and the brat after all these years of searching. Well, yer did a good job of hiding till that blonde piece gave the game away.'

'Who gave the game away? What do you mean?' Ruby knew if she kept Dick talking until Noah got back with Reilly, there was a chance she could escape injury. But his face was dangerously close to hers now, and she could see his temper rising.

'That friend o' yours,' he spat at her. 'I was in me usual corner in the pub when I heard her blabbing to the landlord how you was living 'ere in Isfield!'

Dick's eyes bulged and his words were laced with hatred, and Ruby could see the sweat beading his brow as he bore down on her. All of a sudden, she was frightened for her life; she had never seen him this angry. He looked as if he'd gone completely mad, and trying to reason with him wasn't working.

His rage seemed to be sucking the air from the room, and Ruby was finding it difficult to breathe. *Somehow*, she told herself, *she had to try and remain calm*. Forcing her expression to be neutral, she slowly reached out

273

a hand towards him. 'Dick, listen… we can work this out,' she began. 'Let's talk.'

But her words only fuelled his anger and he lunged towards her, grabbing hold of the necklace and ripping it from her neck. 'You owe me, woman!' he yelled. 'So, I'll 'ave that for starters.'

Ruby screamed out at the pain inflicted on her neck, and could feel beads of blood trickling down her cleavage, but she knew that asking for the necklace back would be pointless. Dick, it seemed, wasn't finished with her yet.

He pulled himself up to his full height and laughed, an evil mocking sound, exposing a mouth full of rotten teeth. The sound echoed eerily around the kitchen and Ruby could smell the stench of alcohol on his breath as he leaned towards her again, still clutching the precious necklace.

'Well, Mrs High and Mighty, Ruby McCarthy!' he said. 'Everything you own belongs to me, cos I'm still yer husband. And don't look like that. You're still married to me and don't you go forgetting it!'

Dick stared down at the large violet coloured stone in his hand and muttered under his breath, 'This is worth a tidy sum,' before slipping it into his pocket.

Ruby wanted to fight him for the necklace but knew it would be useless. *Could she make a dash for the door? Was Reilly on his way?* Before she could move, Dick grabbed a handful of her long hair, and she stifled a scream as pain tore through her scalp.

Anger, fierce and blind, contorted Dick's face as he shoved her backwards against the kitchen top, and Ruby's head reeled. She was powerless to stop him as he lifted his hand and dealt her a swinging blow.

The slap knocked her off her feet, and as she fell

towards the tiled floor, all she could do was hold her arms out to protect her face. Another punch followed closely behind the first, and by the time the third one landed, Ruby knew no more.

Chapter Fifty-Three

Jez was driving like the clappers and had almost reached the church when the sound of a shotgun being fired echoed through the air.

The two men looked at each other in alarm, and Jez drove even faster up the winding, narrow lane. He knew Noah's thoughts would be the same as his own: *Please let us be in time to save India from Teagan.*

Before they reached the church, they abandoned the car so that Teagan wouldn't be alerted to their presence. Full of panic for India, Jez flew out of the car and ran like the wind towards the graveyard. The scene that met his eyes made him stop short.

India was lying face down on the ground, her upper body splattered with blood. Thankfully, he could see she was still alive and appeared to be making a moaning noise, while trying to move her head. Teagan was standing over her with a shotgun in her hand, her face an ugly grimace, and looking as if she were about to pull the trigger.

Taking silent steps towards them, Jez gasped as Teagan glanced up and became aware of his presence. Her face showed such hatred he could feel himself breaking out in a cold sweat. 'Teagan... what the hell are you doing?' he demanded.

She lifted the gun and aimed it straight at him.

'Don't you come no closer, Jez Carlisle!' she warned with cold, flinty eyes. 'There's nothing here for you.'

Teagan's voice sounded different, and Jez knew the young woman had gone completely crazy and meant what she said. As he quickly held his hands up in surrender, Noah came into view behind her, creeping silently, and gesturing to Jez to keep quiet.

'Why don't you give me the gun, Teagan?' Jez said, trying to think of anything to keep her attention off Noah, and knowing that one false move could mean India would be dead.

'No! You're just like all the rest of 'em, you don't care. Leave me alone!'

Jez stared back at her, trying not to let his gaze stray to Noah who was now within touching distance of Teagan. 'Alright, Teagan, I'm going,' he said, throwing his arms up passively and making as though he was turning to go back the way he'd come.

Teagan smirked and switched her attention back to India, who was very still now. Suddenly, Noah grabbed hold of Teagan, making her topple backwards, and Jez lurched forward and grabbed the gun from her loosened grip.

Together, the men grappled with Teagan, who was fighting for all she was worth. But the two of them were stronger and were soon able to force her onto the ground, pinning her arms behind her back.

After making sure Noah had a firm grip of her, Jez sprinted back to his van to find a ball of string. Then, between them, they tied a struggling Teagan up whilst she screamed hatred at India and a string of obscenities at them. Once she was securely tied up, Jez raced over to India whilst Noah called for an ambulance and the police.

Jez's heart was in his mouth as he stared down at India, lying face down and static on the ground. If she were dead, it would break his heart in two. He loved her more than life itself. 'India…?' he whispered her name over and over, as he gently took hold of her shoulders and turned her body over.

India's eyes fluttered open briefly as he bent towards her face, which was drained of colour and deathly white. 'Everything hurts, Jez,' she murmured, then her eyelids closed again.

'Oh, India, you'll be alright now, we've got you,' he reassured her, praying to God it was true. And he took her in his arms and rocked her, trying to ignore the scarlet-coloured stain spreading steadily over her body.

Chapter Fifty-Four

'Da! Da…' Noah's stricken tones forced Reilly to turn from digging to see his son standing behind him, gasping for breath and full of panic.

'What is it, Noah?' Reilly asked urgently, ice-cold fear coursing up his spine. 'Calm down, son, and tell me what's going on,' he told the boy.

Noah pointed up the road and took a deep breath. 'It's… Mama! A man was at the house. You have to come and help, now!'

Reilly immediately guessed what might be happening, and if he were right, their worst fears had been realised. Dropping the spade, he grabbed Noah by the hand and began running like the wind back towards the house.

'Go to Dora's and wait for me there!' he ordered his son, when they neared their house. And he pushed the boy towards the safety of the neighbour's gate.

Reilly dashed up the footpath towards the front door, all the time praying he wasn't too late to save Ruby from the monster she'd run away from six years earlier. But the sight that met his eyes was far worse than he could ever have anticipated.

He flung open the door and raced toward the kitchen to find a man raining blows down upon Ruby's lifeless body. His poor love was lying on the tiled floor with her arms over her face; she looked so still that she could already be dead.

Weighing up the situation, Reilly could see he was much bigger in build than this thug, who was shorter than him and running to fat. He could easily deal with Dick McCarthy.

Lunging towards Dick, he grabbed him by the scruff of the neck and shoved him hard. The sound of his head cracking against the wall echoed across the room. Dick lay there for a second looking stunned, and Reilly took the opportunity to kick him while he was down.

As Dick staggered to his feet and lifted his fist to hit Reilly, Ruby let out a low, agonised moan. Reilly pushed his face into Dick's and issued him a dire warning. 'Don't think you'll get away with this, Dick McCarthy, cos I'm coming after you!' he threatened. 'Now get out!'

Dick froze, then lifted his hands in silent surrender, showing himself for the coward that he was a bully who could beat a defenceless woman black and blue, but couldn't stand up to a real man. Reilly spat in Dick's face before turning his attention back to Ruby.

As he bent towards her, he heard Dick run out of the door. Tenderly, he gazed down at Ruby, blinking back hot tears as he took in the damage that monster had inflicted on his beautiful woman.

Ruby was slipping in and out of consciousness, bleeding heavily from her nose and the side of her neck. Her eyes were red and swollen and she looked battered and bruised all over. *But at least*, he reassured himself, *she was alive*. He quickly stood up, raced to the front parlour, and grabbed a cushion to put under her head.

Stroking her hand, Reilly whispered into her ear. 'Ruby, my love... you're all right now. I'm here,' he soothed. Her brown eyes fluttered open as she attempted to say something he couldn't hear, and he reassured her he would get help. Ruby gave a slight nod then closed her eyes again. Her face was deathly pale against the bright red of the blood, and her hair was in dark, disarray around her head.

'Mama... Oh. Mama!' Noah's hysterical voice echoed across the room.

Reilly looked up to see his son standing in the kitchen doorway, his face a mask of fear. *Why had Dora allowed him to come over to the house alone?*

'It's alright, Noah,' he said, standing up quickly and taking hold of the sobbing child. 'Your mama will be fine. I'll make sure o' it, but I need to stay with her for the moment. Can you go and tell Dora to call an ambulance, please?'

He forced his voice to sound even and calm for Noah's sake. Then from behind him he heard Ruby murmuring something unintelligible, so he bent down again and put his ear to her mouth.

'He's taken... the necklace,' she whimpered. 'Reilly... my amethyst, Dick's stolen it.' Ruby's half-closed eyes locked onto his, pleading with him to get the necklace back.

Reilly stood up and straightened his shoulders. 'I'll get it back for you, honey, don't worry 'bout that.' Anger burned inside him that Dick McCarthy had not only beaten Ruby senseless but stolen her precious necklace.

Just then, Dora appeared in the kitchen doorway. 'Oh, good grief!' she said, her hands covering her mouth at the sight of Ruby lying bloodied and injured on the floor.

'Dora! Did Noah ask you to call the ambulance?' Reilly began looking around for the boy, noting for the first time that he was now nowhere to be seen.

Dora's brow furrowed and her eyes narrowed at Reilly. 'No, he didn't. But I've just seen 'im tearing off down the road, as if the devil himself were after him.'

Panic clawed at Reilly, making him feel sick. The child must have heard Ruby talking about the stolen necklace. Noah could be impulsive and headstrong, and it would be just like him to go after Dick, in order to retrieve the necklace for his mother.

Quickly, Reilly addressed Ruby, who was waking up again. 'Ruby, my love, Dora will stay with you and get you into hospital,' he told her. 'I'll be back soon.' Terrified for his son's safety, and not waiting for an answer, he tore out of the house and raced along the path in pursuit of Noah.

Chapter Fifty-Five

It was four o'clock in the afternoon, and India was sitting in Ruby's kitchen with her feet up on the small comfy settee. The day before, she'd undergone an operation to remove several pellets from her right shoulder, and was now recovering at home.

Noah and Jez had arrived together at the hospital to collect her, and she was feeling a warm glow at all this male attention. She watched her father, who had his back turned towards her, making a cup of tea, and was acutely aware that something had shifted between them.

India felt strange about Noah being back in her life again after all these years. There were tiny slivers of something she couldn't place fighting for space in her heart, but it was too soon to let them see daylight. She could barely let herself hope that the wounds he'd inflicted on her tender four-year-old self all those years ago, could ever truly be healed.

In the long years of yearning for things to be different, India had always imagined what Noah would say if he were alive and sitting in front of her. But hearing him heap blame on her mother had been a bitter pill to swallow, and wasn't what she'd wanted to hear.

Since their reunion, the crushing fear that he would

one day leave her again had remained, effectively blocking any feelings she had for him and making her feel insecure and vulnerable. But today, for the first time since his return, she was looking at her father with new eyes. Perhaps he hadn't meant to hurt her all those years ago.

There was so much more she wanted to know, though. *What happened to Reilly? Why was he convicted of murder?* Despite her anger at Noah for the past, it occurred to her that she might not be the only casualty in this family.

After she'd arrived home this morning, Noah had popped out for supplies and Jez had filled her in on events from the day before. She knew now that without Noah's quick thinking, she would probably not have survived Teagan's attempt on her life. This made her feel differently towards her father. It was as though, in that one act of bravery, he was proving to her how much he did love her.

'We need to talk, India.' Noah interrupted her reverie, cup of tea in hand, advancing on her with his dark eyes full of concern. 'But where to start?' He ran his fingers through his grey hair.

'How about at the beginning?' India ventured, lifting her eyebrows. Then she relayed what Teagan had told her about Reilly Brownlow and Dick McCarthy.

Noah stared at her with a conflicted look. 'Okay. Well, you need to know the truth, because that is all lies. Also, the beginning is where I tell you that Reilly Brownlow was my father, and not Dick McCarthy. I didn't know my father when I was very young, but my mother told me about him.'

India thought about the photo she'd found in Ruby's snakeskin bag, and gave him an understanding nod.

She reached into the kitchen drawer and held it out to her father. 'You look a lot like him,' she said.

Noah took the picture and gazed at it longingly, looking lost in a far-off memory.

'Noah... Dad,' she said quietly, 'you don't have to talk about this now.' Then she added quietly, 'I can wait to hear the rest of the story. There's no rush.'

When Noah looked up, his face was full of torment but he lifted his chin determinedly. 'It's fine. I feel now is the right time to tell you their story,' he said sombrely. Then he sat down at the kitchen table and turned towards her.

'Ruby and Reilly had a love affair while Ruby was living in Ambleside during World War 2. She was recuperating after a bomb explosion outside Hanningtons store in Brighton, staying with a friend who was studying with the Royal College of Art.'

'Was Reilly a student at the college? Did he paint the portrait of Ruby hanging in the kitchen?' India asked, thinking how talented he was if he had.

Noah shook his head. 'He did paint the portrait, but he wasn't a student. He lived in Ambleside and worked at Ambleside Manor.'

'It's a beautiful painting, and they must have been very much in love,' India reflected, thinking of the softness of the colours in the portrait.

'They were, but Reilly was called up, and unfortunately within a few weeks of Ruby returning to Brighton, she heard he'd been killed in action.' Noah lowered his head for a moment as if gathering his thoughts.

'Ruby was left heartbroken and pregnant with me, and no means of supporting us both. And Dick McCarthy offered her a way out. But she only realised after she married him what his true character was,' he said sadly.

Just then, the doorbell went, and Noah went off to answer it. When he returned with Jez, India's heart thumped out of control at the sight of his handsome figure.

'Here's the milk Noah forgot to get earlier,' he said, placing the carton on the table and gazing across at India. 'How are you feeling now?' he asked her tenderly.

'I'm okay, thanks, Jez,' India told him, and because everything had happened so quickly and she hadn't yet spoken about his mother she said, 'If there's anything I can help with when it comes to the funeral, let me know. And Jez, you know how sorry I am, don't you?' India felt tears prick the back of her eyes at the thought of Annika's death.

'Course I do, and thanks, but you need to rest.' Jez's smile wobbled as he spoke. 'It's a difficult time for me, but sometimes I think… that maybe it was a blessing in disguise,' he added quietly.

India didn't really believe that, but if it helped Jez get through the grieving process then she would agree. So, she merely nodded, trying not to notice how bone-tired he looked.

'Anyway, I'll see you both soon,' he said, winking at India and making her heart do a somersault. 'I need to crack on.'

'Okay. Don't work too hard, will you?'

Jez's face lit up as he leaned towards India and dropped a light kiss on her cheek. 'I won't, although I have a backlog of work to do, and later I need to give Daisy-Duke a good run out. Wish you could come with me, India,' he said wistfully.

'I definitely will another time,' she replied under her breath, while gazing at Jez's retreating back. Then she looked across at Noah, who had a strange expression on his face. 'What is it?' she asked, her mouth twitching into a smile.

'You do know you're in love with him, don't you?' he said, looking at her intently and leaning back in his chair.

'I'm not sure how I feel about Jez any more,' India said. She knew that her feelings for Jez were blossoming like flowers in springtime, but it was still hard to see past his and Noah's closeness.

Besides, nothing altered the fact she couldn't trust men any more, she reminded herself, *even handsome and thoughtful ones like Jez*. 'I'd rather not discuss this,' she said, staring evenly at Noah, as he shifted uncomfortably in his chair and before she knew it the words were out of her mouth. 'Why did you choose him over me? I'd like to know,' she said, feeling her heart begin to race.

Noah shook his head and sighed. 'I thought you might ask me that,' he said uncomfortably.

'Was it because... you'd forgotten about me?' India's voice sounded a bit shaky as she spoke.

'I never forgot about you, India. Ever. Please understand that,' Noah said, firmly holding her gaze.

India waited, knowing that she desperately needed an explanation as to why he had loved Jez and not her, and she knew that explanation had to be a good one.

Chapter Fifty-Six

Pausing breathlessly by the gate, Reilly stared up and down the road for a sighting of Noah. Then in the distance he spotted the child running northwards towards the mill and immediately gave chase.

As he ran, he couldn't see beyond the bend in the road, so there was no way of knowing whether Noah was running after Dick or was just running scared. Either way, the boy was in grave danger.

As Reilly rounded the bend, he was just in time to see Noah entering the side doorway of the mill. What the hell was he doing going in there? Even if Dick was in the mill, perhaps hiding from Reilly, it was a dangerous place for a child to be.

Arriving at the door, Reilly had to stop to catch his breath. As he stepped inside and squinted into the darkness beyond, he began to shout loudly, 'Noah! Noah!' The sound of his voice, however, was lost above the noise of the working machinery, which was clanking, banging, and echoing throughout the mill.

Knowing it was useless to keep shouting, Reilly's mind was in turmoil. *Who was working in the mill today? Maybe it was Ned, as he was here most days. Would he be able to enlist Ned's help?*

Wasting no time, Reilly ran past the animal feed which was pouring down a spout into sacks from the floor above, and being operated from the noisy machinery whirling above. Then he shot up the steep wooden steps at the side of the mill. When he reached the stone floor, the noise from the millstones grinding together became near to deafening.

He covered his ears to shut out the sound, whilst his gaze searched the stone floor. Then he spotted Noah. His son was cowering in the corner of the room, the necklace dangling from his fingers. Dick had his back to Reilly and was clutching Noah by the scruff of his neck, effectively pinning him against a wooden beam. Dick's other hand was flailing about as he tried to get hold of the necklace.

Reilly inhaled deeply and paused on the top step, and in that moment of hesitation, he sensed someone watching him. His gaze was drawn upwards to the ceiling of the bin floor to see a pair of eyes staring at him through the cogs. But before he could signal to the person above, Noah cried out, and Reilly's attention was drawn back towards the unequal struggle taking place ten feet away.

As Dick was still unaware of Reilly's presence, he began tiptoeing towards them. The clanking of the engines echoed through the air, amid the sound of the sack hoist as it raised a sack of feed. Reilly knew he must proceed with caution, as both Dick and Noah were dangerously close to the working machinery.

Suddenly his son's gaze whipped round, and he noticed his father for the first time. Their eyes met. Reilly placed a silent finger to his lips to quieten the boy but, panic-stricken, Noah shot out of Dick's grasp and darted towards him, dropping the necklace as he ran.

Reilly heaved a sigh of relief and stepped forward

with his arms held out to Noah, just as Dick spun around to face them. The two men's eyes locked across the room, and loathing for each other hung heavily between them.

In that split second, instead of running straight into his father's arms as Reilly was expecting, Noah did something which was to change the course of all their lives forever. The boy turned back towards Dick, who was bending down to retrieve the necklace from the floor, and quick as lightning gave his attacker a hard shove.

Noah was slight, compared to Dick; a mere boy. But in that moment, Dick was caught off-guard, and Reilly watched in complete shock and horror as Ruby's wicked husband lost his balance and tumbled backwards into the moving machinery.

Dick's screams could be heard echoing across the mill just as Ned emerged from the steps leading up to the bin floor. Reilly was holding Noah close, shielding his eyes from the grisly sight of Dick McCarthy dying an agonising death, while Ned was standing staring at him accusingly.

Chapter Fifty-Seven

August 1951

Ruby's eyes fluttered open and she squinted against the intense bright white light above her bed. As her mind whirled in all directions, she struggled to remember what had befallen her. A vague memory surfaced of Dick's face, contorted in anger, and bearing down on her as ice-cold fear clutched at her heart.

She looked around to discover she was in a hospital ward, and any attempts to sit up were met with agonising pains shooting across her head. Closing her eyes, Ruby slowly lowered her head back down onto the pillow, feeling totally exhausted.

Every single muscle in her body hurt, but especially her head and neck. What had Dick done to her? Ruby lifted her hand and felt around her neck area where it was sore, and the feeling of alarm intensified when she realised her necklace was missing.

A nurse appeared by her side and Ruby turned her head towards the woman, wincing in agony at this very slightest of movements. 'Nurse... can you tell me if my son's alright?' she whispered through a dry, parched throat.

'I'm sorry, dear. I don't know anything about your

son,' replied the nurse as she took Ruby's temperature.

The cold finger of dread was chilling Ruby's bones, and a scream threatened to spill out of her mouth. An image of Dick and Reilly fighting flashed through her mind. 'Can I have some water, please?' she rasped, pulling herself up by her elbows.

The nurse nodded sympathetically and then disappeared behind Ruby, where she helped her sit up by adjusting the pillows, then poured water from a jug beside the bed and handed her a full glass.

Ruby drank greedily and then tried out her voice again. 'Please,' she said, thankfully sounding more normal. 'I need to know about my son,' she pleaded. *Where was her beautiful child? Was he lying dead from wounds inflicted by the evil Dick? And where was Reilly?* Ruby tried to quell her rising panic at all these questions running through her head.

The nurse stared mutely back at her before quickly going off to attend to another patient. Frustrated, Ruby let out a long, weary sigh. Remembering the frightening scene in the kitchen, worry for her son and for Reilly consumed her.

In her mind, she saw Dick at the front door and Noah running out of the house, just as she'd ordered him to do. Dick had advanced on her then, hitting her repeatedly, then she'd heard Reilly's voice come from far away. Her precious Reilly had fought with the evil Dick, and she could do nothing but lie helplessly on the floor. She remembered struggling to open her eyes, and drifting in and out of consciousness, before hearing Noah's young voice calling out to her in distress.

Now, racking her befuddled brain, Ruby knew there was something else. Then in her mind's eye, she saw Dick ripping the necklace from her neck, and remembered Reilly running out of the house after Noah.

Hot tears slid down her cheeks and her heart raced. She knew what a terrible man Dick McCarthy was, and Ruby was terrified that he might have killed both Noah and Reilly in his violent rage. Why, for the love of God, wouldn't someone come and tell her where they both were?

'Nurse! Nurse!' Ruby at last allowed the scream to be free from her tortured lungs, ignoring the pain in her neck as she swung her legs out of bed. If nobody came to her, then she would have to go to them. She simply had to know that both her precious boys were alive and well.

Instantly, it seemed, the nurse was next to her bed again, but this time she was accompanied by a man dressed in a grey suit. The man stood back whilst the nurse tut-tutted at Ruby, lifting her legs back into bed and pushing her down onto the pillows.

Without explaining the man's identity, the nurse retreated to stand next to him, and now they were both looking at her with intense sympathy in their eyes.

Ruby clenched her jaw and forced her racing heart to quieten. 'Where the hell is my son?' she began urgently, and as the man stared at her, her hopes faded.

'Calm yourself, Mrs McCarthy. Your son is safe and with your neighbour, a Mrs Dora Smith?' The nurse pulled up a chair as he spoke, allowing him to sit next to Ruby's bed. 'My name is Detective Constable Reed,' he said.

Ruby lay back on the pillows and let out a long exhale. 'Oh, thank God,' she whispered. *Dick hadn't harmed Noah, after all. But what about Reilly?*

Before she could ask after Reilly, the detective

leaned towards her. 'Right then, Mrs McCarthy,' he said, opening a black notebook and getting out a pen. 'Can you tell me what you remember about events leading up to your attack?'

Anger burned inside Ruby and she felt her cheeks redden as she looked at the bespectacled constable. 'I'm not answering any questions until I know Reilly Brownlow is alright,' she said, lifting her chin.

With his pen poised, the detective regarded her with annoyance, and then he put down his pen. 'Reilly Brownlow has been arrested,' he said with a fixed stare.

Ruby's heart lurched. 'Arrested? Not Reilly! Surely you mean Dick McCarthy? He's the one who attacked me.'

Detective Reed's eyes hardened. 'I'm certainly not mistaken, Mrs McCarthy. Reilly Brownlow is in custody.'

'What do you mean in custody, why… what's he done?' The question hung in the air and the detective didn't answer straight away. Ruby held her breath for so long she felt a pain in her chest.

Breaking eye contact with her, the Detective Constable scribbled something in his notebook before addressing her again. 'He's been arrested for the murder of Dick McCarthy,' he said, emphasising the words as if she was stupid.

'Murder? Why, that's ridiculous! If he had any part in this, it was saving me and Noah from being attacked by Dick McCarthy.' Ruby glared at the detective, thoughts running amok in her head, unable to believe that this could possibly be true.

What on earth had happened? Dick had come looking for her and Noah, and there was no doubt he had intended to harm them both. In her panic, Ruby had told Noah to go and fetch his father, thereby unwittingly involving Reilly in the violence that followed. *But surely whatever the police had based Reilly's arrest on would prove to be false?*

Ruby prayed it was all a misunderstanding and they could clear his name once she spoke up. She feared that after his terrible experience in a prisoner-of-war camp during the war, her beloved Reilly wouldn't survive long locked up in a tiny prison cell.

***

Scarlett stared at Ruby with tears in her eyes. 'Bloody hell, Ruby. I'm sorry I couldn't warn you,' she said, dabbing at her eyes. 'The thing is, you see, I had to get Annika to hospital quickly after she fell down the stairs.'

Ruby's heart was racing out of control and she felt dazed, as if Scarlett was miles away from her instead of standing in her front parlour. But then her friend's words hit home.

'Scarlett, did you know about Dick's intentions?' she said, feeling a jolt of something like panic.

Scarlett's brow was furrowed with concern. 'I did know what Dick intended to do. But, Ruby, Annika was in a such bad way. It was an emergency.' She rubbed at a point on the bridge of her nose, and muttered almost to herself, 'She looked so vacant and confused, I knew something was seriously wrong.'

Ruby heard Scarlett's words, but couldn't take them in. Something about Annika being taken to hospital. But she could only focus on one thing: Scarlett had known about Dick's intentions and had somehow failed to warn her.

Feeling completely numb, Ruby thought how different things would be if they'd had a warning about Dick that day. Reilly would not be in prison accused of murder, and Noah wouldn't be upstairs sobbing into his pillow and traumatised by recent events. She watched Scarlett stand up and pace the room.

'Oh, Ruby, you're obviously still in shock.' Scarlett stopped pacing, then sat down opposite Ruby and began wringing her hands. 'Don't you think I would have flaming warned you if I could have?' she said beseechingly. 'My poor little Annika could have died. She needed urgent medical attention.'

Scarlett's words took a moment to sink in. 'God, Scarlett, I'm so sorry. I wasn't listening properly, was I? Poor little girl. How's Annika now?'

Scarlett gave a sigh of relief. 'She's better, thank you. Still in hospital, but on the mend. It's blinking strange when you think about it. She must have been brought into the hospital at exactly the same time as you.' Scarlett's whole body seemed to slump.

Ruby rubbed at her throbbing head and took Scarlett's hands in her own. 'I know you would have warned me if it had been possible. I just don't know what's going to happen to Reilly now…' Her voice broke on the words, and she dipped her head, struggling against the hot tears.

Scarlett looked completely forlorn. 'Oh, Ruby, you wouldn't believe it, but I had the telephone in my hand to ring you. I was just dialling your number… when Annika had the accident. I told myself I would still have time,' she rubbed at a spot between her brows, 'but it completely slipped my mind in the emergency.'

Ruby lifted her head and nodded sadly. 'Don't worry, Scarlett. It was one of those things which can't be helped,' she reflected sadly. 'What happened this time, though? I mean, how did you see what Dick's intentions were?' It didn't really matter now, because it was too late, but Ruby still wanted to know.

Scarlett's face was white and she looked stricken, and for a moment she didn't answer Ruby. 'It was a dream, Ruby; a nightmare, really. I saw Dick attacking you and then Reilly seeing him off. Then I saw them in the mill, saw Noah push Dick…'

Ruby waited for Scarlett to ask her why Reilly had admitted to Dick's murder when it was Noah who had committed the crime. However, Scarlett didn't ask any more questions, and Ruby thought that perhaps she already knew the answer.

Chapter Fifty-Eight

December 1954

The cold had penetrated so deep into his bones that Reilly knew he would never feel warm again. But the cold was nothing compared to the mental anguish he had suffered these three long years since his conviction.

It had manifested itself in a desperate need to claw at the walls of his cell, and the overwhelming urge to scream and shout at the grey metal door keeping him captive. But it had all been in vain.

He shivered as he listened to the jailer's keys in his cellmate's door, echoing down the corridor outside. In a moment they would unlock his own cell, then expect him to line up with the others to partake in physical exercise in the yard. It was a daily ritual, and at first it had brought him a sliver of comfort, but not any more.

The yard was enclosed in rigid, high, stone walls and was where he could smell the fresh air and see the blue sky and clouds above him. Everything was out of his reach, though, and it was pure torture. He wanted to survive, he really did, especially after Ruby visited, which she did as often as she could.

For the short time they spent together, her beauty and smiling face brought him hope and lifted his spirits. While she was here talking to him about normal mundane things, he could truly believe that one day he would walk free from this hellhole. He could have faith that the day would come when he would be safe again in her loving arms.

But visiting time passed so quickly, and once she was gone, all hope faded and the demons returned to haunt him. The day his friend Sidney was executed for attempting to escape from the POW camp, played out over and over in his mind. The two of them had survived operation Creteforce together, and been captured at the same time.

Sidney had tried to persuade Reilly to attempt escape, too, but he had been terrified he would be caught and shot, which was exactly what happened to his friend.

Night-times were the worst for the flashbacks and terrors, although lately the days were merging into nights. In his dreams, he was back in Crete, or in the POW camp during WW2, reliving the horrors. And when he did wake up, his nerves were ragged and he couldn't stop his hands from shaking.

Ruby constantly tried to instil hope in him, telling him how the days would fly by and very soon they would be reunited again. She said they would be a family again, and he would take Noah out on day trips on his precious train rides.

Reilly didn't have the heart to tell her that every single moment in here felt like a whole year, and that time stretched ahead of him like a black, never-ending tunnel, with no escape in sight.

When he was first convicted, Reilly felt strong, physically and emotionally. He knew with a deep certainty that one day he would walk free from prison and resume his life with his family. But slowly the despair had taken hold, dragging him down into its dark depths.

Sadness had enveloped him into its dark cloak, and though he fought it valiantly for Ruby and Noah's sake, he was slowly beginning to succumb.

His body was weak now, too, and he couldn't remember the last time he'd eaten. Every time he tried, his throat closed up, making food stick in his gullet. As a result, Reilly was weak in both body and spirit, and was becoming too fragile to fight the dark times.

The thought of Ruby's visits had always helped, but they no longer rallied him or gave him hope; he found he was merely putting on a brave face for her. The feeling that he must escape had now become so intense, so all-encompassing, that he knew the day was dawning when that escape would happen... whichever form it took.

With his head in his hands, Reilly sat on the thin mattress of his bed and rocked from side to side. He felt bereft and so completely alone as the hot tears began to fall onto his hollow cheeks. The sound of his sobbing filled the tiny cell, and for a moment he gave into it.

Knowing his time would soon be up, Reilly wondered how his poor Ruby would survive without him. Thinking of her must have brought her closer, because suddenly, as he lifted his head, he became aware of her scent filling the tiny room. Opening his swollen eyes, Reilly could see the cell looked different as the scent became stronger.

The clatter of the iron door shocked him out of his thoughts, and even though the light in the room had now faded, he was comforted by Ruby's presence in the room. Her voice was telling him she would be fine without him.

As the door opened, Reilly turned to face the prison warden, knowing with complete conviction that one day he would be reunited with his precious Ruby again; if not in this life, then in the next.

Chapter Fifty-Nine

August 2017

Her tears were making the pillow wet; Ruby could feel it sodden and cold beneath her head. But tears were useless, as she well knew, because they couldn't change the past. She felt as if she had been grieving for so many years, and was still grieving. Not for herself, but for her lost love Reilly.

She remembered the last time she had seen him in his prison cell all that time ago. They had sat in front of each other, and the look on his face had spoken volumes. This same scene had been replayed in her mind many times over the years, because Ruby knew in that moment that Reilly had given up the fight.

Ruby saw that the hope had died in his beautiful ebony eyes. She'd reached out to him, tried to tell him to find his way back to her, but it seemed it was too late and he was lost and far beyond her reach.

Feeling helpless, she had questioned why she had let him take the blame that fateful day in 1951. The truth was that Reilly had convinced her it was the best course of action, and at the time Ruby had agreed. But as time went on, she had doubted the wisdom of his decision.

Reilly had idolised Noah, and didn't want his son to suffer for his impulsive action. But if any of them could have foreseen the outcome, seen what a devastating effect prison was to have on Reilly, would they have chosen the same path?

Even if Ruby had been the one to decide whether to tell the truth or not, how could she have made that heart-breaking choice between her son, who at the time was only a child, and her true love? In reality, Reilly made the choice to take the blame, but she wondered if she could have changed his mind? Now she would never know the truth.

Ruby had walked away from Reilly that last time with her heart broken, filled with a deep sense of foreboding that something terrible was about to happen to him. Sorrow and regret filled her head on that journey home, making her feel sick with worry.

Maybe she should have tried harder to find Reilly again, in that dark place into which he had retreated. There was so much she wanted to say to him, but no time left to tell him how much he meant to her.

When she was told of Reilly's death in his prison cell, the day after her last visit, her first thought was she wanted to join him. The thought of being parted from Reilly was just too painful. Her torment since then had been so agonising, and her sadness so deep, that nothing had ever alleviated it. Her deep and all-consuming love for Reilly had been an eternal flame, burning forever inside her heart, never to be extinguished.

At the time of his death Ruby didn't know how she would go on living without him. However, she couldn't give up living or retreat inside herself the way poor Reilly had. Her child needed her, and desperately. Drying her tears, she had turned towards her son and given everything to him. She had nurtured him enough for herself and Reilly, and tried to ease his pain by helping him cope with the terrible guilt of not only what he had done, but of the death of his beloved father.

Many times over the years Ruby had yearned to tell the truth, to reveal to the world what had really happened that fateful day. And while Reilly was serving his time for the crime, she often came close. *But once Reilly was dead, what possible good could it do?* she had asked herself over and over again. She came to the conclusion that it would only serve to ruin young Noah's life.

Suddenly, the amethyst necklace caught her eye where it was lying on her dressing table. She desperately wished she were wearing it today, on this final day of her life, but it was just out of her reach, and she didn't have the energy or strength to lift up her body to retrieve it.

In the increasing darkness of the room, the necklace's colour shone a vibrant purple hue, catching what little light there was left. Gazing at it brought Scarlett into Ruby's mind. Her colourful friend had given her the necklace to keep her safe all those years ago at the start of WW2.

Reilly's death had brought Scarlett closer to Ruby once again, making everything more bearable, but these last twelve years since her friend passed away had been the hardest years of all.

In the beginning, she had not believed in the necklace's powers in the way Scarlett had. Then gradually she had come to think of it as a good luck charm. She thought maybe it did have the power of protection, especially after she survived the bomb blast outside Hanningtons store. But the necklace, she knew, had become a curse as well as comfort to her over the years.

After all, on the day Dick attacked her, if Noah hadn't overheard her heartbroken sobs telling Reilly Dick had stolen the necklace, he would never have run after her wicked husband. And that evil man would never have died in the mill that awful day, so Reilly would have lived a long and happy life.

Noah hadn't been the only one to carry the deep clawing guilt around for so long. And despite these terrible events brought about by the necklace, Ruby loved it passionately. And she would be leaving it for her granddaughter, India, along with the house.

India. What a beautiful name, Ruby thought. *Inspired, it seemed, by the necklace because it came from the country of the same name.* That was another big regret in her life, having no contact with India over the years. But maybe by leaving her this house, her granddaughter would somehow find her way back to her father.

Ruby wished with all her heart this would be the case, because the two of them needed to find each once other again.

Noah had always told her he didn't want her house when she was gone, and had tried to persuade her to move once he was grown up. He said it held bad memories for him, and said they needed a fresh start somewhere away from where it all happened.

However, Ruby felt closer to Reilly here, even though it was where Dick had attacked her. Reilly was buried in the local churchyard and every day since his death, she had visited his grave. She could never move away from him and the precious memories she had of their time together in Isfield.

The room was now almost in total darkness, and Ruby was fading fast. She had told the carer she wasn't needed today to give herself some privacy. She didn't want to be carted off to hospital, to be poked and prodded in the sterile brightness of a busy ward.

Ruby could die alone here, in the bed she had shared with Reilly all those years ago. Knowing that death was near now, she tried not to be frightened; she could feel it closing in on her and hovering nearby. Closing her eyes, the blackness began seeping into her very soul, while she longed to see her darling Reilly again just one last time.

The atmosphere in the room suddenly changed and she shivered, knowing it was almost time to go. Then, through the pitch darkness, she sensed a presence and heard a familiar voice whispering to her.

'Hello, Ruby, my love.'

Forcing her leaden eyes open, she gave a tiny gasp. There he was, as handsome as ever, beckoning her to join him.

'Reilly, you've come back to me,' she whispered through parched lips. And with renewed strength, she lifted herself up from the bed and walked into his loving arms.

Chapter Sixty

'It began with Scarlett asking me to help her daughter, Annika, who was a single parent and struggling with her two teenage boys,' Noah explained to India.

'The boys had grown up without a father, which wasn't a problem until they hit their teenage years. Jez and Pete were as different as chalk and cheese. Pete was placid and an easy child, but Jez was different, more headstrong and harder to reason with. He reminded me of myself as a boy, and I'd always had a soft spot for him.'

Noah looked down at his lap and dusted an invisible speck of dust from his trousers. 'He'd just turned seventeen when I stepped in, and by the time he was eighteen going on nineteen, I finally got through to him.'

'He started listening to me then, and came good, so we became very close.' Noah looked up at India. 'He knew how things were with me. Saw that I was gay.'

'You're gay?' India didn't have a problem with her father being gay, but she just hadn't expected it. 'So, why did you marry my mother?' she asked. And for the first time in her life, India felt sorry for Miranda.

Noah shrugged. 'Things were different then,' he said. 'I was in denial and only wanted normality, but it's true I should never have got married. However, no-one can live a lie that like for very long.'

For a moment, Noah gazed at her with a thoughtful expression on his face. 'I'm sorry for what happened, though, India. It was unforgivable to leave you and not retain some contact, even if Miranda discouraged it.'

India's heart lurched when she thought of Miranda's selfish actions over her father's letters. 'Why would she do it, though, that's what I'd like to know? She still hasn't explained her actions properly, except to say she was protecting me.'

Noah gave India a long steady look. 'She did it because I'm gay, India. Miranda couldn't accept the way I'd hidden it from her when we were first married. I presume she thought it would have a bad influence on you, therefore she was protecting you by hiding the letters.'

India could see that her mother, in her own misguided way, had thought she was doing what was best for her daughter.

She looked across at Noah's downcast face and felt as if a weight had been lifted from her shoulders now that he'd explained about her mother and how things were with Jez. 'I think maybe saving my life yesterday went a long way towards you being forgiven. Wouldn't you?' she said tenderly.

India saw the love reflected in Noah's eyes for her, and couldn't help remembering Jez gazing at her in the same way. It seemed they both loved her, and it gave her a warm tingling feeling.

'You're my daughter, and I only did what anyone else would have done in the circumstances,' he said softly.

India smiled at this understatement. 'I'm not sure that's true. After all, you risked your life for me.'

Noah suddenly stood up, came around the settee, and gently pulled her into his arms, being careful of her damaged shoulder. India felt like that little four-year-old girl again, whose daddy was her whole world.

They both stood that way for a moment, and then India shifted out of her father's embrace, feeling the tears not far away. 'I'd really like to know what happened between Reilly and Dick, if you've got time to tell me?' she asked, scrubbing a hand across her face and looking up at him.

'You've told me how Ruby thought Reilly was killed in action during WW2, and then found out she was expecting you. I presume she married Dick McCarthy after this happened?' India felt her shoulder aching, and sat down on the settee to rest it against a cushion.

Noah leaned against the kitchen worktop. 'Ruby did marry him, mainly because she didn't know what else to do,' he explained, 'but he was violent towards her and had an unpredictable temper. She was frightened of him and worried for my safety. In 1945, when I was two, she left him.'

India's heart went out to Ruby for choosing the wrong man to marry, although it didn't sound like she'd had much choice given the predicament she was in. It was a time when pregnancy outside marriage was severely frowned upon, and there was little or no help for single women finding out they were expecting, other than to give up their baby for adoption.

'Good for her,' India said, feeling proud that Ruby had had the courage to escape Dick. 'Is that when she moved here?'

Noah nodded. 'It was a few months before the war ended, which sounds terrible because he was still fighting. The thing is, she hadn't really known him when they married. It was only after the wedding that he showed his true colours.'

Noah looked into the middle distance as if remembering how it was. 'In 1947, we met up with my father again. Reilly was working in Hastings and Mum had taken me on a day trip there.'

Moving to sit beside India on the settee, he smiled as he looked into her face. 'Oh, India, I'll never forget my mother's face when she realised he was alive, after all,' he told her, his eyes shining.

India smiled back and touched her father's arm. 'That's wonderful. Did he come from around here, then? I thought they met in Ambleside.'

'Reilly originally came from Toxteth, but he was working in Ambleside when they met. On his return home from the war, he heard Ruby was married and had moved on. He couldn't face living in Cumbria where their affair had taken place, so he moved down south.'

'That must have been a heart-stopping moment,' India said, feeling happy for her grandmother at this turn of events after the war. But the expression on Noah's face had changed again, and the cold chill of dread was working its way up India's spine.

Noah looked down at his hands and sighed. 'We only had four short years together as a family before Dick found us,' he said in a flat monotone voice. 'I was nine years old when he came knocking on the door, full of anger and rage, and acting as if he owned the place.'

India held her breath, instinctively knowing that something terrible had occurred the day Dick McCarthy came looking for his wife.

'Mum ran through to the kitchen to warn me.' Noah

was talking quickly now, as if he needed to get this story out. 'She told me to run and get my father from Isfield Place where he was working at the time.'

India was trembling in anticipation of what came next, and hardly daring to imagine how scary that had been for a nine-year-old child.

Noah stood up again and paced the room, fists clenched, then he stopped and looked across at India. 'I managed to escape, but Dick was beating hell out of Ruby. Desperation to save her made me run like hell to Reilly, who was at work. He told me to go to the neighbour's house and hide until it was safe, and then he went to confront Dick and stop him killing her.'

Tears glistened in Noah's eyes, and as he swallowed several times, India felt her own eyes fill up seeing how hard it must have been for him. He sat down at the kitchen table and put his head in his hands as if it were too painful to go on.

'Dad…' she began, but he had lifted his head and was talking again.

'I waited with the neighbour for a few minutes but I was too distraught to stay put, and instead followed my father back to the house. I was just in time to see Dick making his escape and running out of the front door. Ruby was lying on the floor injured, and she was saying Dick had stolen her precious necklace.'

Noah stared at his empty palms and muttered under his breath, 'If only I hadn't followed him to the mill… if only.'

India could hardly breathe now. Her stomach was churning, making her feel queasy. 'Do you mean Ruby's amethyst necklace? What happened?'

But Noah hadn't heard India; he was lost in the memory. 'Dick was running from the house with the necklace and I desperately needed to get it back. She really loved it, you see,' he said, with a pleading look in his eyes.

'Oh, Dad, you poor thing. You were so young,' India said, her heart going out to him. 'You took such a risk, and were just a child.'

Noah nodded, as if he understood this for the first time. 'It didn't occur to me that I was no match for Dick, or that I was putting my father in danger by pursuing him. Honestly, India, I still remember how I was gripped by anger so fierce it overrode everything else.'

'What happened next?' India asked tentatively. 'Take your time to tell me, there's no rush.' Noah looked a bit shaky and India could see how painful the memories were for him.

'Dick ran into the mill and I followed him up the stairs onto the stone floor. I could see the chain of the necklace dangling from his trouser pocket, and saw my chance. Pouncing on him, I grabbled hold of it and ran.' Noah winced at the memory.

'I was nine years old and he was a grown man, so as you can imagine, he soon caught up with me. Before I knew it, he was wrestling me to the ground.'

'How awful! Dick McCarthy sounds truly despicable. Why did he want the necklace so much?'

'I suppose it was greed; because it was valuable, he wanted it for himself. After all, a large amethyst stone surrounded by diamonds was worth quite a lot of money even then.'

India nodded and pulled the necklace out from beneath her t-shirt and watched Noah's eyes widen in surprise.

'You're wearing the necklace! Where on earth did

you find it?' he asked, giving her an incredulous stare.

India quickly explained how Ruby had left her the necklace, along with a letter. 'It is beautiful,' she said, 'and I can see how someone like Dick would want to sell it for profit.'

Noah nodded. 'I know that Scarlett gave it to Ruby as a good luck charm during the war years, because I heard that story many times when I was growing up. Scarlett apparently saved a child's life while in Calcutta, and was given the amulet as a reward.'

India was intrigued to hear of the necklace's origins. 'You must tell me all about it soon,' she added, smiling.

Noah smiled affectionately back at her. 'It's why I wanted to call you India, insisted on it, actually. Even though your mother never really approved, she agreed in the end, but it was a name close to Ruby's heart.' Noah dipped his head and sighed then he looked up at her. 'The necklace is beautiful, but it's been a curse over the years.'

'What happened next, I mean, after you pounced on Dick?' Noah's expression was far away again. 'Dad, are you alright?'

Noah shook his head. 'Course I am, but it's hard to remember all this without bringing back the feelings of fear and heartache again.'

'Don't tell me any more for now then,' India leaned towards her father, and touched his arm, worried at how upset he looked.

Noah met India's eyes. 'I have to tell you everything, India. It will always be painful for me to recall these memories, but you need to know the truth about what happened.'

Chapter Sixty-One

'While Dick was trying to overpower me in the corner of the mill, Dad appeared. He'd followed me into the mill. Dick wasn't aware he was there, and I could see Dad signalling for me to keep quiet.'

For a moment, Noah covered his face with his hands, as if he couldn't go any further with the story. India waited patiently, knowing this tale had been bottled up inside him for many years.

He swallowed and continued. 'The thing is, I was headstrong and didn't see the danger, and I suppose that's why I did it.' He shook his head. 'Somehow I got away from Dick and ran towards my father. But I'd dropped the necklace, you see. That was the problem.'

India's whole body went hot and then cold in quick succession. 'Do what?' she whispered, then louder she said anxiously, 'What happened, Dad?'

Noah's face had gone white and a vein throbbed in his neck. 'I was almost in Reilly's arms, but I had to get the necklace back for Mum,' he explained. 'I tried to retrieve it from the floor, but Dick was reaching for it, too…' his eyes were wide, then he shut them tight as if to close out the memory. 'There was another tussle… and I gave him a shove… and in a split second Dick had toppled backwards into the moving machinery.'

India gasped, and a shocked silence filled the room.

She had to force herself to take a deep breath while the word 'murderer' echoed in her mind.

Noah was looking past her now with tears streaming down his face. 'Reilly confessed to the crime immediately, and wouldn't let me take the blame. Mum backed him up, so he went to prison. It was as simple as that.'

He wiped the back of his hand across his eyes and looked at India. 'I've heard Dick's dying screams in my nightmares so many times over the years,' he said, his voice breaking.

India listened as Noah told her how he had desperately wanted to confess his crime, and how Ned, who had been working on the bin floor above that day, had watched events unfolding. But at the very moment Dick fell to his death, Ned had been hurrying down the steps towards the stone floor so hadn't seen who pushed him.

India could hardly believe the sacrifice Reilly had made, or that a nine-year-old boy would do such a thing. But she understood that Dick McCarthy had been an evil man and Noah had been desperate to get hold of the necklace for his mother.

'So, I take it that Ned assumed Reilly did it?' she asked, lifting her brows.

He nodded. 'That's right. That made it easier for Reilly to confess to the crime, and also to convince Ruby it was the best course of action in the circumstances.'

'What about the people living in the village who knew Ruby and Reilly. Did they blame him, too?'

Noah nodded again. 'They all thought he did it, even more so after Ned said in his police statement that Reilly had told him in the pub one night that he wished Dick McCarthy were dead.' Noah's eyes looked dull and his shoulders were slumped.

India's heart went out to her father. 'It must have been so painful all these years carrying this around with you, and not able to tell anyone,' she sympathised.

Noah nodded sadly. 'Only Scarlett, Annika, and Jez knew the truth.'

'Jez knew all this?' A jolt of shock went through India as she realised that was why he had been reluctant to tell her anything.

'He did, but honestly, India, the guilt has been the worst thing imaginable, especially as my father died in prison three years later.'

India felt an ice-cold shiver run up her spine. 'What happened?' she asked hesitantly.

'Reilly escaped the death penalty because he was convicted of manslaughter, after it was decided in court that he was protecting me from Dick. But because he'd already suffered so much in the POW camp during the war, the incarceration destroyed him.

'It brought all those memories back, and he didn't survive in prison. That was what really broke my mother's heart.' Noah's voice cracked on his words, and once again he covered his face with his hands.

India waited patiently, knowing that her father needed a moment to gather his thoughts, but her heart wrenched for him. Poor Noah. As a result of his impulsive action, her grandmother had lived out the rest of her life without her one true love.

As she watched him sobbing quietly, she realised how he must have suffered all these years. After a moment, Noah stood up and blew his nose, then looked at India with a new determination etched on his face. 'Now that I've told you, I need to right the wrong, India,' he said firmly. 'My father needs atonement.'

'But how? Surely it's too late for that?' India was confused.

'It's never too late. I've decided to go to the police and admit to the crime he confessed to, in order to clear his name. I may even have to go to prison and serve time, but if so, then I will.'

India was shocked. Having at last found her father, was she about to lose him again? 'Are you sure? I mean, no-one need know it was you who pushed Dick to his death.' But as she said the words, India knew Noah was right and it was selfish of her to try to stop him.

'I know, India, but it's time the secret was revealed. Everyone needs to understand that Reilly was innocent of the crime he was convicted of all those years ago.'

'I understand, of course I do,' India said, and for a moment they were both deep in their own thoughts, then she looked across at him. 'What about Teagan?' she asked. 'Where does she come into all this? Why did she tell lies and want me dead?'

Noah gave her a knowing look. 'I became suspicious of Teagan after you told me what she'd said about Dick and Reilly. I just knew something wasn't right there.'

'Okay, so what did you find out about her?' India asked.

'As you know, I'm not good with technology,' Noah grinned at her. 'But I got my partner, Adam, to search on the internet for me. It took a while, but we finally came across a newspaper cutting with her photograph on it.'

India listened intently, as Noah told her how Teagan had been convicted of armed robbery in London, and that her surname was Teagan McCarthy – not Hayward. On further investigation, he discovered she was Dick McCarthy's great-niece.

India's eyes widened at this revelation. 'That's awful! So she's actually a criminal.' She shook her head. 'And she's related to Dick? She told me in the graveyard she was avenging his death.'

Noah nodded thoughtfully. 'Teagan must have got it into her twisted head that Ruby's house should have gone to her.'

'It's all making sense now,' India said, thinking how Teagan's attack on her could so easily have ended in tragedy.

Noah agreed. 'Teagan must have been desperate with jealousy and revenge and came here to befriend Ruby, then get what she saw was her due. When that didn't work and you appeared... well, the rest, as they say, is history.'

Chapter Sixty-Two

'Where did Teagan get the shotgun from?' It was a Saturday morning six months after the attempt on India's life, and Noah was about to have a cup of tea with her in the kitchen in what had become a regular ritual for them.

Teagan's plea hearing had come up the day before, and India, Noah, and Jez had all been in court to witness Teagan plead guilty to inflicting grievous bodily harm on India. A date had been set for two months' time for sentencing.

Watching the young woman hang her head in shame whilst standing in the dock, India felt sorry for Teagan, even though she could easily have killed her that day in the graveyard. She couldn't help thinking how being related to Dick McCarthy couldn't have been easy, as it seemed they were a rough family.

'Apparently she stole the gun from Isfield Place and hid it until she got you alone in the graveyard.' Noah shivered as he spoke. 'Teagan harbouring a grudge about how her great-uncle died was yet another consequence of my actions in the mill that day,' he said sadly.

India touched his arm. 'You must let go of the guilt now,' she told him. 'You were only nine years old and had been tested to the limit by what you saw Dick

McCarthy do to your mother.'

Noah exhaled slowly and met her eyes. 'You're right, India. I have to accept what happened all those years ago. After all, I can't change anything. But at least now I've done the best I can to right the wrong for my father. It's such a shame my parents didn't know at the time of Dick's death that I was under the age of criminal responsibility, and therefore couldn't have been prosecuted.'

India stood up and began getting teacups out of the cupboard. 'Surely it wasn't just about you being prosecuted?' she said, as she filled the kettle up and switched it on. 'They wanted to save you, their only child, the shame of being labelled a murderer.' India placed the cups on the table. 'Your father loved you very much and that's why he took the blame,' she told him.

Noah nodded solemnly. 'The police told me that in the light of my confession, they will take the information to the Home Secretary, and ask that Reilly is pardoned.'

India's heart lifted at Noah's words. 'That's great news. It means you've done everything you can to see that justice has been done for your father,' she said, as she poured hot water onto the teabags.

Noah looked past her across the room. 'I'm so sorry I wasn't there for you all those years, India,' he said solemnly.

Following her father's wistful gaze, India saw him looking at the photograph he'd taken at her fourth birthday party. It was the picture she'd found in the Brighton Flea Market, and which now hung proudly on the wall next to the portrait of Ruby.

She tore her eyes from the red ribbons and candy-pink dress. 'It doesn't matter now,' she said, knowing the seeds of forgiveness had been sown the minute he saved her life. 'We won't lose touch again, so we'll put all that behind us and move on now.'

Noah's face lit up with a beaming smile and he reached down to pick up a rucksack which he'd placed beside his chair earlier.

'What have you got in there?' she asked him, looking puzzled, but Noah didn't answer. Instead, he took a small object out of the bag, unwrapped it, and set it upright on the table. It was a small vase-shaped pot, with a beautiful painting of a Japanese figure in a colourful kimono on the front. 'Where did that come from?' she asked, admiring its delicate beauty.

Noah glanced from India to the vase. 'Your grandmother left you this. It's worth a lot of money, and I've been keeping it for you for a long time,' he told her.

It seemed a million years ago now, but India recalled the day she had walked into this house for the first time and read Ruby's letter. Her grandmother had promised her the 'valuable' something if she was reunited with her father, and India had completely forgotten about it until now.

'Ruby said in her letter it was valuable,' she said, lifting her eyebrows.

Noah gave her a crisp nod and held her gaze. 'It *is* very valuable, India. In fact, it's worth around ten thousand pounds.'

India gasped at this tiny pot being worth so much. 'Ten thousand pounds? That's an awful lot of money. Where did it come from then?'

'Apparently, Ruby found it while clearing out her parents' house after they died. She had no idea how much it was worth then, but she had it valued several years before she died. It is a rare Royal Worcester pot, which her mother bought for five pounds in a local antique shop.'

'Were her parents antique collectors?' India couldn't take her eyes off the small pot.

'No, far from it. They were deeply religious and very frugal people, but Ruby's mother took a liking to it, so bought it. Ruby always admired it while growing up, but was never allowed to touch it. I remember her saying it was the only colourful thing in the house.'

'But surely, Dad, you should have it, not me?' India felt bad about taking the vase. After all, Ruby had left her everything else.

'Mum was adamant you should have it,' Noah said firmly, closing the matter. 'By the way, how's Izzy getting on?' he said, changing the subject.

'She is doing very well, thank you, Etta's such a beautiful baby,' she told him. In her mind's eye, India recalled Izzy the last time she'd visited, looking happy and contented in her role as a new mother.

'No problems with the baby then, after that scare she had while pregnant?' Noah ventured, sipping at his tea and lifting his eyebrows.

'Thankfully, the baby is healthy and everything's fine. Also Dimitri has turned out to be a very caring dad and a great help with little Etta, so that helps.'

'I'm sure it does. Etta? That's a nice name. Very different, and quite old-fashioned really.'

India agreed. 'She named her after the sixties' singer Etta James,' she explained. 'Izzy's always been mad keen on sixties' music.'

A knock at the back door made them both jump, and India turned to see Jez on the doorstep, looking as handsome as ever. Her heart was doing somersaults as she let him in. 'Hi,' she said, smiling. 'Like a cup of tea?'

Noah stood up and greeted Jez, then declared he had to get going. Apparently there was a lot of photography work waiting for him at home.

'Why…' India started to say, but stopped when she saw the look that passed between the two men. 'What are you two up to now?' she asked.

Noah didn't answer but hugged India warmly then headed towards the front door. Once he'd gone, India turned back towards Jez, her heart thumping and her cheeks flushed with heat.

He was standing in the middle of the room gazing at her with such a look of love in his turquoise eyes that she was unable to move. Taking a step towards her, he pulled her into his arms and kissed her passionately.

For a moment she was lost in his embrace as he deepened the kiss, but then she pulled abruptly away from him. 'What are you doing?' she said breathlessly.

Jez grinned and raised his eyebrows. 'Sorry, but I love you, India,' he said simply. 'I thought you felt the same… also Noah says…'

India was shocked at his audacity. 'You and Noah have no right to make decisions for me. You two have been conniving behind my back.' She turned away to stop herself weakening at the sight of his loving looks.

India, listen, I didn't mean to upset you. I just think it's time we put the past behind us and moved on from our little misunderstanding. After all, it's been six months now and we love each other, don't we?'

She swung back around to face him. 'It's too late, Jez,' she told him, feeling the tears sting the back of her eyes. 'I can't do this again.'

323

Jez looked confused and ran his fingers through his thick, gold-streaked hair. 'Too late?' he asked. 'And what do you mean, can't do what again?'

'I can't go through all the pain and heartache of what happens afterwards... when it all goes wrong.' India's voice broke. As Jez took a step towards her again, she held up her hand to halt him.

'I wouldn't do that, India. I really love you and would never hurt you.'

To Jez it was simple, but India knew it was anything but. 'I hear what you're saying, but that's rich coming from someone who's been married before, and is still married to his precious bike.'

India couldn't help wondering what chance they could possibly have to make this work, and she hadn't yet mentioned his betrayal with Noah.

Jez shrugged then looked at her determinedly. 'It wasn't like that, India. We were too young, me and Annie... it was a big mistake to get married. I realised that years later.'

India folded her arms across her chest, then heard Jez mutter something under his breath. 'What was that?' she asked, narrowing her eyes.

Jez set his jaw and pushed his shoulders back. 'I said, I would even give up Daisy-Duke for you.'

India felt a tightness in her chest and her mind whirled, questions spinning in her head. 'What about not telling me about my grandfather and what happened to him? You knew all about Reilly's fate, but you refused to say anything.'

Jez tilted his head in a side-to-side movement and held his hands out. 'You have to understand, India, I'd promised Noah I would keep his secret. Only a few of us knew the truth, and that's the way your father wanted it. I'm sorry if you feel let down by me not being honest, but I couldn't let him down.'

She took a deep breath. 'I understand that,' India told him. 'But I still feel strange about how close you were to Noah while I was growing up.' There, she'd said what was in her heart at last, and felt better for it.

Jez shook his head sadly. 'There's nothing I can do about that, India,' he said resignedly. 'Like you, I was young and had no control over the actions of adults around me. Noah was good to me, but he's your father not mine. Perhaps now things are working out for you both, you need to let that go, too.'

He turned and began walking towards the door, and India felt conflicted. *Why did she think she couldn't have a relationship with Jez? The reasons she'd built up inside herself were crumbling before her eyes, and Jez was talking sense.*

Since being reunited with Noah, things had changed. She felt differently, not only about Noah but about herself, too. The feeling of searching for that elusive something had disappeared, and she knew things were so much better. Jez and Noah's closeness was nothing to do with her, she realised now, because at the time she had no contact with her father.

Knowing now that Noah did care had made all the difference. If Jez hadn't told her about Reilly because he was being loyal, then how could India penalise him for that? If she did let Jez into her heart, she was taking a huge risk. *But maybe the risk was worth it*, a voice in her head said. There was such a deep attraction between them, and they had something precious. Could she let that go?

What should I do, Ruby? India closed her eyes and her fingers automatically curled around the amethyst stone. She could hear soft whispering in her ear. 'Go after him, India,' it said, and the exotic scent of *Soir de Paris* wafted through the air.

India's eyes flew open, searching for the source of the perfume. 'Ruby?' she whispered back, but the room was empty.

India's heart thudded out of control. *Was Ruby trying to help India find success with love?* Her grandmother's own happiness had been snatched away when Reilly tragically died inside his prison cell all those years ago.

The sound of Jez's van door slamming jolted India out of her reverie, and quite suddenly she knew what she had to do. 'Thank you, Ruby,' she said to the perfumed air, and ran out of the house after him.

We hope you have enjoyed reading The Amethyst Necklace. Please take a moment to leave a review, even if it's a short one. Your opinion is important to us. And don't forget to look out for the sequel to this book, which is to be released the early part of 2021.

Sign up to Susan's newsletter, which is only sent out when there is something special to communicate – such as a new book release, special promotions, and price reductions.

Use the link below to be taken to the sign-up page. Your details will not be shared and you can unsubscribe at any time.

www.susangriffinauthor.com

Other Titles By Susan Griffin

Bird in a Gilded Cage
Scarlett's Story (the sequel to The Amethyst Necklace to be released in 2021)

About the Author

I live in East Sussex on the edge of the Ashdown Forest with my husband and a cat called Dave. I love writing romance with a mystery at its heart, and weaving secrets of the past with the present. I use my passion for history to research my novels, and am interested in how pioneering women in the past have managed to overcome adversity.

When I'm not writing I'm either painting a portrait of one of my children, singing with my local Rock Choir, or going for long walks in the nearby countryside.

For more information on Susan and her books visit
www.susangriffinauthor.com

You'll find regular news and updates on Susan's Facebook page:
www.facebook.com/susangriffinauthor

Printed in Great Britain
by Amazon